THE KINDRED FEW

THE KINDRED FEW BOOK ONE

HEATHER KINDT

Published by Midnight Tide Publishing

Cover Art by BRoseDesignZ

Edited by Megan Dailey

❦ Created with Vellum

CHAPTER ONE

$\mathcal{T}$he bell tolls for the dead.

I straighten my back as I follow the Citadel guard to the court. The blue feathers attached to his tall white hat sway back and forth as he leads me through the maze of hallways. A single tear traces a path down my cheek, but no one is there to wipe it away. The solitude amplifies the ache in my chest.

I clutch my mother's ledger, not wanting to part with her delicate script filling the pages. Everything else she owned has been turned over to the government.

We approach the towering white doors of the Council Room. Its imposing presence is meant to intimidate, entry reserved only for those with the proper credentials or court-ordered purpose.

"Name." The courtroom guards take over, dismissing the burly man who led me from my apartment in the Vitalis Sector.

My gaze is on his shiny black boots rather than his steely eyes, intent on malice. This will not be a pleasant visit to the court. They hold my fate in their hands.

I swallow back the lump in my throat. "Maribel Nexis Windsong." I leave off my father's hyphenated name, no longer identi-

1

fying him as kin. With my mother's death, I'm officially an orphan.

"Age." His harsh voice echoes through the great hall, causing bystanders to stop and stare.

I dare to look up at the man, his chiseled jaw composed of sharp angles, shaved clean with a razor as it is with all men in the city. He wears the white-and-blue uniform of a soldier, the men and women who cleansed the capital city of Avren over three decades ago. Today, they're more ceremonial, using the most handsome specimens to adorn the streets of the city in their fancy uniforms.

"Seventeen." I bite down on my lip, my admission punctuated by the subtle taste of copper. It is a capital offense to lie, so I tell the truth. My age will seal my fate. If my mother had waited three more weeks to succumb to the ravaging sickness, things could have been much different. I draw in a deep breath, my mind swirling with self-loathing for holding such thoughts.

The guard points to a stone bench inside the door. Two others are there already. One a teenager and one a man. "Wait here. The Council will call you up when they are ready."

The bench is cold beneath my skirt. An appointment with the leaders of the city means I'm dressed in my finest garments, tailored for Citizens of Avren: pale green shirt that matches my eyes, along with a white skirt with flowers embroidered throughout the material. The only real flowers we see in Avren are brought in from the wilderness by the Undesirables.

I crack my knuckles in a nervous habit and glance at the two sharing the bench with me. The boy beside me wears dark trousers and a crisp shirt, freshly pressed and laundered. He is a Citizen like me, no more than sixteen. His face is damp with tears.

The other wears brown trousers, a dirty shirt that may have been white at some point in its existence, and a cap. The clothing of an Undesirable. He is well built, with tousled sandy-blond hair. His chiseled jawline and light scruff on his face suggest a man in his mid-twenties. Without warning, his eyes meet mine, and he winks, causing my face to flame.

I scoot closer to the edge of the bench, trying to avoid the sickness that took my mother. Undesirables carry it, but it only transmits by touch.

My mother was too careless. Our house cleaner, Caron, became a good friend to her. She'd even take her to coffee in the neutral zone, a place that shut down once the sickness spread. Caron died two weeks before my mother.

A guard appears in the courtroom's doorway, a clipboard in his hand. "Grayson Elrod."

The Undesirable at the other end of the bench stands and follows the guard. The government usually reserves court proceedings for Citizens. Undesirables are shot, not tried.

I don't talk to the boy beside me. His tears tell me he's here for the same reason. Orphaned Citizen children not of age have only one destiny.

Instead, I stare at the heavy straps of my heels, clicking the toes together. In three weeks, my eighteenth birthday would have allowed me to move into an apartment of my own. The city requires parents to set aside credits for the children they choose to raise. Many Citizens decided not to have children because of this rule and the arduous process of growing their baby in a test tube.

My mother told me parents used to have babies naturally, when two people fell in love and created a new life together. This process, she said, now belongs to the Unseen, forbidden in our society. If an Undesirable woman becomes with child, she needs to hide it or get rid of the baby. A pregnant woman cannot work in the later stages of her pregnancy. If the child goes to full term, the Council forces the parents to give it away to a Citizen.

The night my mother told me about the way people had babies in the Unseen, I laid on my bed and stared up at the ceiling for hours. As a lady, it is unacceptable to have a man in my bedroom, but something about the idea sent a rush of heat through me. The Citizens of Avren are humane, not forcing their women to carry babies. Growing them in the laboratory makes a lot more sense. The ladies of Avren don't have to lose their figures and can carry on with their lives. If they choose to have a baby, they can hire an Undesirable nurse to care for it.

"Maribel Windsong." The guard reads my name as if he is reading a dictionary from Avren's library.

The weight of the boy's eyes bears down on me as I stand and follow the guard into the chamber. My heart thuds. My fate is already sealed. This is only a formality.

Five Council members occupy thrones at the front of the room—three men and two women, all adorned in blue ceremonial robes with white embellishment for the solemn occasion.

I walk to the front, propelled by the guard's insistent hand on my back. The guy with the sandy-blond hair is still in the room, leaning against the wall. His dark eyes flash to mine.

"Maribel Windsong?" the head woman calls out from her prominent position at the center of the dais.

I tip my chin. "Yes, Lady Raven," I respond, adhering to the proper term of respect for any adult within the city.

Lady Raven peers down at me, her long gray hair braided and wrapped on top of her head. Only those not of age wear their hair down. "Your mother, Celia Windsong, passed to the beyond."

My heart clenches at the sound of her name. It is a statement. Nothing I need to respond to.

The head Council member continues, "Two hundred and ten credits sit in your mother's account, left to you. It is five credits short of the two hundred and fifteen required for residency. Do you have any kin who can gift you these credits?"

I do not. The Council knows this. They know everything about each citizen within the city walls—what they eat, what time they wake, how many lovers they take. With my father gone, I have no kin. "No, my lady."

With her lips pursed, she looks to the left and to the right to her fellow Council members. Each gives a nod. "Then we have no choice but to banish you to the Unseen. Without the proper credits, you lose your rights as a Citizen of Avren." She brings a giant wooden hammer down on a pulpit in front of her. "Our decision is final."

I hold my chin up in a rigid attempt to keep the tears from flowing. The healer gave me a double dose of the daily vitamin we take to stabilize our brain chemistry and prevent displays of emotion prone to cause unwanted disturbances. Avren raised me soft—a perfect Citizen. I can dance, employ proper utensils, and use flowery speech, but jobs like cleaning, building, and cooking are for the Undesirables.

"Maribel, it is time to go." Lady Raven's words cut into my thoughts. I wander through the room, unsure of what to do. While I was here, the workers have cleaned out my home and taken every credit from our safe. The only thing they allowed me to keep was my mother's ledger.

A hand clutches my arm, dragging me to a side door near the front of the room. It's the Undesirable with the sandy-blond hair, the one the guard called Grayson, the one I tried to avoid on the bench.

Outside the courtroom, I shake my arm free from his clutch. "Don't touch me, urchin." If the sickness clings to my clothes, there is nothing I can do now.

Grayson laughs, his gaze raking over my dress clothes. "They all start out the same—too high and mighty for the rest of us. I remember that feeling well. It won't last long, my lady." He gives a mocking bow.

I straighten my shoulders. Before today, an Undesirable like Grayson could have faced the death penalty for treating a Citizen in this manner. "Three weeks, two hours, and fifty-seven minutes, and this would have been different."

Grayson sits on a bench and removes his cap, flipping it in his hands. "One week, fifteen hours, and thirty-nine minutes." He rolls up his sleeve and reveals a tattoo of the numbers 11539. "It's a constant reminder of the life I lost."

Still hesitant, I position myself on the opposite side of the hard wooden bench. Part of me is repulsed by him. Part of me feels the pull of his pain. "What happened to your parents?"

He clears his throat. "Tanner will be out here soon. We don't have time to bond over our tragic stories, Mari."

"My name is Maribel."

"In Avren, your name is Maribel." He pulls his cap back on as the door to the chamber opens and Tanner walks out with a guard. "The Unseen is my realm, and your name is Mari."

Of all the presumptuous, arrogant ideas.

Grayson stands to greet Tanner, holding out his hand. The younger boy stares at it but doesn't reciprocate. I don't blame him. More than likely, Tanner's parents died from the sickness too, and touching the unsavory likes of Grayson Elrod feels like a death sentence to him.

"As a former child of Avren, the Council has tasked me with guiding orphans into their new lives in the Unseen." Grayson walks down the hall, and we follow, knowing we have nowhere else to go.

"But why would they hire an Undesirable like you?" Tanner says, tears still visible on his cheeks.

Grayson whips around, grabs Tanner's shirt by the shoulders, and pins him to the wall. "First, never refer to the people of the Unseen as Undesirables. That's a slanderous term used by Citizens. We call ourselves the Redeemed." He releases Tanner's shirt, letting him drop to his feet. "I branded my skin to remind me of my past and how far I've come."

The boy scowls at Grayson. Tanner is too small in stature to act on the anger he feels toward our guide to the Unseen. The helplessness we both feel, untrained in anything of importance, grows like an insurmountable wall. If we don't join the people who live beneath our feet, we might receive a worse fate: banishment to the wilderness.

I shudder. "But who would choose the life of an Undesirable —I mean, a Redeemed, over the life of a full-fledged Citizen of Avren?" I ignore Grayson's brusque ways, expecting nothing less from an Undesirable.

"Someone who has tasted both and realizes one comes up lacking." He removes a key from a chain at his waist and unlocks a metal door. One of the many doors keeping Undesirables without working papers out of Avren. "Have you ever tasted a beer, Mari?"

I draw in my eyebrows and shake my head. "No. It is forbidden to drink alcohol in Avren. Why would you ask such a question?"

Grayson swings the door open and ushers us inside. The passageway smells of must and germs—everything kept far away from the city. I want to back against the wall, but fear of what might crawl along the damp surface keeps me at the center of the stairs.

"Or have you met a boy and shared a passionate kiss?" Grayson lights a match and holds it to a torch affixed to the wall.

My body burns like the torch in his hand. How could he expect me to answer such a question? "Life partners may exchange chaste kisses. I am only seventeen." But I had experienced this type of kiss—behind a utility wall and out of sight of the cameras. The memory of the touch of his hands still warms my skin.

"And a whole new world is about to blow your mind, Mari Windsong." He glances at Tanner, sizing up his slight form. "You will both need to undergo strength training."

"To hold a broom?" I conjure images of Caron sweeping our floor, humming songs. "Or to bake a pie?"

Grayson holds his torch up to another door, using a key to unlock it. "The Redeemed do a lot more than wait hand and foot on the Citizens of Avren. And the Supes will eat you alive."

The Supes? The concept sounds foreign to my ears. The history books in Avren's library only talk about the stories of the removal of the Undesirables thirty years ago, saying the soldiers met little protest. It was as if the other side knew they didn't belong and there was only one possible outcome.

The air beneath the surface stifles, and I suddenly feel as if an invisible force curls around my neck and squeezes. This is not where I belong—in a dank world surrounded by obnoxious characters like Grayson. He was a Citizen. If I spend too much time in the Unseen, will I lose myself too?

"In the short term, neither the Redeemed nor the creatures of the wilderness like Citizens. Orphan or not, your life is on the line the second you leave the tunnels." He holds the torch close to his face, casting an eerie shadow. "Stick close to me."

Great. A place where I don't want to go doesn't want me.

"I'll go back and plead with the Council." I am positive I have a solid case for a rebuttal. My mother held a respectable position in the Circle, publicly condemning my father the day he left for the Unseen.

I reach for the handle to the metal door and find it locked. Turning around, I stomp my foot, clenching my fists. "Open it now."

Grayson shakes his head. The corner of his lip lifts as he appraises me. "It's no use, Mari. The Council's determination is final. I learned that eight years ago."

Beside the next door, canvas bags hang from hooks on the wall. Grayson removes two, tossing one to me and the other to Tanner.

"What's this?" Tanner opens the mouth of the bag to peer inside.

"Government standard issue," Grayson says as Tanner removes a dingy, long-sleeved shirt. "They will identify you as newbies, but once you earn a credit or two, you can change them out." He drags his eyes over our outfits. "One thing's for sure, you don't want to set foot in the Unseen in *those* clothes."

"What's wrong with these?" Tanner's defiant jaw juts out. "My dad's the mayor of the Third League and he'll…"

"You mean, your dad *was* the mayor of the Third League." Grayson arches his eyebrow, then turns to unlock the door, not bothering to watch Tanner's face fall.

I'm there for the entire show. Emotion is a sign of weakness in Avren, although I've let my own guard down several times already. Tanner should know this. Composure, discipline, grace, and beauty separate a Citizen from an Undesirable. He holds back the tears, clutching his bag to his chest before letting it fall to the floor. Our parents are gone. We can't bring them back.

As Grayson rifles through his keys, I reach out in the darkness and take Tanner's hand. The human connection we both crave after losing our parents.

He is the younger brother I have never had or knew I wanted, and I'll protect him with my life.

Grayson lets the door swing open to the Unseen.

CHAPTER TWO

"It's not a cave." Tanner states the obvious as we both stare into the Unseen.

My breath catches in my throat, and time seems to stand still as I step into the forest behind Grayson. All the stories we'd heard growing up at home and in school were false. This isn't a vast underground cave system but a scene of pure enchantment. The trees bear leaves that emit a soft glow, casting a gentle, otherworldly light upon the forest floor. The air is alive with the mesmerizing dance of fireflies, an insect I've only read about in books. Their luminescent tails trace intricate patterns through the serene darkness.

"But trees... insects, they're only found in the wilderness." And that is impossible. The government locked the iron doors to the outer world decades ago. The humans banished to the harsh landscape experienced untenable conditions.

"I was fed the lies too." Grayson reaches above his head and plucks a piece of fruit from a tree, holding it out in his hand. "Take a deep breath. Taste the fruit. Let out the scream you've held inside for so long."

For the first time in my life, the air doesn't smell like the chlorine used to disinfect the germs left behind by Undesirables. There's a heady scent I'd describe as *woodsy* even though this is my first time standing beside a tree. It's the soil of the plant Caron brought my mother.

Tanner takes the red fruit from Grayson's hand and inspects it. "It's an apple, like slices we get in plastic bags in the cafeteria. I didn't know what a whole one looked like." He bites into it and the juice runs down his chin. "Tastes like one too."

Fear strikes my heart. Everything I have ever believed as true is false. I had anticipated Grayson leading us to rooms in an underground cavern where we'd live out our lives serving the citizens of Avren, but here in the forest, I don't know what to expect.

Grayson bends over and removes a coat from behind a tree and puts it on. It appears heavy and loaded down with weapons. "This way." He leads us down a trail where brilliant stones guide our path through a mystical labyrinth.

The peacefulness lulls me into a trance. My goal is to place one foot in front of the other and remain upright. Grayson is a spider, leading us to the center of his web, and I can do nothing but follow.

"Look at the water, Mari." Tanner breaks my foggy state of mind. He points to a stream beneath a bridge we cross.

The glistening waterway whispers secrets of the Unseen, mirroring the stars above in their luminous ripples. It is as if Grayson has led us through the portal of dreams where magic and reality intertwine.

A hooting noise comes from above, waking me from my trance, as a giant winged creature dives at my head, narrowly missing it as it lands in a nearby tree. I cling to the railing on the bridge, worried about more diving beasts.

Grayson laughs. "Come on, Mari. It's only an owl. There are much greater things to fear in this world."

Like what? If the adults in Avren didn't tell us the truth about the caverns, what else did they lie about? What made a person undesirable enough to drive them from the city to this savage world?

"Was this your reaction?" I walk beside Grayson, my heels clicking on the smooth stones. His quick gait and straight back hold a confidence I can't imagine achieving.

Grayson continues his pace, not slowing down to answer. "Of course. We are all fed lies by the Council. Your parents didn't know any better when they told you stories of the Unseen—a place they never visited. We face instant death if we breathe a word of the true nature of our world."

"And how does Avren keep you under their control?" I stop and bend to buckle my shoe. Grayson's strides are too much for my best heels. "Can we rest for a minute?"

"Yes, but not for long." He leans against a tree in the shadows.

Not caring too much about my white skirt, I sit on the grass and unbuckle my shoes before removing a pair of socks and boots from the government issued bag. Tanner plops down beside me and shakes out the contents of his sack.

"When you leave Avren, the government issues an ankle bracelet. This tracks you." Grayson rolls up his pants to reveal a glowing blue ring around his leg. "If you don't show up to work, the soldiers find you. If it happens too many times..." He runs his finger across his neck.

I rummage through the bag and remove my tracker. It glows in my palm, casting a luminescent blue over my skin. "And what if Tanner and I refuse to put them on?"

There's a click, and Grayson points a gun at my head. "It's not a choice. If the two of you don't comply, they come after me."

The only ones allowed to carry guns within the city are the guards. It is a capital offense if a Citizen is caught with one.

"Where did you get a gun?" Tanner has as many questions as I do.

Grayson doesn't move the barrel. "Put on the trackers, and I'll answer everything."

As much as I don't like the idea of Avren's soldiers tracking me, it's not much different from in the city. There, they track us with cameras. This started in public places—stores, schools, and parks—but then the Council passed Law 291. Each household needed to install a camera in every room. There were protests at first about privacy. But what did Citizens really have to hide? We were all loyal to the High Council. We shared all resources equally. And from what I heard from my friends at school, the government provided every household with a black cloth to cover the camera during private times between a husband and wife. These were limited to ten minutes, and a soldier would come knocking if they went longer.

With the blue trackers clicked around our ankles, Grayson drops the gun and holsters it at his waist. "There are ways to get things in the Unseen that aren't available to us in the city. As an Undesirable human, you work as a servant for the people of Avren. As a Redeemed, you earn credits to use here. In the city, you're given the same things as everyone else. Here, it's survival of the fittest."

"It sounds terrible." Tanner stands, his boots laced up. "And what's stopping people from stealing?"

Grayson taps his holster, and a devilish grin spreads over his lips. "Weapons... locks."

"You have locks?" I scramble to my feet. There were locks on the way to the Unseen, but I had expected them. We had to keep what lurked in the wilderness out of Avren.

"Yes, we have locks. It's the price of freedom." He runs his fingers through his unkempt hair. "It will take you a while to understand. The locks keep out the beasts that roam the Unseen, seeking to prey on unsuspecting humans. The Council banished them in the second purge of the city."

"Thirty years ago?" Tanner asks.

"No, that was the purge of the undesirable humans. This was the purge of Arazian and his followers." Grayson picks up my bag, slings it over his shoulder, and starts walking. "The original founders of Avren had opposing views to Arazian. When they banished him, they erected the iron doors to keep out those they saw as monsters."

Tanner takes my hand again as we both struggle to hold on to reality. "Are they real monsters?"

Grayson doesn't turn to look at us. "Mutated humans built into Arazian's army. He prefers Citizens over Undesirables. Also, vampires, fairies, dragons, nymphs, werewolves, mermaids—basically anything you read as a myth in the city exists just outside of your perfect little world."

My body goes numb. He's messing with us. It's a way of scaring the new recruits—hazing. "So, if what you're saying is true... the Council sees fit to throw orphans, the elderly, and mentally and physically disabled people literally to the wolves?" A fire burns deep inside me as I think about how many *Undesirables* the Council expunged from Avren each year.

Grayson whips around, his eyes burning with fire as he stares into mine. "And before you knew this, you thought sending people to work camps was ok?"

No, not really. But it was part of our life.

"You must learn to navigate this world. Most want to live in peace, but they don't want city-dwellers to interrupt it. About ten percent of Avrenians make it past the first night."

Tanner grips my hand tighter as we absorb this new piece of information.

"But don't worry." Grayson lifts the side of his jacket, revealing his arsenal of weapons inside—silver blades, wooden stakes, bottles with swirling potions. "That's why the Council requested me as an escort. As orphans, I'll take you to my cabin with the others of our kind."

"How many are there?" I ask, still rifling through my knowledge from fairytales about which weapon kills which creature.

"There are four of us right now." He removes a piece of paper from his pocket as we approach a split in the trail. "With the two of you, it will make six."

One trail follows the stream, meandering through the luminescent forest. The other takes a dive into a world where the light doesn't dare go. A screech echoes through the ominous valley, reaching my ears and sending a rush of cold down my spine like an icy river. I drop Tanner's hand, clutching my arms to my chest.

"What was that?" It is too dark to see anything in the valley.

"Only a banshee." Grayson folds the paper and sticks it in his pocket, then lifts his torch. "We'll take the high road this time. Less of a chance of losing either of you... but there's always a chance. Ninety percent according to most."

"You already told us that," I say through gritted teeth. "It's not like we need the reminder." By now, I can hear my pulse in my ears. My footsteps struggle to keep up with my heart beats as I take in short breaths. There's an electricity in the air, prickling my skin, and threatening to suffocate me. When we first entered the Unseen, the wilderness appeared mysterious and, in a way, lovely. With the new knowledge from Grayson, unknown threats seem to lurk behind every tree.

The path continues to follow the stream, which bubbles and gurgles beside us. Tanner's hand is in mine. His skin is clammy, but we both refuse to let go. Any of the monsters Grayson mentioned could devour us as a late-night snack.

"We're about twenty minutes away." Grayson scans the forest as we walk, his fingers dancing on the hilt of his revolver. "Don't expect a grand welcome. The other orphans grew up in the Unseen. Their parents were part of the human expulsion." He stops and looks back at us holding hands. "And don't use any of the *higher than thou* language you've used with me, because they'll slit your throat quicker than a vampire."

I never expected that moving to the Unseen would be a fun adventure, but I hadn't anticipated the hatred the Undesirables feel toward the Citizens. "How long did it take you to be accepted?"

"When I made my first kill." Grayson's boots clomp over a bridge, then go straight through a mud puddle. Dirt and mud are about as welcome in Avren as the Undesirables.

Tanner's eyes widen, sparkling in the moonlight. "Was it a vampire or a werewolf?"

"Neither." Our guide keeps walking through the puddles Tanner and I are desperately trying to avoid. "He was a Citizen."

"That's a capital offense." Tanner drops my hand, moving back from Grayson. "If I turn you in, you will face the firing squad."

"Do you really think I give a shit about capital offenses here?" He glances at the moon, stops, and removes a silver dagger from his coat. It glistens in the warm glow from above. Silver daggers are for...

A low growl reverberates from the bushes to my left. I freeze. Other than the sharp end of the heels in my bag, I'm defenseless.

The creature springs from its hiding place, knocking Tanner to the ground. His screams echo through the forest, and all I can do is cover my ears and close my eyes, knowing I'm next.

Please don't eat me... please don't eat me...

I silently pray to the distant gods of the wilderness, unsure of what else to do. Grayson shoves past me, knocking me out of my frozen trance. He dives onto the back of the creature and sinks the silver blade into its back. The wolf lets out a deafening howl as it whips its head around to glare at the intruder behind him. Blood drips from its mouth, and I think I'm going to be sick.

The creature bucks to dislodge the man from its back, but Grayson is too quick. He pulls the dagger from its body, and with one swift movement, slides to the wolf's underside, driving the weapon into its soft skin. Grayson rolls to the side and onto the ground, away from the wolf and Tanner.

A howl comes from its mouth before it whimpers and falls to the ground.

Shrieks fill the air, and then a hand covers my mouth. I'm looking at the scene from a faraway place, unable to control my body. Blood is everywhere, the smell overwhelming me. I taste it fresh on Grayson's hand, metallic and bitter. In Avren, healers encounter bodily fluids, not everyday Citizens. The sight of it makes me dizzy, and I struggle to stand, only his hand holds me up.

"It's alright. It's over." He keeps his hand over my mouth; his other one steadies my waist.

"Tanner." We need to help him. There's a pool of blood by his body beneath the wolf. Which one does it belong to?

His hand moves from my mouth to my forehead, smoothing back my hair. "He's gone. I couldn't move fast enough before the creature delivered its deathblow to his neck."

My body shakes, and I'm unable to control it. Violence doesn't exist in the city. Other than my mother's slow descent into the sickness, I've never seen another human die.

Grayson turns me toward him, pulling me into his blood-stained shirt, and wraps his arms around me. It's an odd mixture of comfort and horror. My head spins with the weighty scent of the carnage as everything goes black.

WHEN I WAKE, my eyes focus on a canopy of lights above me. Tiny creatures and insects dance among the boughs and fronds of the trees, blissfully unaware of the turmoil in my heart. It doesn't surprise me that only ten percent of Citizens make it in this cruel world. Our parents raise us to be sophisticated, valuing knowledge, manners, and discourse over strength and combat abilities. For Grayson to change his entire way of thinking in a matter of years seems unfathomable.

"Do you think you can walk?" He sits with his back to a tree, sharpening a stick with his knife. He must see me as a weak girl, more accustomed to balls and tea parties than hikes through the wilderness. And he's not wrong.

I hold back the tears, not ready to show any further weakness. "How did you do it? Change, I mean."

He sighs, leans his head back against the bark. "A damn good teacher. Someone who wouldn't give up on me. And I'm sure he wanted to throw me into the Lake of Glass multiple times and never look back." He stands up and holds a hand out to me, pulling me up. "I know this might be difficult to believe, but I was worse than you. With such a short time until my birthday, I thought I was on the track to follow in my father's footsteps, and I had the arrogance to show for it."

He still holds his arrogance, but it's different than that of a Citizen. With Grayson, he has earned a right to be proud of his accomplishments.

"What is your percent of successful deliveries of new Undesirables?" I brush the grass from my blood-stained skirt in a useless attempt to appear presentable.

He shrugs on his coat and rolls back his shoulders. "Currently? Zero percent. If I get you to the cabin, it will be fifty-fifty."

I touch his sleeve, not believing what I've just heard. "We're your first deliveries?"

"You've got to start somewhere." He flashes me his dazzling grin and heads down the trail.

I jog behind him, out of breath, trying to keep up to his long strides. "Why didn't you tell us you were new to this?"

He spins around, his eyebrows drawing in. "I killed a werewolf to save you, so stop whining about my credentials."

"But Tanner died!" And I could die before we reached safety. "What makes you qualified for this job?"

"Maverick Donnely was the greatest trainer to walk this wilderness. I learned from the best. And now you will learn from the best, so stop thinking you know better than I do because you lived in a walled city and wore fancy clothes." He stops and points to a two-story cabin nestled in the trees. Smoke rises from the chimney and warm lights welcome us in. "If you insult the others like you've insulted me, you'll wish you died with Tanner on the way here."

CHAPTER THREE

"*C*an I change into my other clothes?" I look down at my blood-stained blouse, skirt, and combat boots. Whatever garments are inside the bag must be better than what I have on.

Grayson stands watch in the woods behind me as I unbutton my silk shirt. It was a gift from my mother on my seventeenth birthday. She saved her credits to purchase it at the fancy store all the teenage girls frequented. I let it fall to the ground in a heap of memories. I wore it on my first date with Flynn—the one where he stole a forbidden kiss, out of sight from the cameras.

The government-issued shirt is made from a rough canvas material, scratching at my delicate skin. The two garments mirror my former life and the new one I am stepping into with a hesitant toe.

"Are you almost done?" Grayson whispers. He has his hand on his revolver.

"Almost," I hiss back as I pull up the pants. Never in my life have I worn a pair of pants. They feel foreign to me, like the material of the shirt. I sit to pull on my boots. "Why won't they like me? Besides the fact that I'm a Citizen?"

He laughs, a little too loud. "You're a princess. Not literally, but you think it's another's duty to take care of you. I understand where you're coming from, but they won't. So, for now, stay quiet and do as you're told."

Without another word, I follow him to the front door of the cabin, eager for the safety of the locks on the doors. He raps his knuckles in a secret code and waits. An eye appears in a tiny hole in the wood before we hear the telltale click of the lock.

A man a year or two older than me, with dark hair and glasses, opens the door. He has a slight build and wears a dark shirt and brown pants. He grins at Grayson, and I like him already.

"Levi." Grayson signs with his hands as he says, "This is Mari."

Levi signs his response as he speaks. "It's nice to meet you, Mari. I didn't know you were so pretty." He faces Grayson. "Where's the other one?"

My guide hangs his head and draws in a breath. "It was a werewolf." His hands work the sign for what I assume is wolf.

The younger man ushers us in and locks the door. "A fifty percent success rate is not bad for your first run." He touches Grayson's shoulder after he hangs up his coat, then slides his hand down to sign. "I know you were hoping for a hundred."

"Smells good in here." Grayson walks to the kitchen, ignoring Levi's comments, and glances inside a pot cooking above a fire in the hearth. "Where are the others?"

"In their rooms—sulking." Levi scoops a heaping ladleful of soup into a wooden bowl and places it on the table. "Four's enough for them, but I say, the more the merrier."

From Grayson's assessment of the other orphans, I did not expect Levi's welcoming attitude. I relax my shoulders and sit at the table, ready for warm food in my stomach. The shock of Tanner's death is wearing off, and I want nothing more than a good meal and a warm bed.

Levi sits opposite me and smiles. "It's nice to have a pretty face around here. The others scowl all the time."

I'm thankful that he talks as he signs. The teachers never taught me sign language in school because the deaf are promptly sent to the Unseen. I only read about it in books.

"Why are they so unhappy?" I speak slowly and make sure he can see my mouth, unsure of how to act around him. If this is my life, I'll learn to sign for the man who made me feel so welcome in this strange world.

"They aren't," he replies before spreading butter on a piece of bread. "They're only tired of serving the people of Avren. You aren't on their list of favorite people."

But they haven't met me yet.

And back in Avren, I'd done the same thing. I'd freely used the nickname *Undesirable* for people I didn't know, and even with those I did, like Caron. I couldn't expect anything more from them. I was a stuck-up Citizen who only cared about herself.

The sound of boots stomp on the stairs, and Grayson enters, followed by a woman who appears to be in her early twenties. She has fire-red hair and a smatter of freckles on her cheekbones. Her green eyes are anywhere but on me.

Grayson walks to the hearth and ladles out a bowl of soup, nodding his head in my direction. "Mari, this is Everleigh, my girlfriend. Everleigh—Mari."

"Where's the other snot-nose kid?" She takes the bowl from Grayson's hand. "Bastian and I told you not to take this job. Fresh Avrenian blood will lead them right to our doorstep."

"She's an orphan, like us, Evie." He sighs and places his bowl at the table beside me. "Can you show an ounce of compassion?" Sitting down, he takes a piece of bread and places it on a napkin beside his bowl. "The boy didn't make it. I had to kill a werewolf in the highlands."

Still not looking at me, Everleigh sits beside Levi and digs her spoon into her soup, stirring it. Wafts of steam rise from the surface. "See. They attract the supernatural like flies to rotten meat."

I bite into my lip, wanting to ask her why she'd compare me to a dead carcass. But I stick to my agreement with Grayson and remain quiet. These people—Levi and Everleigh, along with someone named Bastian—are being asked to accept a person who is from a city that oppresses them. Their hatred makes sense.

"We'll start training tomorrow. If she is to be one of us, she'll need to know how to defend herself." Grayson elbows me, causing the soup on my spoon to spill on the wooden table. "If there's one thing I'll agree with, it's that she's about as useful as a dead carcass."

"Hey!" I set my spoon down and cross my arms. In Avren, they trained me as a seamstress before my mother died. Caron also helped hone my skills with a needle and thread. The plan was that I would supervise Undesirables in my clothing shop when I had a place. I tread the fine line between the others liking me and standing up for myself. "It's not as if I like the situation any more than any of you, but the Council arranged it and we're stuck together."

Everleigh smirks and brushes a strand of curly hair out of her face. "Maybe we can feed her to the wolves, or even better, the fairies. It's not like anyone's going to miss her in Avren. Her parents are dead."

I close my eyes. "My mother's dead." I run my finger along the woodgrain of the table. The unpredictability of the knots and grooves reminds me of my current situation. "My father left for the wilderness of his own accord."

"Oh, I stand corrected." Everleigh narrows her gaze on me for the first time. "Your mother's dead and your father rejected you. I don't know what's worse. Must be a beast to live with." She turns to Levi and signs as a huge smirk crosses her lips.

"Knock it off, Evie," Levi says, eyebrows drawn in. "You need to give people a chance."

"Where's Bastian?" Everleigh scrapes back her chair and cups her hands over her mouth. "Bastian! Get down here, you big baby. I'm outnumbered."

A door creaks open at the top of the stairs, and I hear his boots, heavy on the floorboards, before I see him. He's dressed differently than the others, wearing more formal fighting gear—leather straps crisscross over his enormous chest. His long brown hair falls like a curtain over his face, where a deep scowl carves into his full lips. I can't see his eyes.

"You woke me from my nap, Evie," he growls, pushing a strand of hair to the side and revealing a crystal-blue eye.

My breath hitches.

"I need support on this one." She plops back into her chair and holds a hand out to me. "Gray and Levi think it's ok to drag this stuck-up werewolf magnet into our home without our consent."

Bastian wanders into the kitchen and rests his hands against the counter, mumbling something under his breath. I stare at his massive shoulders. They move up and down as he breathes. Never in my life have I seen someone as strong as him. Even Grayson doesn't measure up, and he killed a werewolf.

He turns to us, tucking his hair behind his ears and staring at me with his mesmerizing eyes, then flicking them to Grayson. "I've got enough to worry about with the attacks on the southern edge of the city, and you want me to train her too? A weakling? A Citizen raised as a princess?"

I square my shoulders, hostility running through my veins. I want to jump up and attack him, but he could squeeze the life out of me with one hand. So, I use the only weapon I have—my words. "And I suppose a big oaf like you turns to barbells instead of books because you struggle to string a complete sentence together?"

Grayson's eyes widen, and he shakes his head. A foot kicks me under the table.

Bastian pushes off from the counter and crosses the room, pulling out the chair from the end of the table and flipping it around before he sits in it. He rests his arms on the back, placing his chin on them and stares at me. "You brought us a smart mouth, Gray. Maybe I'll enjoy whipping her ass into shape."

Everleigh laughs and tosses her hair over her shoulder. "This might be fun. Build her confidence before we throw her to the wolves."

"Enough, already." Grayson shoves his bowl to the center of the table. "We discussed this before I took the job. The Redeemed in the towns will eat her alive, and the only other options are for her to try her luck with the Supes or become one of Arazian's zombies, and like Bastian said, she's in no shape for that."

"Citizen or not, she's like us," Levi signs before he stands and picks up his bowl along with Grayson's and brings them to the sink. "Another mouth to feed won't harm us too badly."

I slump in my chair as the four carry on a conversation as if I'm not there. I miss my mother and my friends in Avren— Samryn, Ferrah, and Mel. With Tanner gone, no one really understands what I'm going through. For Grayson, it has been many years since he left the city. He's acclimated to his life as a *Redeemed*—whatever that means.

"And what about the sickness?" Everleigh crosses her arms. Freckles pepper her bare skin, the same as the ones on her face. "Her mother had it. Who's saying she's not contagious? One thing's for sure. There's no way I'm touching her or getting any closer than this." She motions between the two of us.

Hot tears well in my eyes. With talk of my mother, she's hit a nerve, bringing up feelings I tried to push behind me. I long for my bed with the soft sheets and the music box my father bought me when I was five. After my father left us, I'd wind it up each night, its comforting melody lulling me to sleep. This will be my first night without it. Everything I ever owned, except my mother's ledger, now belongs to the government.

"You better get some rest." Bastian inspects me as if he can read my every thought, making me squirm in my seat. He must see the tears I desperately try to hide. "I'm going to drag you out of bed at the crack of dawn. I've got more to do with my day than train weaklings."

No longer caring about what he, or any of them, can see, I straighten my back. "I hope one day someone places you in front of a bunch of strangers and questions you about how your parents died." I scrape back my chair, ready to march out, but I don't know where I'm going. "Where am I sleeping?"

"This way." Grayson stands and glares at his girlfriend and Bastian. He leads me to a door to the right of the kitchen and opens it, ushering me in.

The room is small adorned with two twin mattresses on the floor covered in patchwork quilts, an oil lamp, and a bookshelf. A pair of pants and a shirt are laid out on each bed, folded in a neat package.

Grayson scratches his neck before picking up the pile from Tanner's bed. "I'll store these for now. Your fighting clothes are on loan from Everleigh, and Bastian thought you might like a few books to read. The quilt belonged to Levi's grandmother."

The gifts almost make up for the possessions taken by the leadership in Avren. A deep pang of loss fills my chest with the realization that this is my home, and I'll never see the streets of the city again—at least not in the same way.

"Do you like to read?" Grayson picks up a book from the shelf and leafs through it. "I took it for granted when I was in school. Thought it was a waste of time when I could play Suda with my friends. You never know what you'll miss until it's gone."

"I do." The titles are as unfamiliar to me as my current surroundings. "My mother read to me from the time I was small. I spent many hours locked away in Avren's library, perusing the sewing pattern books and classic literature."

"You mend?"

I should have stayed quiet.

"Before my mother died, I was on track to open a dress shop in the Settlement." I stare down at my hands, ready for the questions to end. "Can we talk about this tomorrow?"

He places the book back on the shelf, shoving it into an open slot. "Yeah, sure." He walks to the door and hesitates before opening it. "Don't become a recluse because of Evie and Bastian. They'll come around."

Do I have a choice?

"Good night, Mari. And please call me Gray." The door creaks as he closes it, and I'm alone for the first time today.

I hold the ledger to my chest, drawing in a deep breath before placing it on the shelf with the other books. I turn down the quilt and slip beneath the covers, pulling them up just far enough that I can look out the window at the stars above. In the city, although the ceiling above was glass, they always kept the lights on, blocking out the starlight. The stillness settles me as I drift to sleep, deflecting nightmares of the creatures that lurk beyond these walls.

CHAPTER FOUR

a rooster crows. It's a foreign sound, but one I know well because my friend Mel imitated it often. I'm not sure where he heard the bird's early morning decree before. I turn toward the wall, keeping my eyes shut tight.

The floorboard creaks before a shot of ice-cold water hits the back of my head. I shoot up. By the light of a match, Bastian's head floats in the darkness, pure joy etched in his smirk.

"Get out of bed. We've got to get an hour's worth of work in before the others join us." He tugs the quilt from me and tosses it onto the other mattress.

I groan. In Avren, no one wakes before the sun is in the sky. And I thought I was going to have a private lesson with Bastian. It is bad enough looking like a weakling in front of him. "The others?"

"The morning is the best time to train others in the village." He hands me a bow as I stand up. It's difficult to see in the dark, but the smooth wood feels comfortable in my hand. "Most of the Supes sleep until twilight, although a few enjoy the long shadows of the afternoon."

"And what do you expect to train me to do with this?" I hold up the bow, accidentally whacking him in the shoulder.

"Watch what you're doing!" He steps closer, the sound of his breathing less than a foot away. "You need to protect yourself, so you don't put others out with your complete and utter uselessness," he hisses, clearly annoyed I clocked him a good one on the cheek. "We've got better things to do than babysit you for Grayson."

I'm sure he does—like a couple hundred reps lifting a rock over his head to continue to build up his arm and chest muscles.

I pull on a boot, wanting nothing more than to lie back down and forget this entire nightmare is happening. Citizens of Avren don't fight. We dance, paint, bake, sing, and read, but the Council has strictly forbidden physical altercations.

Bastian stands near the door from the sound of his breathing and occasional sighs. This is as painful for him as it is for me.

"What's it to you if I die?" I pull on my second boot, wanting nothing more than to lie back down and wait for the sun to rise. "You've made it clear since I arrived yesterday that you don't want me here."

The door creaks open. "I'll meet you outside." And then he's gone.

I mutter several curse words, unable to put up with Bastian's crankiness while dealing with my own issues. I'm an orphan in a strange world where, apparently, supernatural creatures want me dead. If I don't learn to fight, I'll die just like Tanner. The image still makes my blood run cold.

Outside, a flower garden filled with a vast array of colors takes my breath away. The rich perfume of the blooms fills my nose, more aromatic than any of the scents sold in Avren's shops. Bastian sharpens a blade on a rock, his back turned to me. He wears a black, tight-fitting shirt with enough give for his large shoulders. Unlike the night before, he has his hair tied back. Sparks fly as he runs the edge of the metal over the hard surface.

He's a warrior ready to take down an army of supernatural creatures.

I watch for as long as I dare before clearing my throat. Grayson coaxed him into training me, but Bastian's made it clear that he doesn't care if I live or die. I'm a Citizen—as much an enemy to the Undesirables as the Supernatural beings. "Are we going to do this thing?"

He shoots me a sideways glance, sheaths his knife, and picks up a quiver resting against a tree. He starts on a trail into the forest, making me wonder how much I can really trust this guy. If he kills me in a remote place, he can always blame it on a vampire or a werewolf.

I take a step into the forest. What else do I have to lose? My whole life is gone, and I'm a stranger in a place I never knew existed.

He leads me, the gray of the morning lighting our way. There's a peacefulness that I never knew existed hanging in the air. The artificial lamps and bright lights of the city will never reflect the calm of the dawn in the wilderness. Is this what my father left to find?

After crossing a wooden bridge over a stream, we stop in a meadow, where a deer and her fawn bound away. A mist rises from the tall grass, giving the field an ethereal appearance, as if we're walking on a cloud.

I wring my hands, unsure of what to do with myself while he removes an arrow from the quiver. The idea of using a weapon and shooting the real thing are miles apart in my thought process.

"Let me see your bow." He holds out his hand, folding and unfolding his fingers.

I comply. As much as it felt good in my hand at first, it has become heavy and cumbersome.

He lifts the bow, nocks an arrow, and draws back the tight string. My breath catches. Never in my life have I seen someone who fits the true definition of a warrior. The soldiers in Avren are attractive, but it's all a show. Since the removal of the Undesirables, all those years ago, they've never seen combat.

Bastian makes them look like shriveling worms beneath his foot. I clasp my fingers behind my back to keep from reaching out and touching his arm.

With a *twang*, he releases the arrow, and it strikes a tree on the perimeter of the meadow. He removes another arrow, letting it fly into the bark right above his first one.

"Now you're just showing off."

He mutters something under his breath which sounds like a forbidden curse word. "It's called survival. This is a kill-or-be-killed world. You'll learn that soon enough."

"Tanner had his neck ripped out by a werewolf." My heart tears every time I go back to the scene. The Undesirables insist on keeping it fresh. "I didn't know him well, but he was a boy who lost his parents like us. At least, I assume you did. That's what Grayson told me."

Bastian's face is stone as he hands me the bow. "Your turn."

I take the weapon and set my feet the way he did, holding the bow the same way. It feels awkward in my hand, even though I think it's the correct position.

"Which hand do you favor?" He inspects my stance and then the position of the bow. "You look like an old woman with your hunched back and spaghetti arm."

Great. He's a warrior, and I'm an old woman.

"My left," I say, tired and cranky. "Why not take the position as my bodyguard, and we can avoid all this uncomfortable show." I throw the bow onto the ground.

"Because." He bends over to pick it up, giving me a straight-on view of his perfect ass. "This is a favor to Grayson and his sudden *save the orphans* kick. If it were up to me, I'd let a dragon incinerate you."

It's a gut punch to hear such hatred from an Undesirable. If

Caron ever felt this way, she hid it. The ones who worked in the city always addressed the lords and ladies with decorum, respecting our positions. Bastian's open disdain obviously kept him from a coveted city job.

I take the bow from him, wanting nothing more than to throw it across the meadow. "What was your official position in Avren?" From what I see, he's nothing but a muscle-headed bully.

He draws an arrow from the quiver and runs his fingers along the tip. "My father managed the farms in Rushia. Growing up, I learned to use the machinery and work the fields. Ninety percent of the produce grown goes to feed Citizens."

"And now?" I take the arrow from him to fit the notched end on the string of the bow.

"I train the rebellion." He watches as I lift my weapon, the arrow refusing to nock. "That and avoid the Work Patrol." Reaching out, his hand skims mine as he lifts the bow. "You're doing it all wrong."

My skin crawls and tingles from his touch. Images of the sickness instantly take over my mind. Not all Undesirables carry it, but the plague doesn't always manifest in carriers. I back against a tree before running to a nearby stream. Dropping to my knees, I scrub my hand in the water, hoping it hasn't already taken hold.

"What are you doing?" He stands over me, his overbearing presence filling me with dread. "Gray said they brainwashed you, but I didn't know it was this bad."

I stand and glower at him, water dripping from my hands. "I'm not brainwashed. My mother died from the sickness because she touched our housekeeper."

His eyes show a momentary look of compassion.

"Don't touch me, *phaloc*." I use the most derogatory term for Undesirable I know for emphasis. I'm here to survive, not make friends, at least not with people who want to turn me into a dragon roast.

"Duly noted." He kicks at the dirt with his foot, no longer

interested in any eye contact. "Let's follow through with our obligations. Gray can check it off his list for today."

I'm proud of sticking up for myself, but at what cost? Bastian hates me more than he did before, and I'm sure he'll laugh over the entire incident with Everleigh later today. If I must live with them to survive, I need to learn to be civil in this new environment.

"Hold up the bow with your right hand." His voice is gruffer, if that's possible, making me want to crawl into a hole. "Hold your wrist straight." He circles me, inspecting my stance before handing me the arrow. "Nock the end of the arrow on the string, holding it between your thumb and forefinger."

I follow his directions, then pull back on the string as he had when he shot the tree.

"Don't rush it, *my lady.*"

My skin crawls again, but this time it's his words, not his touch, providing the discomfort. It's a mockery of not having reached the age to receive the title. "Never call me that."

He steps close to me, his breath tickling the tiny hairs on my neck. "Don't call me a phaloc, and we've got a deal." He moves back slightly, the whisper of him still dancing across my skin. "You're one of us now. Either that, or you're dead. I suggest you stop acting like you wipe your ass with satin."

"And what?" I spin around to face him, still holding the bow and arrow in my hands. "Act like the class system doesn't matter? Act like your uncouth lifestyle didn't cause my mother's death? Because it did." Feeling the weight of the last week crashing down on me, I let the arrow fly over his shoulder, aiming it nowhere in particular.

The wayward projectile hits a target in the shadows.

I'm overcome with dizziness when I realize it's a person. He drops to one knee and yanks the shaft from his chest, tossing it to the side.

"Vampire," Bastian hisses. "That was an iron tip, not silver."

"What's that supposed to mean?" I ask.

He doesn't have time to answer. The monster is suddenly three feet in front of us, baring his fangs. He's paler than any of the people in the city, though shockingly beautiful. His golden-brown hair catches on a wayward breeze as he holds his nose in the air.

"What have you brought us, Bastian Hale?" The creature circles me, bending his face close to my neck. The feeling is the complete opposite of the tickle of Bastian's breath.

I'm paralyzed with fear.

"Fresh blood before the morning rays?" He lifts my arm, inspecting my wrist with his blood-red eyes. "I always took you for the intelligent one."

Bastian's body is tense, his hand moving to the flap of his coat. "Touch her and die."

The creature laughs, his fingernail running along my neck as I stiffen. Never in my life did I think I'd meet my demise at the hands of a mythical creature. If the stories are true, the vampire is too fast and strong for us to escape. He'll drain every drop of our blood before the first sun rays touch the tops of the trees.

"Do you have a fondness for this one, Bastian?" The vampire continues to circle me, raking his eyes from my head down to my toes. "The ones with auburn hair always got me when I had a heart that cared."

"Honestly, I couldn't care less if she lives or dies." Bastian's hand grasps something beneath his coat, but his attention is on the beast. "But having you kill my trainees is not a precedent I want to establish." Swiftly, a flash of silver is in his hand before it hurdles through the air, burying itself in the vampire's chest.

Veins of deep blue etch the creature's face as he clutches his throat. Like a crumbling statue, his face cracks apart and his entire body collapses to the ground into a pile of dust.

"As I was saying." Bastian crouches and removes his dagger from the pile, wiping it clean of vampire ash on his pant leg.

Several strands have tugged loose from the tie holding back his hair, but other than that, he appears unaffected. "You need to be ready for anything. We watch out for each other, but you never know when they'll catch you alone."

My fingers are numb on the handle of the bow as it shakes in my hand. Without my trainer, I'd be dead. After watching Grayson and Bastian take down supernatural beasts, I've change my viewpoint on my upbringing. Teachers in Avren filled my days with what I now call *soft skills*—etiquette, philosophy, and, in my case, how to craft a killer ballgown. Nothing prepared Citizens for werewolves and vampires.

He sighs as a tear rolls down my cheek. "You're weak. Your mother died. And yes, you witnessed a werewolf attack." The toe of his boot kicks at the pile of ash. "But this was nothing. I had it all under control." He removes a dirty rag from his sack and hands it to me. "Wipe your tears. We've got a lot of work to do."

I throw it back at him, wearing my tear-stained cheeks like a badge of courage for what I'm about to say. "Maybe I'm weak, but I'm compassionate, which I can't say about you. From the moment Gray brought me home, you and Everleigh have been nothing but horrid. Here in the wilderness, you learn to survive. In Avren, we learn to love."

Bastian's eyes flash, his fingers trailing along a silver chain around his neck. He stares into a far-off place before responding. "Ejecting orphans and the deaf, like Levi, is not love. It's building a society of people who think, act, and look just like you. The depths of my love have run through this land without ceasing—a raging river reaching to the inner workings of my soul. You know nothing about me or my people, so stop spouting your self-righteous crap." He glares at the bow. "We're done with our lesson today."

"You call that a lesson?" I raise the weapon, determined to glean a bit of his knowledge. I don't let his rant affect me, knowing he's wrong and I'm right. "A warrior like you giving up so easily on a lost cause like me?"

He grumbles more obscenities under his breath, stooping to pick up his sack. "I'm not giving up. Others are waiting for me in the Grove. Are you coming?"

I need to jog to keep up with his long strides as he marches through the forest, unhindered by the threat of Supes with daylight streaming through the trees. My senses absorb the faint whisper of smoke that lingers in the air, hanging in the canopy like floating gossamer. Birds call out to each other with unfamiliar songs. They swoop from tree to tree above us, alighting on branches, their keen eyes following our path. Tiny land creatures, no bigger than birds, scurry across the forest floor to climb the nearest tree. The fascination with the world around me alongside my shredded emotions from my time with Bastian have my head spinning.

Bastian seems unaffected by the wondrous sights around us, more intent on reaching our destination.

I remain quiet, more annoyed by my companion's heavy boots than anything else he said to me today. To sit on the forest floor and let my senses absorb this forested world would be heaven. But according to Bastian, there isn't time.

The smoke thickens as we approach the Grove—a circle of grass with four or five cottages surrounding it. Each home has a chimney with thick, gray smoke rising to the upper reaches of the trees. A group of people assemble outside a cottage, each decked out in fighting gear and holding a weapon.

"Bastian." A woman with long blonde hair braided down her back approaches, carrying a bow like mine. A wide smile is on her lips until she flicks her gaze at me. "Who's this?"

"Someone Gray dragged in last night." He doesn't look at me as his face holds a bored expression. "Another orphan to train. Susan, this is Mari." He continues to the cottage where the others wait.

I hold out my hand in the customary Avren greeting, but she only stares at me, then turns to Bastian. "I thought you were the Kindred Few. If Gray keeps bringing in spoiled brats, he'll ruin your reputation."

Bastian says nothing in response as he greets the other three trainees lounging on barrels by the wall of the cottage. "Where's Lyden?"

"Didn't show up this morning," one guy responds, standing as Susan and I approach. "I think he heard he had to face me again." He has curly dark hair and a crooked grin, but unlike his female counterpart, he holds his hand out to me. "I'm Rafael, but you can call me Rafe or whatever the hell you want."

I shake his hand as my skin prickles with embarrassment. The laws forbid flirting in Avren. The Council matches you once you turn eighteen. My hope had been for Flynn. We'd known each other since I was six. We went through school together and, as teenagers, mastered the art of eye contact when the teacher wasn't looking. Flynn liked to take the seat next to me in class, using every opportunity to brush his skin against mine if I dropped my pencil and he picked it up—which he always did.

He was my first and only forbidden kiss.

But the Council will match him soon. My heart aches for how much I have lost.

"Maribel," I say, taking Rafe's hand. "But you can call me Mari, and that's it."

"Touché," he responds, holding onto to my fingers for a few seconds longer than I deem comfortable. "I'm never opposed to another pretty face. No offense, Commander Hale, but you and Elrod just aren't my type."

Commander Hale? Is he referring to Bastian?

"Imagine that threesome." Another guy hops from the barrels and holds his hand out to me to shake. "I'm Mav, Lyden's twin brother." He turns to Bastian. "And no, I haven't seen him this morning." He's joined by another woman with short brown hair.

Unlike Susan, she gives me a wide smile as she wraps an arm around Mav's waist. She has a long sword strapped to the belt around her midsection. "I'm Laurel. We're glad you're here."

Bastian, or rather, Commander Hale, stands before us, a thin, grim line creasing his lips. "Our endeavors are more important than ever. Not only do we prepare for battle against the army and Citizens of Avren, but the Supes are also becoming more aggressive."

"What do you mean?" I wring my hands, not believing what he said. "I thought you were training me to protect myself."

"I am." He removes a dagger from his jacket, holds it in his hand, and flings it at a nearby target, hitting a tree. "I'm training you to protect yourself against the soldiers in Avren's army."

While Avren's soldiers haven't faced combat, they greatly outnumber us. It's a suicide mission.

"What happened with the Supes?" Rafe leans against a barrel, his fingers dancing over the handle of a machete strapped to his waist.

"A werewolf attacked one of Gray's targets last night, and this morning, a vamp risked daylight to attack Mari." His eyes meet mine for the first time since we stood in the meadow, the crystal blue sending a chill down my spine. "Let's get to work."

CHAPTER FIVE

*L*oose hay covers the training ground outside the Grove. Someone has propped two canvas dummies on bales, attaching them to sticks in the ground. A small fire burns in a pit with an iron pot above it. Steam rises from the cauldron and my stomach growls. They serve breakfast in Avren promptly thirty minutes after the initial waking music.

Bastian rests a foot on a hay bale, assessing the mess of a training ground. "Whose job was it to clean up after yesterday's session?" He narrows his eyes at the others.

All fingers point to Rafe.

He holds up his arms. "Hey, it's not a one-person job. Laurel was supposed to help me."

"Nice try." Laurel smirks, hands on her hips. "I can't cook and clean up after the lot of you. It was your responsibility to find a helper, and I had lunch to prepare."

"*I had lunch to prepare,*" Rafe mocks her, a look of disgust rolling over his face. He wrinkles his nose and purses his lips. "If I had a loaf of bread for every time someone used that excuse, I could open a bakery."

"Whatever." Laurel unsheathes her sword and faces her commander. "Can I fight Rafe first today?"

Bastian steps forward and takes the weapon from Laurel's hands. "I thought we'd do a little hand-to-hand combat today." He inclines his head in my direction. "In honor of our recruit. It'll let you take out a bit of aggression. Rafe… Mav… you're up first."

Mav pounds his fist into his palm.

Rafe's eyes grow wide, and he backs away with his hands in front of him. "I was hoping to show Mari the ropes. You know, a little rolling around in the grass. A few rounds of that and I'll have her ready to face an army of vamps."

"You know we only use hand-to-hand with Citizens. Don't face a Supe without specialized weapons." Bastian unbuckles his belt and lets it fall to the ground. "I'll fight Susan."

There's a glimmer in the blonde woman's eyes as she assesses her opponent. She sweeps her braid over her shoulder, her hands in fighting position.

"Take notes on Susan's moves." Bastian circles her, but his attention is on me.

I sit down on a log, ready to observe.

"You're up next, so it's important to study what works and what doesn't."

The Council of Avren denounces fighting. It's a method Undesirables use because they are primitive, lacking our advances in technology and mediation. *Our advances*. I'm no longer a Citizen of Avren but an Undesirable. It's as if someone took my worldview and flipped it on its head.

"Are you watching?" Bastian growls. Susan has him in a head-lock, his face red as she adjusts her hold on him. He uses the temporary loosening of her grip to snatch her waist and throw her to the ground, sitting on top of her and grinding her wrists into the dirt. "Never let up, Mari. Your opponent will use your weaknesses."

With his head turned to me, Susan locks her teeth into the sensitive skin of his forearm.

"Shit!" He releases her wrist to shake out his arm.

Using his distraction, Susan shoves him off, jumps to her feet, and dives for his midsection, knocking him to the ground. She climbs onto his chest and uses her knees to pin his arms to the ground. "Give up, Commander."

"You're something else."

When she releases him, he grips the front of her shirt and pulls her in for a kiss.

My stomach flips, so I avert my eyes, focusing on the other fight. Mav has Rafe backed into a tree, keeping the scuffle off the ground. Mav is shorter but has the clear advantage in strength to his wiry opponent, his arm muscles tight within his shirt.

Bastian sits beside me on the log, slightly out of breath. "You think Mav has him beat?"

After seeing Susan kiss Bastian, I can't look at him. People in Avren never showed affection in front of me—not even my parents. I tug on the hem of my shirt, intent on keeping the conversation professional. "He's clearly the stronger of the two."

"Looks can deceive." He scoots closer, leaning in to point at Rafe. "Don't underestimate your opponent."

As he says this, Rafe slips out from Mav's grasp and ducks below his arms with lightning speed. Suddenly, he's behind him, his arm wrapped around the shorter man's neck. After a few intense minutes, Mav stops flailing, and Rafe lowers him to the ground.

"See," Bastian says, placing his hands on his knees as he stands. "He'll have quite the headache when he wakes."

Rafe waltzes forward, his chest puffed out. Laurel shoots him a disgusted look and goes to attend to her boyfriend.

"Are you ready for our scuffle, Mari?" Rafe holds out a hand to help me up, not letting go when I try to drop it. "I promise to let you spend a majority of the time on top."

"Mari's off-limits." Bastian ladles the steaming substance from the cauldron into a bowl and hands it to Susan. "Find another poor urchin to bother."

"I can handle myself." Keeping my hand locked in Rafe's, I'm not sure if I can, but I'm tired of the Commander's constant mothering. In a move I watched Susan use, I swipe my leg around, trying to knock Rafe's feet out from under him. It feels as if I hit an iron pole.

He laughs and gathers me into his arms, deep dimples carved into his cheeks. "You're so cute." He jostles me as my cheeks burn. This is not how I pictured my first fight.

I want to bury my fist in his dimples as I glare at him.

Rafe finally releases me, his face falling as he walks away. His mood swing gives me whiplash. The vitamins I took yesterday no longer feel as strong. I'm beginning to understand where he's coming from.

"Don't mind him." Bastian nods in Rafe's direction. "The guy's used to rejection. Susan, teach Mari how to perform a proper leg sweep while I work with the others."

Susan's eyes widen, and she frowns. "Do I have to?" Her intense gaze rakes down the canvas-bag clothes the government issued me. They are hideous. "Why do the rest of you get to have all the fun?"

My heart rate increases as I roll up my sleeves, sweat prickling my neckline. It isn't like I chose to come here. Grayson delivered me into these circumstances. A new feeling rolls through the pit of my stomach, stretching out until my extremities grow numb. The urge to punch someone has grown tenfold, and Bastian is the closest punching bag. Maybe the meds have officially worn off.

With everything I have, I slam my fist into his chest, which I'm sure was unexpected, because he never would have allowed me to do it. Before I can do it again, his hands are around my wrists. He twists me around and pulls me into his chest. His hot breath is tickling my ear, causing me to shiver. "We are *not* enemies."

I struggle to free myself, but he won't release me. "Let me go. It's no wonder Avren rejected you. You reject everything we stand for—order, nonviolence, peace. And to fornicate in public in front of everyone?"

"What?" Susan quirks an eyebrow. "You mean our kiss? Seriously?"

"That is for the bedroom," I whisper, not believing we're talking about this in public. "When you're married."

Bastian's lips move close to my ear again, and I struggle against him. "Baby, you haven't seen anything." He lets go of me, and I move to my spot on the log, trying to calculate my next move.

"Take me back to Gray." I lift my chin, trying to procure an inkling of authority.

Bastian leans against a tree and crosses his arms. He pulls something from a bag attached to his hip and sticks it in his mouth. It's a cylinder of paper. He strikes a match against the tree bark and a flame appears, which he brings to the paper. Smoke rises from the end of the cylinder and again from his mouth when he opens it. "Gray will not take you back to the city. One, you know too much, and two, they'll never accept you." Smoke exits his nostrils after he sticks the paper into his mouth. "You can either learn to fight with us or try your chances with the Supes. We all know how that worked out for the boy."

As much as I want to tell him to take his training and shove it, he's right. This is my life now. A world where sin reigns. Disorder and lawlessness are preferable to civil obedience. If I am to survive in this place, I need to learn to defend myself.

I turn my attention to Susan, who stands with her hands on her hips, taking in the entire exchange between Bastian and me. "Will you teach me to take Rafe down with a leg sweep?"

She smirks, whipping around with her long braid down her

back. Her black fighting gear shows off her trim hourglass figure, making me envious. "If I teach you my tricks, you'd better take that oversized oaf down."

By this time, Mav is on his feet and holding his head, with Laurel by his side. Rafe's nowhere to be found, which doesn't bother me at all.

Susan leads me to the far corner of the Grove. Without warning, she sweeps her leg out and knocks me to my bottom. "Stay away from my boyfriend."

I shake my head and crawl on my hands and knees to stand again. "I'm not…"

Her leg knocks me back on my bottom. Is she going to let me stand?

Without getting up, I shield my eyes from the rising sun. "You know my story. I live with Bastian. It's not like I can stay away from him. Gray's making him train me. If it was up to me, I'd live on the opposite side of the wilderness from him. He's a bit difficult to get along with, don't you think?"

She jumps on top of me, slamming my head into the ground. My head spins. I thought they wanted me to learn how to fight.

Her face is inches from mine. "Rafe is yours, Mav is Laurel's, and Bastian's mine. You better start learning how things work around here."

"Don't I have a choice in the matter?" I stay still, not wanting the larger woman to think I'm on the attack. In Avren, we had no choice on who the Council chose as our life partner. From what I'd observed, I thought things were different in the wilderness.

With her hands balled up in the front of my shirt, she seethes, "I see the way you look at him."

"I didn't mean to look at him in any particular way." Bile rises in my throat, and I swallow, unsure if I should make the next statement. "I can't stand him, really. He's a pompous ass who thinks he's better than everyone else."

A sharp sting spreads across my cheek as her fist connects

with my face. Another pummel hits my nose, and a warm rush of blood runs over my lips, the tangy, metallic taste entering my mouth. It wakes me up.

With all my strength, I push Susan and twist my hips, determined to throw her from me. Her fists continue to beat at me. I hear shouting in the distance as I yank her braid, drawing a scream from my opponent.

After a few more fear-filled moments, her weight is off me, and a groan escapes my lips. In Avren, I was on the road to become a designer, crafting dresses for balls, weddings, and other important life events. Here, I'm worthless, a weakling in a world full of titans.

"Mari, are you ok?" A hand touches my shoulder, and I look up at Bastian through my blurry vision.

All I want to do is sleep. This is all a nightmare, and when I wake, the comforts of my bedroom in Avren will surround me. Closing my eyes, I block out the noise and focus on what my life could have been.

The life three lousy weeks stole from me.

CHAPTER SIX

Six handsome suitors vie for my hand in marriage in front of the Council. One is Flynn, dressed in a fine suit I made him in my shop—the one I would have opened if I'd stayed. He looks dashing with his golden hair shining in the lights of the Council room, a warm smile across his lips as I enter wearing a yellow gown. Surely the members of the Council will see we are the best match.

Out of curiosity, my attention drifts from my crush to the other five men, each seeming qualified in his own way. When I reach the last of the suitors, my jaw drops. "There's been a mistake."

"We don't make mistakes in the choosing of the suitors, Maribel." Lady Raven glares at me from her perch high above us. "The Council chooses each suitor based on DNA testing, personality surveys, and observation. These six are the best matches for you." She folds her hands on her podium. "We will now decide which of the six is your perfect match."

I can't look at him. My cheeks flame in embarrassment. How can the Council let an Undesirable stand beside five worthy Citizens? I crack my knuckles and look up at Flynn, the one person keeping me sane in this situation.

Lady Raven brings down her gavel as the Council reconvenes. "We made our decision. Your perfect match is Bastian Hale."

My heart pounds rapidly as I sit up in my bed and take in my surroundings. It's dark except for an oil lamp burning on top of the bookshelf casting shadows around the tiny room. My head is pounding, and I touch a bandage crossing my forehead. A dark-haired man sleeps in the other bed beside me, a pair of glasses on the floor by the mattress.

"Levi," I whisper. When he doesn't stir, I try again, but throw a rolled-up sock at his head. "Levi."

He turns and sits up when he sees I'm awake.

"How did I get here?" I know the answer, but I need to fill the silence. Talking with my friends always got me through tough times, like when my dad left. The dream still echoes in my soul, filling me with an odd combination of longing and dread.

He lifts his chest and raises his shoulders to give himself the appearance of a large man. He curls his arms and puffs his cheeks, making me laugh.

"And where is he?" I trace a pattern in the quilt, knowing his presence and not Bastian's, in the other bed is intentional.

He points at the ceiling. "Sleeping."

Is Susan with him?

He drops to his knees on the floor beside my mattress to touch my bandages. Concern creases his forehead.

"I'm ok," I say, laying a hand over his. Scarring mars his skin, something rarely seen in Avren. "I need to take my training seriously, or this might turn into an everyday occurrence."

He provides a weak smile as he drops his hand and holds onto mine.

"Why are you so good to me?" I grieve my friends in Avren, so he is a comfort to cling to in this strange world. "I'm a Citizen. You're supposed to hate me like the rest of them."

He sets his lips in a pout and shakes his head, holding his palm over his heart. First, he points to me, then forms two fists, holding them above his chest and pulling them apart as if he is a prisoner breaking free from his chains. "You are Redeemed."

"I hardly think any of your housemates would call me that." In my eyes, the word is a badge of courage to them—one that is earned after hundreds of fights and thousands of bruises. "My life was much different from yours. I don't belong here like you do."

He furrows his brows and takes my hands in his, pulling me to my feet. Pain screams at me from my head and lower back. I bite my lip to keep from revealing it. He tugs me across the room, opens the door, and leads me to the kitchen.

When he lifts his foot to the first stair, I pull him back with my hand. "What are you doing?"

He frantically spells something with his free hand, his tugging insistent. I stare into the darkened stairwell, drawing in a breath. No one wants to be disturbed up there.

Not willing to stop, he continues to pull me, one reluctant step at a time, to the top of the stairs. Three closed doors branch off from the landing. He reaches for a handle, and the door opens with a loud creak.

Something rips him from my hand. A large arm wraps around his neck, connected to Grayson.

"What the hell?" Grayson drops his arm and signs to Levi, speaking out loud so I can hear him. "You know better than to sneak up on us at night. I thought you were a Supe. I could have ripped your head off."

Levi signs to Grayson.

Grayson turns to me, his eyes still heavy with sleep despite the scare. "He wants me to interpret for you. He doesn't think he can communicate it the right way. Says it's important and can't wait."

Levi conveys his message to his older friend. The two

exchange looks I don't understand, like the ones I used with my closest friends in Avren.

"He wants you to know you're kin. You've lost your mother and father, so we're your family now." Grayson glances at the other two doors in the hallway. "You know Evie and Bastian don't want to hear you talking that way." He holds his hand out to me. "She's only been here a little over a day."

I watch Levi sign something else to Grayson, who nods along with their conversation.

"Yes, I feel the same commitment to the orphans of Avren." Grayson gives me a sideways glance. "And yes, I feel the connection too."

What connection is he talking about? I hate only hearing one side of the conversation. "Can you translate what he's saying so I don't feel like you're talking behind my back?"

"He's talking right in front of you. It's not his fault you don't sign." Grayson pinches the bridge of his nose and closes his eyes. "This is a conversation for another time, not in the middle of the night when I need my beauty sleep." He turns and walks to his bed.

Levi laces his fingers in mine and pulls me out of the room, closing the door. "I'm sorry. There's so much I want to tell you."

My heart warms looking at him, feeling his fingers in mine.

We are kin.

"I've never had a brother," I say into the darkness of the stairwell. "I always imagined what it would feel like to have someone to confide in besides my parents." Tears sting my eyes. This man, who barely knows me, wants to embrace me as his sister. I'm not sure what to think of that, but it ignites something deep inside me.

He keeps his hand in mine as we descend the stairs to my bedroom. The oil lamp burns on the bookshelf, casting a warm glow. He settles on the other mattress.

I crawl onto my bed and rest my back against the wall, watching him lay his head on the pillow. "Where do you usually sleep?"

He props his head up on an elbow. "This is my room."

"You gave up your bedroom for two Citizens?"

He nods and gives me a smile.

"I don't mind sharing with you." I twiddle my thumbs in my lap, feeling more like the intruder than the owner. "Where did you sleep last night?"

He quirks the corner of his lip and points to the ceiling. "Bastian."

A strange feeling of jealousy hits me as I wonder what it's like to sleep in the same room as the Commander. Does he snore? Talk in his sleep? My mind drifts to what it would be like to share his bed, and I immediately put a stop to my internal wanderings. "I'm sorry you had to go through that."

Levi waves a hand at me and lays his head back down on his pillow. It's late, and we're both exhausted. After my beating, Bastian will have to let me sleep, even though I've been out for hours.

I stare up at the ceiling. All my life, I've known who I was— Maribel Nexis Windsong, future seamstress and owner of an upscale shop. Without the identity Avren, my parents, and the Council bestowed on me, I feel lost. The protection of the walls of the city is gone, leaving me exposed. Who am I without others telling me about my future?

Maybe I'm afraid to find out.

THE SOUND of feet shuffling on the wood planks of the floor wakes me. I wrap the quilt tighter, building a cocoon and trying to block out the chilly morning air. I peek out through a break in the blanket. It is still dark, but I can make out Levi walking to the door and Bastian standing at the threshold. He clamps a hand on the younger man's shoulder as he passes. Levi only hangs his head.

Bastian's heavy boots clomp over the floor, and he stops at the foot of my mattress. "Wake up, Mari."

"Go away," I grumble as I bury my head beneath the blanket. The aches and pains from my injuries the day before are out in full force today. My left eye feels almost swollen shut.

When I don't hear the retreat of his boots, I peer out.

"You can't hide from a Supe." Without warning, he rips the quilt from my body. "You need to train."

Shivering, I clutch my pillow, trying to stay warm. "You're an asshole. Leave me alone."

"And you're a stuck-up princess who'd rather lie around and degrade our lifestyle than learn to save her own life." There's no passion in his voice, only a matter-of-fact tone, as if he's telling me about the weather. "Get yourself together and meet me in the yard."

I mumble curse words, shoving my foot into my boot and lacing it up. This is not the life I want to live, but I have no choice. Either I walk away from Grayson and his band of orphaned misfits, or I embrace them. It's all I have.

My fingers pull my hair into a messy ponytail as I walk across the yard to Bastian, who is sharpening knives again. "If you don't use them, don't they stay sharp?" Everything with him is a show.

"Who says I don't use them?" He doesn't look up from his task until he's done. When he lifts his head, his eyes bore into mine. "You've been out for fifteen hours, which doesn't make you the best authority on how I spend my time."

I bite my lip to prevent any more quarreling with my trainer. "Thank you." My pride is at basement level, and I've never really been good at expressing my feelings—not like Levi. "Thank you for saving me from Susan."

He turns and lifts a quiver from its spot beside a tree. "She was out of line. I train people from the Grove because they're our neighbors and we've got to look out for each other." He adjusts the strap of the quiver across his chest, where it looks as natural as any other feature of his body. "She's not kin and knows better than to threaten my family."

A rush of cold sweeps through me, sending an electrifying shiver down my spine. When did this change happen? I don't know what to say.

"Just because you're kin, doesn't mean I like you." He lifts his head, hair sweeping over his eyes. "Levi might think you're Redeemed, but with me, you need to earn it. The only thing you've shown me so far is how to get your face beaten into the ground. The city's made you weak."

"And you think that's my fault? Life Givers created me in a test tube with the right mixture of my mother's and father's DNA. From the second I was born, people waited on me hand and foot." Tears build as I recall my childhood—good times with my parents, my father leaving, learning to sew from my mother, my friends. "You're asking me to do things that were forbidden in Avren." I clench my fists, feeling an emotion building like fire in my veins. "You've got to have patience with me."

"Yeah, well, it's never been my strong suit. You've been here for less than two days, and you've already had a werewolf and a vamp on your trail." He lifts the bow and hands it to me. "Be thankful I'm not the patient type."

He tromps through the woods to the training ground. Afraid to follow too close, I keep a ten-pace distance, just far enough that he can hear me scream if I'm attacked. When we reach the open meadow, he digs into his pack and removes two apples, tossing one to me.

I sit down on a log and take a bite, still amazed by the freshness of the food in the wilderness.

"Gray will take you to your assignment this afternoon. We already received a warning because you didn't show up yesterday. If you're not there today, soldiers will come knocking on our door sooner or later. You won't know your duty until you check in." He takes one last giant bite of his apple and chucks the core into the woods, sending squirrels and various birds scattering. "My guess is dish duty."

"Dish duty?" I take another bite and contemplate his words. So much has happened since I left Avren. I haven't had time to think about the blue ring around my ankle and what it means. If I don't arrive at my scheduled time, soldiers from Avren will come looking for me. "They have to recognize my skills as a seamstress."

He quirks an eyebrow as he brushes his hands on his pants. "You sew?"

"Yes." I stand and throw my apple core. It lands with a satisfying thump beside Bastian's. "The official plan drawn out by my parents and approved by the Council was for me to open a shop when I turned eighteen."

"Oh." He tugs on the bottom of his shirt, exposing a gaping hole in the material. "Do you think you could help me out? You know, I give you a vamp ass-kicking lesson and you mend my shirts?"

"How about I teach you how to mend your own shirts? A Supe's bound to kill me one of these days, and you'll have to rely on yourself." I kneel beside him and lift the material to inspect the hole. "The seam's come undone. It won't be difficult to fix if you can find me a needle and thread."

He watches my fingers dance along the material. "I won't let *anything* happen to you, Mari."

I'm suddenly aware of how close we are, and my hands freeze. With one swipe of my finger, I could touch the bare skin of his stomach through the hole in his shirt.

He sucks in a breath and stands, leaving me alone on the ground and ashamed of my thoughts. "I mean, Levi seems to really like you, and I can't have him moping about for days on end because a werewolf tore you to shreds."

I stand and brush the dirt from my pants. "No, we wouldn't want that." The bow is resting against a tree, so I pick it up, ready to hit a target today. After being so close to him, I half-wish Rafe and his entourage would show up to distract me.

The angle of the sun tells me it's later than when we stood in the meadow yesterday. Bastian's not taking any chances. I take the stance he showed me, determined to demonstrate improvement.

He circles me, his gaze moving from the position of my feet to the angle of my arms, making my traitorous heart flutter. My dream was just a dream and nothing more. The Commander is only assessing my position like he would with any other recruit.

"Your spaghetti is a little firmer today." He nods and holds out his hand, and I place the bow in it. "I want to show you a couple of things." Bow and arrow in hand, he raises them to shoulder level, once again looking like a god. His piercing blue eyes never waver from his target as he releases the arrow and hits the center of a tree. "Keep your back as straight as your arm. Never let your eyes wander from your goal—hitting your enemy. Don't drop your weapon until you hit your mark." He hands me the bow and draws another arrow from the quiver.

I raise the weapon, notch the arrow, and pull back on the bowstring, setting my sights on Bastian's arrow buried in the tree. Before doing anything else, I straighten my back and root my feet into the ground. I imagine the tree bark is the living, fluid being who killed Tanner. This is my one shot.

Keeping my body as stiff as Bastian's, I release the arrow, only closing my eyes after it whizzes through the air.

"Why are your eyes closed?" he says, tapping me on the arm. "Look what you did."

I open my eyes to find my arrow buried in the tree right next to Bastian's. I smile, more out of a nervous shock than anything else.

He rubs his hands together and shoots me the first smile I've ever seen on his face, elevating his appearance tenfold. "She can be taught."

CHAPTER SEVEN

"*Y*ou need to fib a bit here." Grayson swipes a dab of the concoction Evie made under my eye to help mask the bruising. "As amazing as Evie's abilities are with natural elements, the guards of Avren will still notice it. Your sole purpose as an Undesirable is to serve Citizens. If they know you've been in a fight, they might place you in solitary."

The idea of safe alone time is tempting.

"You tripped when you arrived in the wilderness because you were unfamiliar with the rugged terrain—perfectly understandable for someone raised in the city." Grayson provides one last swipe and smiles at me. "Our privilege is our downfall. The Council can track us. With those born in the wilderness, they can avoid work duty unless caught by Avren's soldiers. Redeemed parents hide pregnancies all the time because the alternative is too devastating to think about."

"So that's why Levi, Bastian, and Evie don't have to work? They don't have anklets?" I glance at my reflection in a silver serving plate. I didn't see my eye before, but I'm sure it looks better.

"They do work, but on the side of the Redeemed, not the Citizens. It's how we earn credits to survive. You already know that Bastian is training resistance members. And it's against three different forces, you could say—the dark and the light. On one hand, we have Avren, the tower of civility and perfection. On the other, we have Arazian and his counter-resistance—a city of darkness—snatching the Redeemed to join his army of mutants. Lady Raven is well aware of his plans but shields the city from the darkness's very existence by lying to her people. As you know, in the city, fear leads to chaos. They value order above everything else. And then we have the Supes."

No one ever mentioned Arazian in the city. And when people went to the wilderness instead of the Unseen, it was considered a death sentence. I didn't know they were one and the same. The existence of a whole other city is mind blowing. "What is the other city called?"

"The First City." His lip quirks, and he shoots me a sideways glance as he places a lid on the jar of makeup. "Ironic, really. Arazian really has it out for the people of Avren more than anyone else. He was a powerful member of the Council, and a rumor surfaced at the time that he was Lady Raven's lover."

Lady Raven never married, choosing to commit her life to the city. The Council had erected a statue of her in the city square, an example of purity for the rest of us to look up to. Grayson's accusations seem sacrilegious. I no longer hold any loyalty to the leader, but denial flows through my veins. "You lie."

"It's only rumors. The further you're removed from a situation, the clearer you're able to see it. You'll find this in time, especially when you start your assignment." He covers my hand with his. "We are in a unique position. The others don't understand what we've been through. I'm glad you're here."

I can't yell at him after this. As much as I want to defend our leaders, Grayson has my best interests at heart—or at least I think he does. Changing the subject is my best course of action. "What's Evie's job?"

He rolls the jar of makeup between his hands. "She works at a Supe watering hole."

"You're definitely a liar." I rest my arms on the table, shooting one out to stop the hypnotic rhythm of the jar. I clutch it in my palm. "Humans don't work for monsters."

Grayson raises an eyebrow as he pitches back from me, a menacing sparkle in his eyes. "They do when they need insider information."

I swallow back the bile rising in my throat. This man, who seemed so caring a moment ago, allows his girlfriend to risk her life for information. My suspicions are true—Levi's the only sane one in the bunch. "Why isn't she dead?"

He leans the back of his chair against the wall, resting his boots on the table with a thump. "Mari, Mari. It's a symbiotic relationship. They need us for occasional feedings during dry season... to provide entertainment... as lovers. In return, they give us information about the two cities and keep us alive. Only the newbies are open for killings. If they can make it past a year, they're usually left alone."

"And that's why I'm in danger." I had thought Evie was only kidding about the Supes smelling my blood, but there is more truth to it than I had originally thought. "What does Evie do at the watering hole?"

"A bit of everything—sings, plays the piano, serves up drinks. Whatever the owners need that night." He removes a slip of paper from his pocket and tosses it on the table. "That's the newest information from last night."

I stare at the piece of paper, waiting for him to tell me what's on it.

"Go on," he goads, pointing at the parchment. "Open it."

Wrinkles crease the paper from its time in Grayson's pocket. I unfold it, taking in the flowery script before reading it aloud. "Arazian is on the move." I toss it to the center of the table. "What's that supposed to mean?"

He shoves the note back into his pocket. "Most of the time, Arazian keeps to himself, choosing to hole up in his throne room. He sends his mutants to do his dirty work while he sits back and reaps the benefits." The chair creaks as he moves his feet to the floor and stands. "He doesn't leave his city unless there's a damn good reason."

"And do your sources hint at this reason?" I shrug on a cloak Evie loaned me from a hook on the wall. The inside is lined with three daggers to use as a last line of defense. Grayson and I must cross through the luminescent forest to get to my work assignment.

He lifts a battered gray cloak from another hook and puts it on before inserting a key into a locked cabinet. "No, they're tight-lipped on the matter or have no clue, but that's highly unlikely." The cabinet is full of weapons—swords, knives, machetes, maces, bows and arrows. He removes one after the other, placing them strategically within the lining of his garment. A knife clatters to the floor. "Damn holes."

"I can help," I say, walking over to inspect the damage to the material. Moths and months, or even years, of placing sharp objects within have damaged the integrity of the fabric. "It will only take me five minutes if you have a needle and thread."

"No time for that." Grayson peers out the window at the setting sun. "And besides, we don't waste our credits on things like needles and thread."

"But you waste it on more weapons." In Avren, clothes make the person. That was part of the reason I'd trained to become a tailor. When someone looks good, they feel better about themselves. Here, in the wilderness, clothes have a more practical use. "The mighty Kindred Few will look pretty silly loaded down in weapons and rags."

He shoves one last dagger in his boot and tugs on the sleeves of his cloak as if he's suddenly self-conscious about his attire. Like he said, he'd understand better than the others. "Tell you what. You earn credits, and I'll let you buy material to make me a new cloak."

"And the others?" I already have designs running through my head, but where will I find the time? A lot of my day will already be full of training and work duty for Avren.

"You'll have to talk to them." He opens the front door of the cottage, blade in hand. The forest is quiet with the oncoming twilight as animals settle in for the night. "They'll probably want you to fix what they already have."

While my father worked for the Council, my mother was a mathematician, spending her days among like-minded individuals. They used their calculations for the betterment of the city by advising architects, engineers, and scientists. I inherited creativity from the Barellis side of the family. In his free time, my father painted exquisite landscapes of what he dreamed the wilderness looked like. It wasn't against the law to use his imagination in such a way, only to act upon it. When he left to see the wilderness he'd dreamed of, the Council exiled him from Avren.

The hike along the trail is different this time, partly because every small noise makes me want to run back to the cottage and partly because I have a weapon in my pocket. It provides me a small sense of security. I glance at Grayson walking beside me. Although he is slightly smaller in stature than Bastian, his presence and weapons settle my nerves. He took down a werewolf, so that must give him some badass credits.

He walks with conviction, and I struggle to keep up. But I don't complain. The forest sets every nerve on edge. "Besides your training with Bastian, Evie and I will work with you to reverse your brainwashing."

"I can think for myself." I stop. His statement offends me more than anything said so far in the wilderness. "You think you're so high and mighty because you've lived here for seven years. It takes time to adjust. We both lived for many years in Avren—our friends are there. You can't say it's all bad."

Grayson hangs his head, sunlight casting shadows on his face.

"How can you forget what it was like having everything you need, the comfort of a temperature-controlled apartment, and the peace permeating our lives?" I don't understand how he sees the wilderness, with its dangers and discomforts, as preferable.

He raises his eyes to mine. A fire burns behind them. It's a phenomenon I've never seen in another human. The only way I can describe it is passion. "The founders built the city on the backs of others, Mari. *Your* luxuries, *your* comfort, and *your* peace directly result from thousands of other people working for nothing and without a choice. We were no better than Arazian's zombies. The Council orchestrated our careers, our marriages, our sex lives with our spouse, our free time. To me, freedom means more than any kind of comfort or peace the city brings."

He walks ahead of me, and I remain quiet, chewing on his words. Within no time, the spires of the city come into view, rising from the darkening landscape like a pillar of golden hope. Seeing it again ignites a flame in the pit of my stomach, but I squash it as quickly as it rises.

I'm here to work.

As an Undesirable.

"After enough training, you'll make this trek yourself. For now, one of us will escort you. The others won't take you directly to the door since they're not tagged, but they can get you close enough so you're safe." With a quick glance around, he removes his cloak. I hand him mine, and he hides them both beneath a bush. He leads me along a trail that runs down a hillside to the opening of a massive cave. Dozens of Avren's guards keep watch at the entrance.

"Brought us a new one tonight, Grayson?" A shorter guard elbows the one beside him, who flashes his buddy a devious smile. "And a pretty one."

Grayson stiffens beside me but relaxes as he approaches the guards. "Mack... Kyle... this is Maribel Windsong." He waltzes past them, removes a clipboard from a metal box, and scans the paper attached with his finger. "Says here she's reporting to the Sweet Street Bakery." He tosses the clipboard onto the box. "I'll escort her there."

"Wait a minute." Kyle, the taller one, approaches me and lifts a finger to my hair. My stomach curls, but I remain still. "How do we know she isn't carrying a weapon?" His hand moves to my waist, and it takes everything within me to keep from trying out the leg sweep move. With his breath hot in my ear, he says, "I think I'm going to have to frisk her."

I don't know what I expect from Grayson. They have guns. He doesn't. The group also outnumbers him twenty to one.

"I'll vouch for her." Grayson snatches my arm and pulls me away from Kyle. "If anything happens, you can string me up in the city square and remove the blocks yourself." He doesn't let go, clutching me hard against his chest. "Ever since they kicked me out of the city, you've looked for an excuse. Maybe today's your lucky day."

"The Council knew you were an Undesirable from the day you were born." Mack spits, hitting Grayson in the face.

As the saliva runs over his cheek, he wipes it away with his sleeve, not bothering to give Mack any reaction to his degrading act.

"You can protect her this time, phaloc, but she won't always have you by her side." Kyle laughs as we pass, his eyes trailing me the entire way into the cave. Bastian's training seems more important than ever.

"I went to school with Kyle and Mack," Grayson says through gritted teeth. "There's something about being in the wilderness that brings out the worst in the people of Avren. They think that once they cross the line where they're no longer in the city, they can act like animals." He finally releases me as we enter an enormous cavern filled with machines and furnaces.

Men and women work the machines in oil-stained uniforms.

Some workers are missing an arm or leg; others have darker skin colors, or sign to their coworkers. Sweat covers their faces. The heat and noise within the cave are almost as intense as the turmoil brewing inside me.

The noise dims from the machines as we press farther into the hillside and closer to the city. Streets lined with shops materialize, still within the cave but providing a more pleasant atmosphere. Lanterns light the cobblestone walkways where people gather after a hard day's work. Couples sit at tables eating an evening meal with friends. Laughter and music come from a building where people are dancing inside. It's a mixture of Undesirables and Citizens. This is the neutral zone—a place my mother knew well. It surprises me to see it open with the current worries about the sickness.

Grayson lifts the corner of his lip. "This is the closest thing to freedom the people of Avren can experience. They still outlaw alcohol and dating, but the Council can't stop the people from having fun." He clasps a lamppost and spins around it, coming face-to-face with me. "Do you have a favorite song?"

The question strikes me as peculiar. In Avren, there is one song that is everyone's favorite. "The National Anthem." How could he expect any other response?

He taps the side of my head with his finger. "And that right there is brainwashing." Grayson dances over the cobblestones to the rhythm of the music coming from the nearby building. "Songs are supposed to be a matter of preference, not what you're told is your favorite by leadership." He dances up to me and places a hand over my heart. "What moves your soul, Mari?"

No one has ever asked me that question before. The Council appraised my skills and talents to determine my career path, to choose my leisure time activities, and eventually, they would have found my perfect match. It didn't matter what I wanted. My own thoughts and desires weren't even secondary in their decisions. To create the perfect society, we had to give up our destructive free will.

Thoughts of Flynn come rushing in, but they quickly morph into Bastian. My heart, and maybe soul, flutter at the memory of his touch. My cheeks warm as I push away my traitorous thoughts. "I don't know."

A wide smile pulls at his lips. "Then I will help you discover it."

The mouth of the cave opens to the pillared white walls of the city. My breath catches seeing it again. I search the fifth floor for the entrance to our apartment, but the buzz of the city draws my attention. Gorgeous people in exquisite dress, so familiar to me but seemingly a world away, grace the streets of Avren. My friends and Flynn are among them somewhere, and a fresh horror hits me. They might see me in my new role as an Undesirable. They will look at me the way I looked at the outsiders in the past. Guards stand watch, taking papers from workers.

"They won't let me go any farther without my own working papers." Grayson hands me a black wallet. "Do you know where Sweet Street is located?"

I roll my eyes. Every kid in Avren knows where the confectionary wonderland is located.

"Never mind," he says, brushing a wisp of hair from my forehead. It's endearing in an older brother kind of way. "You've got this. Don't let the hatred get to you." He places a hand over my heart. "Your worth is in here, and like Levi said, you're kin now. Someone will be at the entrance of the city to pick you up when your shift's over." He pats the top of my head and then he's gone.

I draw in a breath, aware of how Evie's clothes make me stand out among the elegantly clothed people of the city. The linen pants and cotton shirt are plain among the velvets and silks of the Citizens. Straightening my shoulders, I hold my head high, ready to learn the ways of the Sweet Street Bakery.

The bell above the door jangles as I walk in. A man behind the counter draws in his dark eyebrows. His countenance quickly changes as he turns back to his customer and hands her a bag. "Enjoy." As soon as she leaves, he sweeps around the side of the counter and all but shoves me to the back of the shop. "Never enter through the front door again."

"I'm sorry," I stutter, practically tripping over my shoes as he ushers me past workers kneading dough and pulling loaves of bread from hot ovens. "I didn't know there was a back entrance."

"There's always back doors for *phalocs* like you," he hisses. He opens a cupboard and removes a bundle of clothing, shoving it into my arms. "Get changed, and Kit will show you the ropes."

A woman with olive skin and beautiful brown hair assesses me from her workstation. She frowns.

He opens a door to a supply closet, then stomps away to serve another customer with a smile. I lay the clothes on a barrel and slump to the floor. My heart drops at the idea of having to prove myself yet again to a bunch of strangers. I gaze at the blue-and-white striped uniform, reluctant to take on another identity.

CHAPTER EIGHT

I pull my hair into a ponytail as I exit the supply closet, finally ready to take on whatever the Sweet Street Bakery will throw at me. This is not my skill set, but I'm willing to learn. Thoughts of the men and women in the cave remind me I'm lucky to procure a job assignment within the city.

The woman named Kit wipes her hands on her apron and crosses the kitchen to greet me. "You must be a former Citizen," she says, glancing at my hand as I hold it out to her.

I quickly hide it behind my back. "I'm Maribel. My father was on the Council about five years ago. Daxon Barellis?"

"Never heard of him," she says as she turns and marches back to the counter where she was working. "I don't keep up with politics or matters of state. They expelled my family when I was three."

"What for?"

The expulsion of an entire family is extremely rare.

"My parents had me without permission." She offers me a satisfied grin as her hands dive into a pile of dough. "The old-fashioned way."

"What?" My mouth hangs open. "But women take pills for that, and if it happens by accident, there are places to correct it."

"My parents didn't believe in those kinds of places." Kit frowns at me. She portions the dough in half and slides it toward me. "Here. Wash your hands and help me knead the dough. We're preparing the bread for tomorrow morning."

I stick my hands under the stream of water, still chewing on Kit's words. The Undesirables defy the Council, but to hear of Citizens actively going against orders is unheard of. When it comes to making babies, the Council always knows best— growing babies in test tubes, where things like hair color, eye color, and personality can be controlled, makes the most sense. Anything could go wrong if parents brought a naturally born baby to term.

But here I am standing beside a woman who was born the natural way and I see nothing wrong with her. In fact, she's beautiful with her dark almond eyes, straight brown hair, and shapely figure. She'd fit in with the people of Avren, but she's baking their bread. Other than Levi's hearing impairment, I've seen nothing wrong with the people born the natural way in the wilderness either.

I slide beside Kit at the counter, placing my hands in the dough. It feels cold and elastic, but the sensation of forming and reforming it over and over with my knuckles relaxes me.

"Guy is the owner." Kit tosses the dough into the air and slams it back down on the counter. "He's a Citizen. Bit rough around the edges, but once he knows you're a good worker, he'll warm up to you." She points to a man beside the oven. "That's Felix."

The man gives me a quick salute and returns to his job.

"And that's Robert." She nods her head toward a younger man squirting icing out of a tube onto a pan of rolls. "Guy was in line to receive the newest person expelled from the city, so the officials sent you here."

"Do you ever switch jobs?" When I lived in the city, the

workers in the shops and Caron came to mind when I thought about Undesirables. I never imagined the harsh working conditions in the caverns for the people who keep the inner bowels of the city running.

Kit smirks and pounds her fist into the dough. "Got your first glimpse of the Unseen." It isn't a question. She knows I had to come that way to enter the city. "Nothing you need to worry about unless you cause trouble. You're an Untouchable."

"What's that mean?" I slow my hands in the dough.

Kit places her dough into a ceramic bowl and covers it with cloth. "Although we're considered Undesirable, there are different classes within the system. Only the highest class may work in the city. We were Avrenian as children. We know their ways." She carries the dough to a windowsill, and when she returns, takes mine and works it. "The next class are those who the authorities expelled in good standing. They at least know how the city operates, but for some reason, didn't fit in. The children of the Undesirable come next if they're caught. Because they don't have a tracking anklet, the guards seldom catch them." She slows her kneading and looks me in the eye. "The last group are the criminals. People the Council expelled for crimes against the higher order. They wear red anklets so others can identify them. The Council assigns them to the worst jobs. With no rights or protections, the guards work them to their limits using corporal punishment."

It's the Council's heavy hand that keeps crime out of the city. Although I don't agree with abusing the criminals, it makes sense to keep them in line.

"Do you know what the number one crime in Avren is?" She places my mound of dough in another bowl.

I can't imagine what it might be because I never saw a crime happen within the walls of the city. "Stealing?"

She laughs as she carries the bowl to the windowsill. "In a place where they give you everything you'd ever need? No, Mari."

She leans against the counter, lowering her voice. "It's plotting against the Council."

Inhaling sharply, I furrow my brow and shake my head. "Why would anyone want to threaten the Council?"

"Think about what happened to you... to me... to Felix and Robert." Her gaze rests on the other two workers. "We did nothing wrong. I was *three years old*. What kind of human expels a toddler to the wilderness, which they know is full of Supes? Can you answer that question?"

It isn't something I ever questioned—it's the law. My conversation with Grayson from earlier floats to the forefront. *Reversing your brainwashing.* "Do you think the Council expels someone at the first hint of dissension?"

"That's exactly what they do. If you don't fit into their perfect world because you look or think differently, you're gone." She joins Robert at the icing station, picking up a bag of confectionary sugar and emptying it into a large bowl.

I chew on her words before following. It doesn't make sense to me. "But what about the orphans? They did nothing to deserve the wilderness."

Robert raises a dark brow his eyes meeting Kit's. He's ruggedly handsome, and I sense a connection between them. "You're an orphan for a reason."

"Yes, my mom got sick." The feelings run fresh through every nerve in my body. "An Undesirable like you brought it into the city and infected her. She did nothing wrong."

"The healers have the antidote," Robert says flatly as he carefully creates a delicate swirl on a cinnamon roll. "The Council instructed them not to use it."

"How do you know this?" My voice rises, and the others glance at the door. I lower my voice, knowing they are fearful Guy might walk in. "Why wouldn't they save her?"

"What happened to your father?" Kit asks.

My father. The one who walked away from his family because of his fascination with the wilderness. "He left on his own."

"And you said he was on the Council before?" She stares at me as if she wants me to connect the impossible dots.

"Are you saying my father committed a crime and was expelled to the wilderness, so the Council punished us?" It's an outrageous claim—one I never considered before. As a member of the Council, he'd know things he wouldn't share with me.

She sighs and places a hand on my arm. "We don't know what really happened." Her eyes meet Robert's, his lips purse. "But we know what the Council is capable of. They released the sickness into select portions of the wilderness. Places where the rebellion percolated. But they used it more as a weapon against their own people, blaming the Undesirables for the ramifications. If they used it against your family, there must be a reason."

"How do you know this?" The immensity of her claim is almost too much to handle. If it's true, the Council, in whom I've always trusted to care for the people of Avren, are the enemy.

"Unless you find out the truth, you can never see things the way they really are." Robert lowers his lips close to my ear and whispers, "We are part of the rebellion." He passes his tray of cinnamon rolls to Felix to place in the oven. "The Council sent me to the wilderness with my mother when I was eleven because the guards caught my father in his bedroom with another woman. It tore our family apart—my father with a red anklet and my mother and I with blue. Two different classes in the fallen world."

"Maribel! Get up here! I need your help!" Guy barks at me from the front of the shop.

I almost trip over my feet trying to please my boss, an unfamiliar situation. A line stretches outside the door, snaking to the right, making me wonder if Guy is adding a secret sauce to the bakery items.

My boss's face is red, perspiration slick on his forehead as he ducks into a glass cabinet and removes two cinnamon rolls. "Here." He gives me the rolls wrapped in paper. "Put these on a tray and deliver them to table seven."

Tray? Table seven? I think he forgets this is my first day.

Beneath the counter, there's a stack of blue trays, so I remove one and set the rolls on top of it. I scan the store for table numbers.

"Put them on a damn plate, phaloc," Guy hisses as he removes three more pastries. "The rolls are going to Citizens, not vermin like you. I swear, all they send me are imbeciles."

My cheeks flame as my heart races with the shame of his words. Never did my parents speak to Caron like this. It was almost as if she was a member of the family. My hands shake, placing the paper-covered rolls on a gold-lined plate.

Table seven. I don't want to ask Guy anything.

The tray wobbles in my hands as I cross the floor, weaving in and out of patrons, trying to find the correct order. Customers lounge at the tables, laughing and talking—like I used to do with my friends—clueless to what lies beyond the walls of the great city. Small placards with pink borders stand in the center of each table, identifying their numbers. Seven is by the window.

I freeze.

Flynn sits beside Rosie, his arm draped over the back of her chair. He has a wide smile on his face, his attention on the guy opposite him. He laughs, and my stomach clenches remembering how we used to laugh together.

I skirt around the edge of the table, slightly behind Flynn, hoping he won't look up. He can't see me as an Undesirable. I need him to remember how it used to be—long talks in the city park, *accidental* brushes of skin, and heated kisses in secret. If he sees me this way, I don't think I can take it.

Without a word, I place the tray on the table and turn to walk away, ready to leave this part of my life behind.

"Maribel?" a woman at the table calls.

I stop and close my eyes. I could ignore the woman's recognition—continue walking away.

I turn.

Flynn's eyes meet mine. Warm brown pools flecked with gold assess me—the woman he would have really wanted beside him —if my mother hadn't died.

"I'm sorry about your mother," the woman, a distant memory from school, continues to ramble. "It really wasn't fair."

Her voice drifts over my shoulder, lost in the haze filling my mind. I don't move my eyes from Flynn's to acknowledge her, afraid I'll lose him forever if I do. He speaks volumes without uttering a word.

My body shudders, and I feel like I'm going to be ill. I rush to the rear of the shop, intent on reaching the supply closet before I empty the contents of my stomach. The door slams behind me. The vomit splatters into the corner, covering the cement cinderblocks. I lean an elbow against the wall and rest my head as my body continues to shake.

The door cracks open.

"Go away." I don't want Kit or Robert to see the mess in the corner.

The door squeaks as he enters, and I look up. Flynn's blondish-brown hair falls over his right eye. He strings it behind his ear, a move I've helped him with many times before. "Maribel. Can we talk?" He takes a step into the closet, then stops, plugging his nose. "What died in here?"

Our love. Any hope for the future I created in my mind.

"I think you should go." I roll a mop bucket over the puke and hope he'll go away. "Don't want to catch the sickness from an Undesirable."

His forehead creases in pain. "I still love you. It's not your fault the Council banished you from the city." He reaches for my hand, so I slip it behind my back.

"But they did." I take a step backward, intent on keeping our conversation light and professional. I'm the worker, he's the patron. If only he'd stay at his table like the well-behaved customers.

"What if we could change that?" The gold flecks in his eyes intensify as he continues to push for something I'm not sure I want anymore.

Not since seeing the wilderness.

"The same Council has ruled for eight years, never opposed. A vote might force some of them to step down and give us the opportunity to write a new history." He runs his fingers through his hair, giving him the tousled look I always loved. "A group of us meet every week to discuss the changes we want to bring to the Council. They've got to listen to reason."

"The idea is wonderful, but what if you fail? They'll kick you out of the city too." I run a finger along the hem of my uniform shirt. "It's better this way," I say in the strongest voice I can muster. I draw in a deep breath, trying to find the courage. "You have your future with Rosie. I have mine. The Council will never allow a Citizen and a phaloc to be together."

The heat of his stare makes me uncomfortable. He can't let go of what can never be. I hold my arm over my mouth and nose, wondering how badly my breath reeks.

He stops a couple of feet away, stuffing his fists in his pockets. "Promise me something."

"I can't make promises I can't keep, Flynn."

He's close enough that if I raise my arm, I can touch him. "Promise me to never refer to yourself as a phaloc again. You are so much better than them." With one step, he closes the distance, raising a palm to my cheek.

My insides twist in confusion. I'm a wreck of nerves and desire, unsure if I want to kiss him or run away. "Guy will wonder where I am." I brush past him and head out the door, ready to get back to work. Empty hope no longer plays a role in my life.

"Where have you been, worthless girl?" Guy bends over, reaching into the pastry case. His pants slip to reveal a crack.

It's just what I need to relieve my nerves. My lips tug into a smile as I hand my boss two more plates to load for the customers.

CHAPTER NINE

*W*ith my initial training done, I hurry along the streets of Avren, avoiding eye contact with Citizens. The run-in with Flynn has my mind racing. Was he in a relationship with Rosie? Did the Council match them? Did he get the job as a soldier like he wanted?

Get it together, Mari. You've only been gone two days.

With my job at the Sweet Street Bakery, I will see him again. What if he insists on pursuing a relationship that can never be?

I shove my hands into my apron pockets as I approach the neutral zone. I've stuffed four fresh rolls inside. Nervous, I scan the mix of people for a familiar face—one who might get me back to my bed in one piece.

"It's about time you made it out here," Evie grumbles as I approach. Her curly auburn red hair is piled on top of her head. She's wearing a short brown leather jacket, which I'm sure is filled to the brim with weapons. My *kin* wouldn't enter the luminescent forest unprepared.

I shrug, trying to act nonplussed by her comment. If I can't walk two steps without a Supe killing me, I'll need protection. "I leave when Guy lets me." I reach into the pocket of my pants to pull out a handful of coins. "At least I can contribute to our household."

She stares at the small pieces of metal in my palm. "Worthless in the wilderness, phaloc. Avren's the only place that takes *meetok*."

Meetok is the currency used to buy smaller things in the city. Credits hold the real value. "Then I will spend my coins on Sweet Street." I brush past her, although I'm unsure of the exact direction of the way out.

She catches up to me, giving a sideways glance. "What's Sweet Street?"

I stop and raise an eyebrow, unsure if I want to share the rolls with Evie and Bastian. "You're dating Gray, and he's never told you about the great things inside the city?"

"Gray doesn't open up about his past life." She takes a slight lead down an alley, so I follow. "It's a bit of a painful subject for him."

"We're orphans. He's not the only one dealing with shitty circumstances." Seeing Flynn this evening conjured a lot of old memories. Not only did I lose my mother, but I lost my friends, my status, my future.

She pauses at a corner and lets a group of Citizens pass, laughing like they don't have a care in the world. They'll head up to their cozy apartments without the fear of rabid werewolves attacking them. Envy over what I lost courses through me.

"Don't judge his circumstances until you hear his story." Her heeled boots click over the cobblestones. "Gray's past makes the rest of ours seem like a fairytale."

I keep quiet as we pass the guards watching over the mouth of the cave. In the dark, I can't tell if the two that gave me trouble on the way in are still here.

"Stick close, Windsong," Evie whispers, tucking her arm into mine. She lifts her hood over her curls. "Lift the hood of your cape. The worst of the wolves guard the mouth of the cave and feed on innocent girls."

"I met two of them on the way in," I say as I raise the covering over my head and keep up with her long strides. Based on her appraisal of the guard situation, I can tell she's been the subject of harassment before.

When we finally reach the switchbacks leading up the hill to the forest, both of us release the breath we held passing the guards. Evie lets go of my arm and removes a long, curved blade from the inside of her jacket. It glimmers in the light of the moons above.

"Have you ever had to use that?" I ask, unsure of how I will ever get to where I can intentionally take another life—Supe or not.

"At least three or four times a month." She doesn't stop her ascent up the trail to wait on my slow, labored steps.

As much as Avren prepared me for academic success, they reserve physical training for soldiers. The climb up the hill Grayson and I descended earlier might kill me before a Supe has the chance. Heart racing, I stare up at Evie, who is almost at the top. I try to catch my breath, my palms braced against my knees as I lean forward. What I wouldn't give for a glass of water.

"Come on, slowpoke," Evie calls from above. "We have a surprise waiting for you at the cabin."

I don't want any surprise Evie has to give me, but if Levi and Grayson are involved, it might not be too bad. All I want to do is flop down on my bed and process my chance meeting with Flynn.

When I finally reach the top, Evie leans against a tree, eating an apple like the one Grayson gave us the first night. Beneath the luminescence of the tree above, with the soft glow highlighting her features, she appears to be an angel, not the demon she's presented to me. Will there ever come a time when I can refer to this woman as my sister?

She pushes from the tree and begins down the trail, not giving me a second to rest. I'll learn to savor the times when Grayson or Levi travel with me to work.

"If you can't tell me about Gray"—I jog to settle in beside her —"tell me more about Bastian. What's his story? He mentioned something about working on his father's farm. What happened to his parents?"

"Bastian's more secretive than Gray." She reaches up and plucks a glowing leaf from the tree above us. Without missing a step, she pulls a small black pouch from her bag and shakes a powdery substance onto the leaf. She rolls it up, finally stops to strike a match against the bark of a nearby tree, and lights the end of the leaf, sticking the other end in her mouth. Smoking— just like Bastian. "You make me nervous. It's a wonder Gray can stand to be around you."

Nervous? Because of me? I'm the one trying to navigate a world that is completely foreign to me. "I can't hit a target five feet in front of me with an arrow. I don't know what you need to be nervous about."

"That you're a spy sent here to infiltrate the opposition. Lady Raven wants to squash the rebellion before they set foot in Avren." She sends a puff of smoke in my direction. "I don't trust you."

"Then why send me to the city for work if you think I'm going to relay information to them?" I grip my hair, feeling the reality of my circumstances crashing down around me. If what Robert said about the Council intentionally releasing the sickness is true, then I understand Evie's concerns. "After all these years, surely someone has removed these tracking anklets."

Evie keeps her head down as she walks, crunching the gravel beneath her feet. "Besides those born in the wilderness, only one person has successfully left Avren, removed his anklet, and lived a life free from the interference of the soldiers." She looks at me, and for the first time, I sense fear in her eyes. The woman holds an air of silent confidence like a shield, warding away those who wish to defy her. "Arazian."

"Gray mentioned how he was on the Council many years ago before I was born. He said Lady Raven took him as a lover." I purse my lips, the wiring in my brain convinced I just uttered a blasphemy. But I want to understand the world I grew up in better, from the outside looking in.

"He witnessed the disgraceful ousting of the man determined to change Avren for the better. Gray was only five years old, but the pageantry of Arazian's expulsion left a lasting mark on him." Evie drops her leaf and grinds it into the dirt with the toe of her boot. "He vowed that day he would never go through that kind of shame. But look at what leading his life as a model Citizen got him."

And me.

I had expected the disrespect from the Undesirables. A person fallen from her high and mighty perch in the perfect city. Maybe we deserve to feel an ounce of what they feel. But in the Sweet Street Bakery, I never expected Guy's barking orders—for him to call me a phaloc. A place where in the past, he had greeted me with a smile and served me as the daughter of a Citizen.

"Tell me more about the First City." Images of a black fortress surrounded by dead trees, dying people, and black birds pecking at their flesh come to mind.

"We don't travel in that direction." Evie ducks beneath a low-hanging branch, letting it swing back and almost hit me in the face.

I duck, annoyed but waiting for an answer to my question. "But you know about it from stories."

"I've lost friends to the First City," she quips. "It's built on the site of the Great Battle where Lady Raven sent her forces in blind. None of them came back. The walking carcasses of Avrenians built his fortress on top of a graveyard filled with their own soldiers. He used the sweat and sheer power of the Redeemed and Supes to create his unholy city, then turned them into his army of unnatural beings, ready to take down anyone who stands in their way."

"In the way of what?"

"The total annihilation of Citizens and taking back Avren." She lets out a soft chuckle as if the idea pleases her too. "He's biding his time, having his zombie crew snatch more unwilling recruits for his army. I honestly think he's afraid of the prophecy."

"What prophecy?" In Avren, I was told to not rely on supernatural folklore. Wisdom, science, and education are the pillars of any successful society.

"The ancient books of the unspoken laws of the fae world reveal what is to come for the two cities. A great fae ruler wrote them before either city existed." Evie lowers her voice as we are now in darkness, the luminescent forest well behind us. "It is said that both cities will fall at the hands of the two who will rise from the center. The center is the wilderness. With the cities gone, the Redeemed and Supes will forge a treaty and live in peace."

"Do you really think that will happen?" In my world, the Council was a stronger force than a multitude of armies.

"It *is* happening." She leaves the words hanging between us as the cabin's warm lights appear before us.

Relief spreads through me. I'm thankful we didn't have any Supe run-ins.

Bastian opens the door wearing a tunic and woolen pants. I'm surprised it's him and not Levi. He gives us a curt smile and heads back to an armchair beside the soft glow of an oil lamp. A book lies open on the ottoman. "How was the first shift?"

I remove two rolls from my pocket but leave the meetok buried at the bottom. I toss him a roll, which he catches in one hand. "As mortifying as I thought it might be."

He bites into his roll, muttering something indecipherable and plops into the armchair, picking up his book.

I hold the other roll out to Evie. "Thank you for bringing me home."

Ignoring my gesture, she turns to Bastian. "Where did the other two go? I thought they wanted to give Mari her surprise."

"Meeting of the minds," he says, not taking his eyes from his book. "The Sillaby Wood Church." He glances at her, and a silent message passes between them, making me feel like an outsider again.

"It can wait until the morning," she says, plopping down in a chair at the table.

Instead of questioning them about the other two or my surprise, I stretch my arms above my head. "I'm tired. I'll see you in the morning."

Without looking up, Bastian says, "Bright and early, sunshine."

I mutter multiple curse words under my breath as I stomp to my bedroom. On top of my late work assignment, I'm still required to train at ungodly hours in the morning. My trainer might be the death of me.

With my head on the pillow, I avoid thoughts of Flynn. What I need right now is sleep, and replaying my time with him might keep me up for hours. The sound of the lonely song of a musical instrument in the other room lulls me into a dreamless sleep.

THE CLOMP OF his boots on the floorboards wakes me before sunrise, but today I don't protest as I roll from my mattress.

Before I can tie on my boots, Bastian reaches for my hand and leads me to the common room. My eyes are drawn to a leather fighting suit, including pants, a long-sleeved shirt, and vest, shining in the light of an oil lamp.

He drops my hand. "It was Evie's idea, but we all agree that you can't wear that horrible canvas getup anymore. It gives us a bad reputation."

I circle the table, running my fingers along the well-crafted seams, the crisscrossing straps to hold weapons I haven't earned, and the soft leather. Never in my life have I worn something that will cling so closely to my body. In Avren, we wear tailored clothing, but it is still modest. The canvas outfit made me look like a sack of coal used to heat the city. But this one outfit might change my entire outlook on my current life—like maybe I can be as strong as Bastian, as badass as Evie, and as crafty and deadly as Grayson.

"Where did it come from?" I ask, daring to lift it from the table to admire the handiwork of the tailor. I want to make new fighting gear for my *family*, but I don't know where to start to get the material. Whatever I can afford with my meetok won't come close to this.

Bastian lifts a shoulder, his dark hair tied back for our early morning session. "We pooled our credits. Like I said, thought you should look the part. Maybe you'll hit a target with your arrow today."

I go back into my room. Levi's not there. His bed is still made like he didn't come home at all last night. My gut twists in concern, not liking the feeling of not knowing where my brothers went for their meeting. I pull on the new clothes, and they fit as snuggly as I had expected.

I step out of the room and head outside, where Bastian waits for me. He has his back turned, sharpening his knife. Once again, I admire him, Flynn miles away in my thoughts.

"Are you ready?" I ask, feeling like I have nowhere to hide in the skintight leather clothes.

He turns and my cheeks flame as he assesses me. "You look good." Then he heads into the forest.

I don't know what I expected. A positive appraisal from someone who detests me is better than nothing.

CHAPTER TEN

"*L*evi didn't come back last night." My statement pushes the boundaries of my relationship with Bastian, but if I'm part of this family, I need someone to open up to about what's going on.

"He didn't." He keeps his back to me and continues his trek to the practice field. Instead of expounding, he changes the subject. "We'll head to the Grove today after our archery lesson."

Fantastic. I can't wait to spend quality time with Bastian's girlfriend and her squad.

"Why can't we continue our private lessons? I need to save my energy for my job in the city." I tug at the leather on my thigh, trying to keep it from riding up my crotch as we walk.

He stops. His shoulders move up and down with his breaths. "The less time we spend alone together, the better."

"Because you can't stand me?" Heat rushes to my extremities as anger builds. I have tried everything to fit in with Bastian and Evie. I've followed their directions, staying out of their way as needed.

"I don't want to talk about it," he hisses, never turning to look at me. "We shoot a few arrows and get over to our group practice.

Believe me, the less time we spend together, the better it will be for both of us."

"I couldn't agree more." How did I ever find this man attractive? He can't stand to look at me, let alone take time teaching me the skills I need to survive in the wilderness. Why didn't he let the vampire drain my blood and save both of us a bunch of trouble?

In the field, he allows the quiver to slide from his shoulder and land with a thud in the tall grass. Arrows scatter. It's unlike his normal calm and brooding disposition. He bends, scoops up an arrow, takes his stance, and shoots. The arrow pierces a hanging piece of fruit and drives it into the bark of a nearby tree, reducing it to pulp.

Holy mother of badasses. I'm sorry. As much as he's not my favorite person right now, that was hot, and at the same time, scary.

I pick up an arrow and tap its shaft against my palm. "How many practice sessions do you think I'll need to do that?"

"About a million." He hands me the bow but doesn't make eye contact. His thick lashes cover the hypnotic crystal blue. It's better, anyway. I don't need to waste my thoughts on a person who hates my guts.

I set my stance, raise the bow, and nock an arrow. The forest is full of wide trees to hit. It can't be that hard. The past two times I tried, I instinctually closed my eyes right before releasing the arrow. Bastian had said to keep my attention on the target— to see the head pierce the wood. I pull back on the string, keeping the arrowhead in line with the center of a tree and my eyes wide. When I release, I keep the bow raised and my attention on my target. It splinters the wood and sticks.

A rush of adrenaline hits me, and I throw my arms around Bastian's neck. "I did it!"

He laughs, but his body is stiff, not reciprocating my hug. "Yes, you did."

I drop my arms, and he backs away slightly, enough to show me he didn't want me entering his personal space.

"Again," he says, lifting another arrow from the quiver. "It's not enough to hit a target once every ten times. When you have Avrenian's army marching toward you, you can't miss."

I nock my second arrow, set my stance, and focus on a tree to the left of the one I just hit. Adrenaline rushes through me with the high of possibly being good at something. I pinch the arrow tight between my fingers, ready to release.

A cool stream of air brushes along my neckline, breaking my concentration, and I release, sending the arrow high into the canopy above.

"What did you do that for?" I whip around to face him.

He's so close, I can feel the heat radiating from his body as we're inches away. I want to step back, but an invisible string ties me to him, and I'm rooted to the ground.

"Distraction." His lips are so full, making me wonder what kissing them might be like. "If you can't keep your focus, mentally and physically, you've already lost."

An awkward half-smile crosses his lips as he steps away and gathers the arrows into the quiver. "I think that's enough for today."

I lift the bow, blood pumping hard through my veins. The rush of having him so close and hitting the tree a second time makes me feel alive in this strange world. "But I want to try again to see if it was only a fluke or if I'm onto something. Give me another arrow."

He lifts the quiver to his shoulder, still refusing to look at me. "The others are waiting. We'll see if you can master your kicks with the same precision."

Although disappointed, I puff out my chest and straighten my back as we walk through the woods to the Grove. For the first time since entering the wilderness, I'm proud of myself. In Avren,

I had plenty of accomplishments, but here it's like I'm starting over.

Bastian walks ahead of me—never beside me. He's the Commander, and I'm the inadequate soldier. I thought I had broken through his icy shield, but that's not the case. Today he has made it clear that we're not to be friends.

The others already wait in the Grove when we arrive. I want Bastian to proclaim my victory, but he remains tight-lipped. The men scuffle in the grass while the women sit on the logs, chatting.

Susan jumps up to greet Bastian as we approach, but not before taking a moment to rake her eyes down my leather outfit. "Looks like the Kindred Few finally accepted the princess." She wraps her arms around his neck, where mine had been minutes before, and pulls him into a kiss.

He keeps it short despite her efforts. "It was Evie's idea. Thought she needed to look the part of our sister."

Evie. Despite her gruff exterior, maybe the idea of another woman in the house is important to her. Between this and my success with the bow, I'll check this off as a banner day.

Rafe approaches and circles me, appraising my new garb. "You brought her wrapped as a present for me today, Commander." Once again, I want to knock the goofy grin from his face.

"Leave her alone," Bastian all but growls, and my stomach tightens. "I know Susan and Laurel plan to have us all matched, but she's my sister, and I don't want her with you."

Rafe holds a palm to his chest and stoops forward as if in great pain. "That hurts, Commander. After all we've been through?"

"Mari will choose who she wants to be with when the time is right, if ever." The authority in his voice puts a period on the end of the conversation for Rafe, who slinks away from us.

My insides are in turmoil. On one hand, he's acting like a protective older brother; but on the other, this is coming from someone who just told me he wants nothing to do with me except our obligatory time to train. "I'm ready to fight."

"Laurel can teach you the leg sweep today," Bastian says flatly, removing his weapons. "She has a little less bite than Susan."

Confusion still clouds my thoughts as the next words slip out. "I want to fight you."

"No." He tosses his weapon belt to the ground, its clatter emphasizing his word.

Ready to leave my old self behind, I shove him in the chest. "Afraid of me?"

He crosses his arms over his massive muscles. Clearly, fear isn't the first word coming to his mind. "No."

I shove him again, and he snatches my wrist, pulling me close. Our faces are inches apart. The intensity of the heat radiating between us as his blue eyes pierce mine brings me back to the meadow. In a matter of seconds, it is as if the entire world around us disappears, and he is all that exists.

"I will not fight you, Mari." He releases me, storming to the center of the Grove to join Mav and leaving me feeling like a pile of mush.

I shake my head. It's a bunch of nonsense conjured by a stupid teenage girl with a crush on a totally unworthy person.

My goal is to survive, and it starts with learning from Laurel. Unlike Susan, who wears tight leathers like me, the other woman has on a green tunic and brown leather pants. She's sharpening a stick with a knife beside the fire. Her auburn hair and sun kissed freckles give her a natural beauty, missing from the people of Avren. A woman born of the wilderness, living like this her entire life.

"The Commander said I'm supposed to practice my leg sweep with you." I sit down beside her to watch her whittle.

She smirks, a dimple forming on her left cheek. This close, I see a smattering of freckles beneath her eyes more clearly. "It's 'Bastian' unless he's in earshot."

"Got it."

"He's already got a big enough head." She tosses her stick to the side, lays her knife on the log, and stands. "But I think you already know that."

I smile, grateful for a friend. "Mav seems like a good guy." In the city, we never talked aloud with our friends about boys. To admit we had a crush on someone might negate them from our match pool if the Council got wind of it. Flynn and I were too reckless.

"He is. And Rafe's decent too." She watches the two of them sword fight along the perimeter. "It's been a while since he bedded a woman, and he's a bit desperate."

I catch my breath, unsure of how to respond. She has confirmed the reality of the rumors I'd heard in Avren about the wilderness. "Well, desperate doesn't look good on him."

Laurel laughs, tossing an arm around my shoulder. "I think I like you."

For the next half hour, Laurel works with me on the ins and outs of a good leg sweep, teaching me every trick she knows. If I can master this move, I can bring my opponent to the ground, where I will have the upper hand.

She stands before me, arms raised and ready to fight. I block her incoming punches, catching her off guard. While she's vulnerable, I bend my left leg slightly to give myself more power in my sweep, knocking Laurel to the ground. Rubbing her butt, she adjusts to her hands and knees, a position where I could easily kick her in the face if this were an actual fight.

I hate that my brain works this way now.

"That was great!" She brushes her pants with her palm as she stands. "I'll let Bastian know you're ready for the next step."

But she doesn't have to. He approaches with a wide grin—one I don't see too often. "Excellent work, Laurel."

What about me?

Laurel loops her arm around my back and squeezes me to her. "She's an exceptional student, Commander."

A man enters the Grove from the far end near the cottages. His face is as white as the snow I've seen in picture books as he approaches Mav.

"That's Mav and Lyden's father," Bastian says. "Maybe he has news." He leaves us and crosses the field to join them.

We follow close behind, not wanting to miss out on anything.

"Hello, Bastian." The man addresses the Commander with as much authority as the rest of his followers. "We think we've found Lyden, but we need to form a reconnaissance team to investigate the trail before it goes cold." His eyes well with tears. "I just don't know what I'll do without either of my two boys."

"Any clue as to who has him?" Rafe hops onto a pile of hay, resting his hands between his knees. "If it's a Supe, I've got his number right here." When he taps his chest, his weapons jangle inside his coat.

"Can't know for sure if it is a Supe, Citizen, or the Miscretes." He lifts his cap and runs a hand over his balding head. "Ganon said an innkeeper saw him about a week ago heading into the Ringlet Forest, accompanied by unsavory hooded creatures."

"What are Miscretes?" I whisper to Laurel.

"What was that, Mari?" Susan raises an eyebrow.

I clutch my hands, not wanting to proclaim my lack of knowledge to the entire group.

"If you have something to say, tell all of us." Susan glares at Laurel as if she is an accomplice to my crime.

Part of me is glad Susan looks so petty calling me out while there are much more important things to discuss. "Who are the Miscretes?"

"The mutants who serve Arazian both willingly and unwillingly. The real term is Miscreations, but we call them Miscretes for short. When Avren's little test tube experiments go wrong, the Dark King has someone there to clean up the mess and deliver more followers to his ever-growing army."

"That's terrible." All my life, I thought growing babies in a test tube was a good thing—more parental choice, less disease, fewer Undesirables. But the idea of having a whole new class of people deemed mistakes makes me cringe.

"And that is one reason the Council needs to be stopped." Bastian is beside me, a stalwart tower, his deep voice resonating through me. With relative ease, he scoops up a sword and sheathes it at his hip. "Have you gathered a group of fighters from the village?"

Mav's father shakes his head, lowering his hat to his heart. "We're simple farmers, you know that. Our pitchforks and shovels will be no match."

"Then we'll go." It's not a question but a definitive statement. "Gray and Evie can join us, making us seven strong. My lucky number."

I silently count the numbers in my head.

"We leave first thing in the morning for the Ringlet Forest. Don't worry, Carl. We'll come back eight strong with Lyden." He rests a hand on the man's shoulder and gives it a reassuring squeeze. "Come, Mari. I have work to do."

As he walks away, I rush over to the logs to gather the quiver and bow. Bastian's ideas differ from mine. Earlier, I hit the tree with an arrow. Maybe it wasn't a tiny piece of fruit, but since leaving Avren, it was the first time I felt proud of an accomplishment. With the bow and arrow, I could help on this mission.

When I finally catch up to him, I'm out of breath and determined to find my place in my new family. "The count back there didn't include me."

He keeps his eyes forward, pulling a square piece of paper and more powdery substance out of his pouch. Stopping, he strikes a match against a rock and lights the end of the paper like Evie had done on the way home yesterday. "No, it didn't."

"With my bow and arrow skills, I can help." I slip an arrow out of the quiver, ready to prove myself again.

He lets out a stifled laugh. "What bow and arrow skills?" He snatches the arrow from my hand and taps it against the bark. "You mean hitting one tree earlier today?"

"Come on, Bastian." I hate begging, but I can't imagine sitting around the cabin with Levi, both of us locked inside and bored out of our minds. "If Gray and Evie go, who's going to take me to work?"

"You won't go. It takes at least a week for the dumbass soldiers of Avren to organize a search party for missing workers. Truth is, they're too scared the Supes will snatch the Undesirables and all they'll find is the blue anklet in their lair seconds before they're the next meal." He takes a long drag on the end of the paper, making me suddenly fascinated with his lips. A small scar is visible on them as they curve around the smoking stick, too alluring to focus on for longer than a few seconds. "There's no telling what has Lyden. You being there puts the rest of us in more danger."

With a little more drag in my step, I follow behind my commander, determined to help rescue Mav's brother somehow.

CHAPTER ELEVEN

*B*astian taps the edge of each boot on a stump outside the cabin, knocking away any loose mud. Voices come from the living area. My shoulders relax at the thought of Levi and Grayson making it back home. I don't like the secrets kept from me, but even I must admit two days is a little soon for anyone to be fully trusted.

With a thud, Bastian drops his bag on the table. "They've found Lyden. Arazian's lackeys dragged him to their hideout in the Ringlet Forest. My crew from the Grove will join us in the morning to assist in the rescue."

Grayson curses, his arms elbow-deep in dishwater. "When will I ever get a decent rest around here? First, I travel to collect Mari, then Levi and I go to see..." He stops, his face pale as his eyes flick to mine. "And now this?"

Unless my two *brothers* went to see the Grim Reaper to plan for my untimely death, I really don't care where they went. What I do care about is not being included in the current mission.

"Where were you?" I settle onto the arm of the red chair where Levi sits and flick him in the arm. "It scared me. You weren't in bed this morning."

"We had some things we had to take care of," he says as he signs. "Nothing big."

"You know how it is, Mari." Grayson dries his hands on a towel before joining us. "Oh, wait. You don't know what it's like to travel to get essential supplies. You press a button, and it arrives on your doorstep."

I glance around the room. "There's a button like that here? You'll have to show me."

Bastian removes his hair tie, and his dark hair tumbles over his shoulder. "I'm going to pack for the morning. I suggest the two of you do the same." He glares at Levi and Grayson in warning.

Translation: *Don't tell Mari where you really went last night.*

It's alright. I'm used to Bastian and Evie's mistrust.

When I hear Bastian's door close at the top of the stairs, I clasp my hands. "You two need to let me go. You don't want to stay here, do you, Levi?"

"Nice try." He crosses one leg over the other and leans back in the chair.

Grayson brushes crumbs from the table onto the floor. "What my eloquent friend here is trying to say is, there's no way Bastian would allow you to go on a dangerous mission yet."

"Why does he care?" I plop down on the bench and tent my fingers. The guy hates me. He'd feed me to a pack of hungry werewolves if he had the chance. *And yet*, he saved me from a vampire and his blood-thirsty girlfriend.

"You're our sister," Levi says, a wide grin on his face. "Family looks out for each other."

It's easy to see Levi, and even Grayson as a brother. Except for keeping their location the night before a secret, they treat me with respect. And Bastian does too—at times. But there are things about him I don't see in a brotherly way at all.

"I saved the two of you breakfast." Grayson lifts a towel from a plate on the table. "Black looks good on you by the way."

My cheeks warm as I instinctively try to smooth out the skin-tight fighting gear like I used to do with my skirt in Avren. It has become so comfortable, I almost forgot I was wearing it. I sit down at the table, my stomach growling at the sight of fresh eggs, bread, and strips of meat. "Thank you for making me feel welcome." I run my hand down the sleeve of my fighting gear. "For this."

Grayson lifts a shoulder and swipes a piece of bacon from my plate. "It was Evie's idea. She didn't think the other woman in the Kindred Few should fight in a recycled potato sack. It embarrassed her."

"Well, either way, it's growing on me." I take a bite of eggs and chew as Grayson goes back to the dishes.

Levi gets up and sits across from me at the table, eyeing my other piece of bacon. I smirk and hand it to him. He devours it in two seconds flat.

"What happened to your family?" I smear a pad of butter on the piece of cornbread. As a member of the deaf community, the Council would never allow Levi to enter Avren, even as an Undesirable.

He hangs his head, palms spread on the table.

"You don't have to answer." Thoughts of my mother's last day swirl in my head. Losing a parent at such a young age is difficult.

"The Council exiled them when Lady Raven rose to power." Grayson dries his hands, faces us, and leans against the counter.

"I can answer for myself," Levi signs furiously, his hands flailing. His face is red. "Stop acting like I'm incapable of anything."

My heart sinks. It's the first time I've ever seen Levi upset, and it spells out a source of tension between my brothers.

I reach out and take Levi's hand in mine. "I asked you, but if it's too painful, I don't need to know."

He grips my hand tighter, his blue eyes drilling into mine. "You're my sister. You need to know. In the short time I've known you, you've held nothing back from me." He draws his hand back so he can sign as he talks. "Both of my parents were deaf, born before the baby experiments started. When the Council changed hands, placing Lady Raven and Lord Arazian in power, they exiled the Undesirables, including my parents. They lived in peace in the wilderness for ten years before I was born. My father avoided the blue cuff because he couldn't hear. They didn't want him in Avren. Instead, he worked the fields for Bastian's father. My mother stayed home with me." The lump in Levi's throat bobs as he swallows. "When I was ten, a swarm of Arazian's Miscretes broke down the door to our cabin. They shook the entire cabin with their violent actions, waking me. I hid beneath my bed as the monsters tore into my parents' bedroom. I clutched a pillow as tears streamed down my cheeks. The next morning, I finally dared to leave my hiding place. When I worked up the courage to look in my parents' room, the only thing the Miscretes had left behind were streaks of blood."

I want to gather little Levi into my arms and tell him he's loved, but he's a man now, and as much as it pains me, I stay on my side of the table. "What happened to you?"

"When my father didn't show up for work, Mr. Hale sent two workers to our cabin to look for him. After a thorough search of the cabin, they found me, pale and shaking beneath a blanket, afraid the Miscretes had come back to finish the job." His lip quirks to the side. "Bastian and I grew up together—the natural and adopted sons of Jaresiah and Sarah Hale."

I don't want to ask what happened to them. It is a story for another time and maybe it's Bastian's tale to tell.

"I hit a tree with an arrow today." I carry my plate to the sink and wash the crumbs away with my hand and a bit of soap and water. It's not a boast, but like Levi, I want to show the others I'm capable of more than they give me credit for.

"When you hit a hundred trees over a hundred days, we'll let you come with us on a mission. For now, you and Levi will watch over the homestead." Grayson rolls down his sleeves, opens a cabinet, and begins putting dishes away. "Consistency is key."

It's no use. If Grayson's not on my side, it's not like I'll convince Bastian or Evie.

"We'll hopefully only be gone a week. Two days there, two days back, and three to carry out the plan. The two of you can't get in too much trouble in that time." He swats me on the bottom with a spatula, making me jump.

I snatch it from his hand and chase him around the room trying to smack him back, knocking over a chair and a bowl of pinecones.

Bastian barrels down the stairs, a frown on his face. He's not wearing a shirt, and his pants are low on his hips. I freeze and hide the spatula behind my back, wishing I could hit him on the backside with it.

"What the hell is going on down here? I'm trying to take a nap," he growls.

Grayson is back in the kitchen, acting like nothing happened. We both say, "Nothing."

Levi pushes away from the table, his chair scraping over the floorboards. "They're both liars." He tattles like Bastian's our father, which is ridiculous. He's five years younger than Grayson. "Mari's a naughty girl."

"Is she now?" Bastian raises an eyebrow, and my heart pounds.

"Grayson hit me with the spatula. All I wanted to do was retaliate. I don't think that's naughty, it's practical. If my older brother hits me, I'm going to get my revenge." I cross my arms, weapon in hand. "I won't let my three brothers gang up on me." As an only child growing up, I longed for an older brother or sister—someone to confide in. Grayson's playfulness allowed me to act like a child, and I realize for the first time, I can breathe. I tap the spatula against my hand. "Do you need a spanking, Bastian?"

Adrenaline rips through my body with the thought of chasing the commander, but he shuts it down with a glare. "One of our comrades is being held by the enemy. I don't have time for games as tempting as they sound." He turns and stomps up the stairs to the room, slamming his door.

I toss the spatula onto the counter, determined to act nonchalant. Bastian gets under my skin in the worst and best ways possible, but I don't want the other two guys to know this. It's a secret hidden in our heated glances, our causal brushes of skin, and in the way he says my name.

"I better get rest too." Grayson climbs the stairs to his room, leaving me alone with Levi.

"Do they always treat you this way? The babysitter?" I flop down on the couch, not ready for a week of boredom locked in the cabin.

He sits on the couch beside me, his shoulder touching mine. "Just because they're leaving doesn't mean we can't have our own fun."

"Whatever do you mean?" I elbow him, excited he's up for getting out of the cabin. "Do you plan to defy the commander's orders?"

He shakes his head and chuckles. "I do it all the time. The secret's not to get caught. Have you ever been to Mafekadi?" His fingers spell out the name of the town.

"The only places I've ever been to are Avren, this cabin, and the Grove. So, no." The name of the town sounds inviting and adventurous, so whatever he has planned is a big fat *yes* for me.

"It's a fae stronghold in the foothills of the Elmridden Range. As long as we can avoid the tricks of the residents, it's a great place to spend a day." He drums his fingers on his leg. "We'll have to overnight in Rumsford along the way."

A secret couple of days away with Levi sounds like heaven. And although I've never seen him kill a vampire or werewolf, I know between the two of us, we can protect ourselves.

That night, I go to bed feeling better about the others leaving us behind. They can go off, save Lyden, and feel good about themselves. I hope to find the material I want in Mafekadi to work on new fighting gear for my family. If I'm nowhere near their expectations of usefulness as a fighter, I want to prove my worth in another way. My expert skills as a tailor are the one thing I can give them.

In the morning, I wake to noises in the main room of the cabin. Levi's bed is empty, so I throw on a coat to block out the chill in the air and walk into the living room. The other four are sitting around the table, laughing and eating. It doesn't look like a crew about to embark on a dangerous mission.

It feels as if I'm a stranger intruding on this perfect scene, but then I see an empty chair with a plate set in front of it. "Good morning."

"Mari, you're awake." Grayson jumps up to give me a hug. "We thought we'd miss you."

The three leaving for the Ringlet Forest wear their fighting gear, which has seen better times. Empty plates sit in front of them. Weapons rest against the wall by the door. My gut twists thinking about them being gone for a week and not knowing if they'll all make it back.

"Come here." Bastian scrapes his chair back and leans over to lift my pant leg. He pulls a knife from his belt and works on removing the tracking device from my ankle. When it snaps open, he stuffs it into his pocket. "I'll hide this along the way."

"Why am I working if it's that easy?" I glance at Evie, who purses her lips. "I thought Arazian was the only Citizen who successfully removed an anklet."

"The only one who successfully removed one without consequences. Somehow, the soldiers always find the offenders. When they find you, you'll face longer work hours and possibly harsher conditions." Bastian shrugs. "But it's your first offense, and we can't have Levi taking you to work. You'll both be dead the second you step foot outside the cabin."

I glance at Levi. His head is down, the tips of his ears turning red. This is one moment when I really hate Bastian.

"You trust him enough to protect me at night while the three of you sleep in your own bedrooms." I square my shoulders, ready to defend my bunkmate. "If you were so worried about his effectiveness, one of you would sleep on the mattress beside me."

"Maybe we don't care enough to worry about your life, princess." Bastian scrapes back in his chair and stands, stretching his arms over his head. "Gray's the only Citizen I've ever met besides soldiers. So far, with you, I'm not impressed."

I glare at him. The hatred electrifies my skin with pinpricks. "It goes both ways, *phaloc.*"

"Enough!" Levi yells. He pushes back in his chair so hard that when he stands, it falls to the floor. He storms off to our bedroom, leaving silence in his wake.

"We were fine until you showed up." Bastian rakes his fingers through his hair, then rests his hands against the table. "I know you're on your whole *save the orphans* kick, Gray, but you need to know where to draw the line. She's in the way of our mission, and I don't care who you think she may or may not be... she's a pain in my ass."

As much as I want to defend myself, I'm tired of wasting words on Bastian. He's made his mind up about me, and it seems literally impossible to change. "I'm going to see if Levi's alright."

Grayson snatches my arm and pulls me into a hug before I can leave. He holds my head against his, whispering, "You're so much more than Bastian and Evie make you out to be. Be good while I'm gone."

I hear the front door open and close before I make it to our bedroom. We're alone. Levi has his back to me, lying down and facing the wall.

Sitting on his mattress, I rest a hand on his shoulder, giving it a squeeze.

He turns to me and blinks.

"Are you ok?"

I expect to see tears in his eyes as he cranes his face in my direction, rolling onto his back and staring at me before he signs, "There are times I'm ashamed to call them my family. But he has a bigger heart than he's willing to show you."

"I'm sure he does." Without asking, I kick my feet out onto Levi's mattress and snuggle beside him. The only sounds in the room are the chatter of birds outside the window and the beating of our hearts. Grayson's words rattle around in my brain. If I'm so special, why do Bastian and Evie treat me like shit? I tilt my head to face him. "Tell me more about the prophecy, Levi.".

"I wasn't completely honest with you. I'm a quarter fae on my mother's side." He props himself up on his elbow. "Imagine that. They kicked my parents out of Avren for being deaf, not knowing my mother was half fae. With my ancestry, I enjoy going to Mafekadi. I feel at home there."

"And what about here with Gray, Bastian, and Evie?" I'm asking him to open himself up to a person he's known for less than three days.

"They're kin, Mari. Like you." He twists a strand of my hair with his fingers, so intimate yet so different from the times Flynn touched me. "We can't leave each other. There might be someone I'm still related to in Mafekadi, but why would I ever need them when I have the Kindred Few?"

The title still holds little meaning to me. Yes, it feels good to have an adoptive family so soon after losing my mom. But I feel like I'm nothing but an anchor weighing them down.

"And the prophecy of the fae?" I try again now that he is looking at me. His green eyes magnified in his glasses, holding onto me like I'm a priceless treasure.

THE KINDRED FEW

Does it have any of the ancient fae magic I've read about in the Avren library?

He sits up straighter, resting his back against the wall before running his hand through his dark hair and setting it askew. "I don't have it memorized like I should." His gaze goes to a faraway place, as if he's trying to remember something from his childhood. "My mother had me memorize it as a nursery rhyme, but that was a long time ago."

"Try for me."

Levi's words draw me into the mythical nature of a prophecy. He rubs his hands together, getting ready to sign. "I'll give it a try." He sucks in a breath and closes his eyes.

"Two cities loom above us all,
one veiled in beauty and the other in darkness.
Both hold death within their walls.
For those saved by Mahogany's gaze
dance among the fairy rings and a fire's blaze.
The great wilderness protects the hidden.
Two will rise from the cities' walls—young and brave and true.
Their sacrifice will save us all
and end the evil reign
of both great cities."

My mouth hangs open. Avren with its pristine streets, towering spires, and scientific and artistic advances seems indestructible. Does it really need to meet its doom for the rest of us to live in peace?

He weaves his fingers through mine. "It's you. We all know it."

My breath hitches as a rush of fear hits me. How do the others think I'm a great savior? It's insane, really. A girl grown in a test tube and raised by a Council member and a mathematician does not qualify as a mighty warrior destined to bring down two great cities. And even if I am one of them, which is highly unlikely, who is the other one? Grayson? He's the only other person I've met from Avren. But there are a lot of Undesirables. It could be anyone. "Why do you think it's me?"

"There are further writings on the prophecy in Mafekadi. Fae scholars have studied the scrolls for centuries. The two saviors will be orphans, one from Avren." He lets go of my hand to hold up a finger. "The other from the First City." He holds up a second finger.

"But I thought only Arazian and his mutants lived in the First City. Do you think one of them will really work with an Undesirable orphan from Avren to destroy its creator?" None of this makes sense to me.

He scratches his head, his warm smile shining down on me. "There are parts of the prophecy which remain mysteries waiting to be deciphered."

CHAPTER TWELVE

*W*ith the others out of the house, we spend the rest of the afternoon in the common room. Levi stacks wood in the fireplace and soon has a crackling fire roaring in the hearth. I carry several books from the shelf in our room, dropping them with a thud on the table.

I inspect the title of a blue book with silver letters embossed on the cover. "Do you think Bastian has read these books?" I flip the title in Levi's direction. "Even *Sowing Seeds?*"

He covers his mouth with his fist to hide a smirk. "Bastian has sown a few seeds both in and out of the garden."

That's what I thought.

Tossing the blue book onto the couch, I settle on a fictional story about fairies to pass the time. The coziness of the red velvet cushion on the armchair and the warmth of the fire and the blanket over my legs have me dozing off.

The front door slams, startling me awake. Bastian removes his jacket. He hangs it beside the door and turns to me, an unfamiliar look on his face—one I've seen on Flynn's face before.

Desire.

What the hell is he doing here?

I look around the room for Levi, but he's gone. Did he go to the bedroom to lie down? Spread on my lap, the book is open to a chapter where the fairy's glamour tricks the main character. But Levi is part fae, not Bastian.

"Where are the others?" I ask, keeping the blanket over my legs, protected from his heated gaze. "I thought it was a two-day journey to the Ringlet Forest."

He crosses the floor in long strides before he kneels beside the armchair. Shadows dance over his chiseled face in the flickers of the firelight, and it takes everything within me to keep from reaching out and touching his skin. "Maribel. One day without you had me going insane. You are the reason I wake every morning—the siren of my dreams." He pitches forward, over the arm of the chair, and closer to me.

I squirm, edging away from him like I did with Grayson on the bench in the Council room.

What's wrong with me? Don't I want this?

It doesn't make sense. This man, only this morning, said he didn't want me around. And it's obvious we can't be alone together. So what's he doing here?

His mouth is dangerously close, and I want to close my eyes to block out the fullness of his lips and that damn sexy scar—but if I close my eyes, he might try to kiss me. "You haunt me, Maribel Windsong." Soft lips brush against mine.

I stiffen. This is not what I want. Not when he treated me so badly.

Bastian cradles my face in his palm, his long fingers caressing my skin. "What's wrong?" he whispers. "You want this too. You know it." His lips trail along my jawline, sending a delicious shiver down my spine. "From the second you stepped through the front door of the cabin, I knew I'd never see you as my sister."

I gaze into his eyes. Fire blazes within his crystal-blue irises.

"But can you ever see me as a Redeemed? As one of the Kindred Few?"

His fingers pause. "Mari... darling." The corner of his lip lifts in a smirk. "Know you'll never be one of us."

I squeeze my eyes shut and shake my head. When I open my eyes, he's gone. It was all a dream, but it revealed my true feelings about him. Commander Bastian Hale will never see me as a member of the Kindred Few. I am an outsider living in his home, taking up space and eating his food.

Placing the book on an end table, I fold the blanket and lay it over the top of the armchair. My stomach growls, so I head into the kitchen to find something to cook for dinner for the two of us. If Levi really plans to take me to Mafekadi tomorrow, I want to make sure I get to bed early.

Not really knowing how to cook, I slice some fruit and arrange it on a plate. I wish I had paid more attention to Caron working in the kitchen of our apartment. She was an excellent cook.

The back door opens, and Levi enters carrying an armload of some yellow flowers that grow in the garden. "You're awake."

"I hope you're not decorating with flowers for me." I hate to discourage romantic gestures, but unlike Bastian, Levi really feels like a brother. "We're leaving in the morning."

He removes a pocketknife from his coat and promptly cuts the head from a flower. It drops onto a plate. Beneath the counter, he removes gloves from the cabinet and puts them on. Taking a stone from his pocket, he grinds the petals into a pulp. Not exactly the romantic gesture I first envisioned when he carried in the bouquet.

"Yarrow." He pinches a small amount of the flower pulp between his fingers and sprinkles it into the open locket around his neck. "It will ward off evil spirits on our journey to the land of the fae." He holds up a second chain with a round locket, filling it with more ground yarrow.

"I know little about the fae. A week ago, I didn't even know they existed." I sit on the bench beside him, carrying the plate of fruit. "You'll have to teach me."

"Mafekadi is the Seelie Court. As a quarter-blood, they don't bother me too much, and they're much more akin to my human side than the Unseelie Court." He pops a slice of apple into his mouth, chomping away as I consider what it means that my best friend in the wilderness is part fae.

I lift the yarrow-filled locket from the table. It's the best gift anyone's ever given me besides my father's music box. I hold it up to the light, illuminating the symbol etched into the silver. Four interlocking circles glow in the afternoon sun. "Is this a fae symbol?" I trace it with my fingernail, curious about Levi's ancestors.

He hooks a finger through the chain. "No, it's the symbol for the Kindred Few. Each circle represents a brother or sister. Separate, we're alone and weak, but together we're strong." He dangles the locket from one finger. "We'll need to add another circle for you, Mari."

As much as I want to cling to his sentiment of bringing me into the fold, it reminds me of how the Windsong-Barellis family line was decimated one circle at a time. And I'm not sure if there's room for another circle in this symbol. "How long have you lived with the others?"

Brushing my hair to the side, he clasps the chain behind my neck. "Bastian's parents took me in after my parents died. We had five happy years. His mother taught me how to bake the best apple pie and how to load and shoot a shotgun." His gaze meets a faraway place, one where a person who has witnessed too many horrors goes to. "Then came the fire. Bastian and I survived while his parents and brothers didn't make it. He took me to another farmer. Said he had to go find himself." He traces the woodgrain of the table with the tip of his finger. "Bastian didn't know any better. At sixteen, he thought he was doing what was best for me. I only wanted to stay with the only family I had left."

My thoughts swirl with his story. Losing two sets of parents in five years in grotesquely violent ways might make anyone lose their mind. How can he be the most level-headed person here?

"I met Gray four years ago. He found me sleeping in a pig pen outside a farmer's cottage near Erith. As an indentured fifteen-year-old servant regularly beaten by my owner, Gray took pity on me and paid for my freedom. When he found out I was an orphan, he brought me to the cabin where he lived with Evie." He stares at the wall behind me as if drawn back into his memories. "Between that time and the time I lived with my parents, I was taken in by the Hales."

"Bastian?" A bolt of excitement mixed with a sick feeling settles in the pit of my stomach.

"He came about a year later." With his hands free, Levi signs his words. "At seventeen, he was almost as impressive as he is now. Strong, lean arm muscles, tall, and much shorter hair. Turns out the Dark King wanted his parents' farm for the land. It's close to the First City. Burned their house to the ground rather than offer to pay for it. That's when we parted ways."

"And will the others travel closer to the First City when they reach the Ringlet Forest?" A protective feeling washes over me, imagining Bastian, Gray, and Evie fighting the Miscretes to free Lyden. And what if it's a trap?

"The Miscretes only travel this close to Avren in the protective shadows of the night, avoiding the soldiers and most interaction. They don't bother the Supes, only the humans, although the Dark King occasionally convinces one of them to join his forces. It's rare." He bites into a slice of apple and sits on the edge of the table. "His second-in-command is a vampire."

All this talk of the First City makes me long for Avren's safety. "And when we travel to Mafekadi tomorrow? Is it in that direction?"

"No." He touches my arm. "Don't worry, I'll be with you. Mafekadi is to the south, while the First City is west. We'll travel when the sun rises and arrive at Rumsford before dark, so nothing dangerous will bother us." He assesses me, his hand warm on my sleeve. The sound of the crackling fire fills the room. "I know you want answers about the prophecy. It's incomplete, so I don't think we'll find them traveling to Mafekadi. That's where Gray and I were the other night."

"In Mafekadi?" What other secrets do my brothers keep?

"No, trying to find the lost part of the prophecy." He hangs his head, and I can tell he's ashamed, but I'm not sure if it's because he did or didn't tell me. "There's another fae village to the north called Frostacre. It holds the Unseelie Court and my Great-Uncle Bracken." He glances up as if he expects a look of condemnation from me. "The grumpy bastard's as cold as the town around him. Only rambled on about how his ancestors ripped apart the parchment holding the prophecy years ago and wiped memories of the knowledge. But we had to go. Gray and I are desperate to find out how you piece into the puzzle."

"The prophecy mentions another *savior*." The word tastes awkward in my mouth, especially if Levi thinks I'm one of them. "From the First City. Do you think the other part of the prophecy holds more clues as to the identity of the two people?"

"That's what we believe. Why would someone go to such great lengths to hide it? There are plenty of Redeemed who will help the process along if we know the identities of the saviors." He places the last piece of apple in my hand. "You'll need your strength for our journey tomorrow. I'll sleep in Bastian's bed tonight, so you don't have to listen to me snore."

"You don't snore," I laugh, then take a bite of the apple.

"You lie and you know it, Maribel Windsong."

I tap him on the nose, thankful for his friendship. "Only to stay on your good side."

BIRDS CHIRP OUTSIDE MY WINDOW, waking me from a restful sleep. I made it through the whole night with no memorable dreams of Bastian. The one from my nap yesterday still haunts me.

I roll out of bed and run my fingers through my hair before bounding into the common room. I'm ready for a journey. Two packs lay on the table. Levi stands by the stove whistling a familiar song way out of tune. He's as excited as I am.

"Good morning," I say, moving into his eye line so as not to scare him.

He smiles his sweet Levi smile, pulls me into his arms, and kisses the top of my head. "Are you ready to see one of my favorite places?

"Beyond ready." I snatch a piece of bacon from the frying pan, burning the tips of my fingers but ready to toss my vegetarian lifestyle to the wayside. Between my lips, it's salty with a savory goodness I never knew existed. My old ways were in my past life —a life regulated by a five-person Council who knew everything and nothing about me at the same time.

"We'll travel past the Grove, along the shores of the Lake of Glass, until we reach Rumsford on the southern shore. The next day, we need to climb into the foothills of the Elmridden Range." He rakes his eyes over my black fighting gear. In all honesty, it's getting pretty old, but besides my canvas sack from the Council, it's the only clothing I have. "Why don't you look in Evie's room for more comfortable clothes to wear?"

I climb to the top of the stairs and face the three bedroom doors. Levi continues his off-tune whistling while he cooks. Biting my lip, I slowly turn the knob to Bastian's room. I don't know why I do it besides trying to quench my curiosity about the commander. The door creaks, but it doesn't matter with Levi.

Inside, I close the door behind me and drink in Bastian's room. Levi made the bed, which is raised up from the floor with a frame. A gray blanket covers white sheets. He's nailed pieces of paper to the wall with the symbol from my locket sketched on them. The only difference is there are five circles instead of four.

On the opposite wall from the bed is a small writing desk with a quill, ink bottle, and a sheet of parchment laid out on top of it. I walk over and run my finger along Bastian's cursive script. With a pang of guilt, I read his words, wanting to know everything about him.

Xavier,

We are closing in on the people and resources needed. The training continues to follow schedule, and we've secured the supposed savior. Grayson and Levi draw closer to finding the prophecy remnant, though the idea of a savior from the First City is still unbelievable to me.

In your next letter, send the guard schedule along with names, ranks, and training. A weaker entry point will allow us to infiltrate the city. Not sure yet how I will raise a useless girl to the rank of a badass savior, but it is a task I must fulfill.

Your brother in spirit,

Bastian

I sink into the chair at the desk, running his words on repeat through my head.

Useless girl.

Tell me what you really think of me, Bastian Hale.

And yet, he includes me in his stupid family crest, or symbol, or whatever the hell it is. He seems to have some hope in my abilities.

I exit Bastian's room, feeling more irritated than anything. Why I wasted space in my brain and heart for this man is beyond comprehension. Sure, he's kind and patient at times. But he's mostly annoyed he's tasked with training me—like it's something I chose.

Evie's room contains more feminine touches: flowing curtains, a shag rug, and a white bedspread with a pale blue coverlet at the foot. I open her trunk, removing a pair of woolen leggings and a tunic. A dark blue cloak hangs on a hook by the door. Unsure of how she'll react to having the newbie touching her stuff, I stare at it for a minute before tossing it over the other clothes on my arm.

I breeze past Levi to our bedroom to change. He must wonder why I spent so much time rummaging through Evie's things, and I'm not ready for the questions.

As I dress, I process Bastian's letter. Xavier must hold a position in Avren's guard to know the answer to the commander's questions. It also sounds like they plan to attack sooner rather than later. If I'm one of the prophesied saviors and they have no clue who the other one is, they're bound to fail.

Why the rush? I'm not a military strategist, but unless there's an outside influence pressing them to move forward, I'd think they'd have everything lined up before their tiny militia took on the full force of Avren's soldiers.

When I come out of the bedroom, Levi doesn't say a word about my extra time upstairs. Maybe he doesn't care.

"I made each of us a lunch of bacon, bread, and fruit." He lifts a backpack to his shoulders before helping me shrug mine on. It feels awkward over the bulky cloak, but it will keep me warm. "Are you ready?"

"As I'll ever be." My instinct is to remain in the safety of the cabin, which reminds me of my apartment in Avren. But after reading Bastian's letter, I want to leave the useless girl behind. From this day forward, I'm determined to fill the role of the savior others claim I am.

CHAPTER THIRTEEN

a strange ache fills my heart as we walk away from the cabin. It's like I'm losing Bastian, Grayson, and Evie all over again. But it's mixed with the excitement of an adventure to a strange place.

Levi stops beside the garden and picks a delicate white flower. He places it in my hair, letting his hand linger beside my face. "My beautiful travel companion."

I purse my lips, feeling my cheeks flush. "You're not too bad yourself."

He takes the familiar path through the woods leading to the field where I train with Bastian. It's empty except for a robin looking for its breakfast. Not expecting trouble, I only carry a dagger inside my cloak, leaving my arrows behind in the weapons cabinet.

There's a group of men throwing axes at a makeshift target in the Grove, laughing and slapping each other on the back when one of them splits the wood. We skirt around the perimeter and pass between two cottages into the primary thoroughfare of the village. A woman lumbers down the dirt path carrying a laundry basket. Beside her, two toddlers struggle to keep up, sometimes tripping on the ruts in the road. An older man holds a board up beside a window, nailing it to the side of the house. The smell of smoke fills the air, rising from the chimneys of the cottages, along with the sound of a lonely rooster announcing the beginning of a new day.

"They are all Redeemed," Levi signs to me as we pass a man chopping wood outside his cottage. "Born to the wilderness, they hold no loyalty to Avren."

A woman exits the cottage, and the man with the ax lays it down. He snatches the woman's waist, causing her to giggle, and pulls her into a kiss. Her stomach bulges to an abnormal size. I try not to stare.

"Good morning, Levi," she calls waving.

Levi walks over to the couple and shakes hands with the man. "Agnes… Cooper. This is the newest member of our family, Mari Windsong."

"Pleased to meet you." Agnes holds out her hand to shake mine, but I can't take my eyes from her stomach. It is the first time I've seen a pregnant woman. "I'm putting on a few pounds," she laughs.

"Mari came from Avren." Levi wraps an arm around my shoulder and squeezes. "There's a lot of new things in our world."

Agnes steps closer to us. Wisps of her dark curly hair, tied back in a flowered kerchief, catch the early morning light. "Give me your hand."

Unsure what to think, I hold it out to her. She grasps my fingers and places my palm on her stomach. I flash my eyes to her in horror. While I did hug my parents, I never touched a stranger in such an intimate way. I want to remove my hand, but she holds it steady, winking at me.

My breath catches as a sensation rolls against my palm. "What was that?"

"She's kicking." Agnes releases my hand, but I keep my palm firmly against her stomach, desperate for more of this new life.

The foot pushes against her stomach again. "Due in about a month."

"Aggie insists it's a girl." Cooper throws an arm around the woman I assume is his wife. "There's a bet running among the men in the village."

Besides the dangers lurking in the darkness, this is the fundamental difference I see between the life of a Redeemed woman and a Citizen: the freedom to choose and express romantic feelings by having a child of her own. It draws me to this life more than anything else.

Walking away from Agnes and Cooper, I slip my fingers beneath the straps of my backpack, lifting it higher on my shoulders. "Why do Bastian and Evie hate me so much? I mean, I know I grew up in Avren, but so did Gray."

"They don't hate you." He takes my hand. "They don't understand you."

"And that's the thing." I skirt around a pile of horse dung in the middle of the road. "You don't understand the Avren mindset, but you welcomed me with open arms."

"I'm a quarter fae, part of the deaf community, and lived in a pigsty for over a year." He stops and takes both of my hands, his eyes large behind his glasses. "I know what it's like to not fit in—to be the one who's ostracized. Bastian and Evie have always held a place among the Redeemed. If I don't accept others after finding my own place to fit in, I'm the worst kind of hypocrite."

I release his hand and hold my palm over his chest. "I think it's your heart. You don't have a mean bone in your body."

His lips tug into a warm smile as he turns to continue walking, still clinging to my hand.

The sun is high above us when we reach the Lake of Glass. It is a massive body of water reaching as far as my eyes can see. Light shimmers on the crests of tiny waves lapping against the shoreline. Other than in books and the stream following the path from Avren to the cabin, I've never seen a natural body of water, and it's as breathtaking as the luminescent forest.

"It's called the Lake of Glass because of the way it looks in the early morning and at twilight. It's so calm, you can use its surface as a mirror." Removing his glasses, he crouches, scoops water into his hands, and washes his face. "I believe there's a magical element to it."

"What do you mean?" I kneel beside him, fascinated by small fish darting in schools through the shallow water.

"Legend has it that if you enter the lake when it's completely calm like glass, the water has transformational qualities. An old woman who submerges herself completely can exit as a young woman again." He raises a shoulder, then signs without talking.

I adjust myself so I'm facing him. "What did you just say?"

"Sorry." He gives me a coy smile. "I don't like to swear out loud. The others think it's a bunch of shit—tales made up by the fae on the other side of the lake so they can drown unsuspecting people when no one else is around."

"And do they?" Maybe Levi didn't tell me the complete truth about the Seelie Court.

"People have drowned in the Lake of Glass, but there's no proof it was the fae any more than there's proof it was a Miscrete or even an accident." He stands, stretching his arms over his head. "We still have a long way to go." In other words, he doesn't want to talk about the drownings. Opening his pack, he removes a piece of bread, slices it with his dagger, and fills it with bacon.

I do the same as my stomach growls for the first time since we left the cabin. Other than the piece of bacon I swiped from the pan, I haven't eaten anything all day. The energy the food brings is evident within minutes as I finish the sandwich.

Levi hands me a canteen, and I wash my food down with cold water.

"Rumsford sits at the south end of the lake. There's an inn I like to stay at when I travel to Mafekadi. It's not too much farther

to get there, but it's safer to stay with humans than with the fae."
He helps me lift my pack over my cloak.

We skirt the edge of the lake along the well-worn trail,
climbing over boulders and wading through offshoot streams.
With the breeze from the lake whipping through my hair and the
sun warm on my face, never have I ever felt more alive. In the
city walls of Avren, I witnessed artificial nature—a fountain,
houseplants, an occasional animal brought in to garner *oohs* and
aahs from the crowd. *This...* this is a whole other level. And in a
small way, it makes me understand why my father left to live
here.

By midafternoon, I see the gables and rooftops of a town
poking out from the trees on the edge of the lake. It must be
Rumsford, but I can't ask Levi because he's too far ahead to hear
me. Foothills and tall mountains rise behind the forest, adding to
the breathtaking beauty of the lake. Mafekadi lies somewhere in
the hills above Rumsford. Exhausted, I add a slight jog to my step
to keep up.

"Keep close to me in the town," Levi says, finally stopping to
let me catch my breath. I hope he doesn't walk so fast when we're
going uphill tomorrow. "People are friendly, but like most places
in the wilderness, there's always a mixture of creatures who pass
through."

Images of the werewolf tearing into Tanner's neck and the
feeling of the vampire's ice-cold breath on my own send ripples
of fear through my body. While Grayson and Bastian are bigger
men, trained to kill, I'm not sure if the same is true for Levi. And
it's definitely not true for me.

Rumsford's buildings are much larger than the small cottages
in the Grove. Brown wooden structures rise two stories beside us
as we walk into the town. People mingle in the streets, some
walking, some working, others standing in groups. The weight of
stares is heavier than the pack on my back.

I lean into Levi, looping my arm through his and keeping my

free hand on my dagger inside my cloak. We need to appear innocent but not easily manipulated. The strict laws in Avren, along with the fear of eviction, keep most Citizens in line. This is the wilderness where those safeguards no longer exist.

A tall man with long, silver hair bumps into me as he passes. Not bothering to stop, he turns his head back and glares at me with eyes of glowing amber. I want to ask Levi about him, but I'm too scared to stop so he can see my lips. It's better if we keep moving.

The Ironhorse Inn lies on the far end of town closest to the foothills. A metal sign with a horse on it sways, squeaking in the breeze.

"Is the name intentional?" I ask, remembering my weapons training lesson with Bastian. Iron kills fairies.

"More like an inside joke." Levi scratches his head after signing. "Mafekadi and Rumsford have a mutual understanding. Don't kill and don't be killed. Both towns live in peace this way."

"Can iron kill you since you're part fae?"

He steps onto the threshold of the inn. "Just like any other weapon can kill a human."

The downstairs portion of the Ironhorse is comprised of a dining area, complete with a bar, and dotted with tables alongside dark secluded booths. As it's not dinnertime yet, only a few patrons sit at the counter.

The woman at the bar looks up as she's wiping down a glass. "Can I help the two of you?"

"We need a room for the night." Levi places a bag of coins on the counter. "My wife and I are here to visit her sister, who's heavy with child."

My cheeks flush with Levi's words. There's a method to his madness, but it inflames me all the same, not with anger but embarrassment. The only man I ever thought about marrying was Flynn. With the Council's matching of eligible singles after they turn eighteen, it was a looming event. Here, in the wilderness, marriage thoughts don't enter my mind as often. It's more about survival.

"I've got two left." The woman places the glass on a shelf behind her. "One at the top of the stairs—the honeymoon suite." She waggles her eyebrows. "The other is farther down the hall with a smaller bed."

"We'll take the second one." Levi counts out the coins to pay for the room. "Will dinner be served down here tonight?"

"Rack of lamb." The bartender's cheeks and chest puff out as she smiles. "Cooked it myself this morning."

"Sounds delicious." Levi takes the key and my hand, leading me away from the bar.

Our room is four doors down on the right from the top of the stairs. It's about the size of our room in the cabin, but the bed isn't as big as our two mattresses pushed together.

"No worries," Levi signs. "I can sleep on the floor. I don't want our room at the top of the stairs where anyone can slip in."

"You're not sleeping on the floor." I fluff the pillows on the bed before jumping onto it. The springs squeak in protest. "I'll sleep on my side. We'll have plenty of room."

We take turns walking down the hall to a commonly shared bathroom to wash up, then take a brief nap before heading downstairs for dinner.

People pack the dining area. It's as if all the residents we saw on the street came into the Ironhorse to continue their boisterous conversations. It is literally deafening, making me jealous of Levi only hearing muffled sounds.

As if by miracle, Levi finds an empty table near the center of the room with three chairs. We squeeze through the patrons to find our seats.

"I'll get us a couple of beers," Levi shouts, turning away before I can protest.

The act of committing sins against Avren will take some getting used to if I want to survive in the wilderness. Drinking, swearing, kissing and doing other things with the opposite or same sex are all forbidden in the city.

It's only a drink, Maribel. Get yourself together.

Levi returns with two mugs of beer and sets one in front of me, the liquid sloshing over the side. "I ordered our dinner, so it will be here soon."

With the surrounding noise, I wish I knew sign language. It would make our conversation so much easier. I lift the mug to my lips and take a sip of the bitter liquid, trying not to make a face as it slides down my throat. It isn't exactly what I expected from a *forbidden* beverage. I must make some kind of face because Levi is trying hard not to laugh.

Instead of owning up to my naiveté, I look over his shoulder, taking in the sights and sounds of the Ironhorse. The man with the silver hair who bumped into me in the street sits at the bar. He's looking right at me and raises his glass when our eyes meet.

I quickly avert mine back to Levi, not wanting to draw any attention in our direction. Why is a man well into his twenties, and extremely good-looking, interested in a seventeen-year-old clearly sitting with another man?

"Don't turn around." I clutch Levi's hands in mine. "There's a man staring at me from the bar."

Levi's first instinct is to turn, so I grab the side of his face and pull him into a kiss, regretting it the second it starts. He responds, reluctantly at first but then moving his hand to the side of my face, cradling my cheek.

I pull away, only far enough that he can read my lips. His eyes are brighter than I've ever seen them. "He's locked onto me, so I needed to show him we're a couple."

My companion drops his gaze, unable to hide his disappointment. I hate that I hurt him. "I'm going to the bar to get another beer so I can get a good look at him."

He leaves, and I feel exposed in a world of strangers. Mr. Tall, Silver, and Good-Looking takes the opportunity of Levi's departure to cross the room and fill his seat. My heart is in my throat, staring into his unnatural amber eyes. I can't look away.

"I'm Quinn Malum." He holds out a hand as if he expects me to kiss it. His fingers are impossibly long and white. "And you are?"

I don't respond to his hand dangling in the center of the table. "Maribel Windsong," I choke out, unsure if I'm addressing royalty. I glance up at the bar. Levi freezes, beer in hand and eyes wide. My pulse quickens, knowing he's afraid to return to our table.

"What a lovely name for such a ravishing woman." Quinn doesn't need to smile to capture my attention. His eyes hold me in the palm of his hand, and I don't know how to break free. "Are you here with your husband?"

"Uh... no," I stammer, feeling like the least eloquent person in the world. "He's only a friend."

Quinn quirks an eyebrow, suspecting my charade. "Ah, a friend with benefits. Or are you always so familiar with your *friends?*" He leans in closer, moving to the seat beside me almost magically. "If this is true, how do we become friends, Maribel Windsong?"

What is it about this guy that has me so enamored? It feels unnatural, like really wanting to eat a ton of desserts from the Sweet Street Bakery but knowing I'll have a massive stomachache afterward. Quinn Malum is a ten-layer cake with buttercream icing.

"Are you from around here, Mr. Malum?" The formal question is a way to avoid his obvious forward intentions. "You seem different than most people in this town."

He scoots closer to me in his chair and gathers my hands into his. An icy chill runs down my back at his touch, but I can't look away. "I've traveled here from the north. I have business in Mafekadi with a distant relative. No one told me the human women are so captivating in the south. There's something about you, Maribel." With him this close, I'm enveloped by a woodsy scent, like moss and rotting leaves on the walk from the cabin to the Grove.

"Are you fae?" I ask. It makes sense. His unnatural good looks, the way he has me almost under a spell, and having relatives in Mafekadi.

"I'm a courtier in Frostacre. Have you heard of it?" He arches a perfectly manicured eyebrow.

"Only recently. I'm new to the wilderness, so I'm only learning." I bite down on my lip.

That was an incredibly dumb thing to say.

His long fingers intertwine with mine as a beguiling smile crosses his lips. "You are from Avren." It's a statement. Obvious with my lack of understanding of the dangers of the wilderness. "Then you need someone to teach you all the benefits of this world." When he pitches forward, his long hair sweeps over my arm and his lips almost touch my ear as he whispers, "Let me be that man."

My skin is on fire. I don't know if it's the brush of Quinn's hair on my arm or registering what he means by "showing me the ways of this world," but it has me burning up.

"You're in my seat." Levi stands next to us, his face sheet white. "I need to ask you to leave."

Quinn looks up at Levi, pursing his lips and trying not to laugh. "You have fae blood, boy, but only a half-, maybe a quarter-blood." He tilts his head to the side, appraising him. "Your *friend* here is bewitching. I'm not sure what it is yet. Make sure you keep a close eye on her for me. Don't want a vamp too curious about what's brewing in her blood." He stands, picks up my hand, and kisses it. "No worries, Maribel Windsong. I will circle back to find you soon."

And then he's gone, and I'm suddenly an empty shell, unsure of how my life will go on without his presence.

"I'm so stupid." Levi takes the seat beside me and places a hand on my shoulder. "Are you ok?"

My skin feels clammy, as if I'm getting sick, but I have too many questions I need answered. One in particular. "Tell me more about who you and Grayson think I am."

He squeezes my shoulder, hanging his head. When he looks up, there are tears in his eyes. "Come up to the room, and I'll tell you everything."

CHAPTER FOURTEEN

The dim light from the hallway spills into our tiny room as we enter. Levi strikes a match to light the oil lamp on the table before I close the door. He doesn't say a word as he skirts the bed, sits, and fluffs a pillow on the far side. Lying down, he faces the wall. I'm not sure if he's more afraid of what I asked him or of sleeping beside me.

"You really don't have to act weird." I unlace and kick off my boots beside the door. "It's not like we haven't slept in the same room before."

Turning toward me, he props his head up on his elbow. "Can you say that again?"

I'm not sure how we'll have the conversation we need to have in a darkened room.

I settle under the covers, trying not to shiver in the cold air. I turn to face him so he can read my lips. "What's so special about me?"

He sighs and runs his fingers through his hair. "The prophecy is only part of it. There's a connection we feel when we're around you. It's almost spiritual if that makes sense."

Spiritual? In Avren, people look down on religion. We exist

because of science. The progress of humankind is all due to what we've accomplished establishing a perfect society. When left to chaos or even religion, we spiral downward into the creatures of the wilderness. "How do you mean?"

He shifts significantly closer to me. "Don't you ever get a gut feeling?"

"I suppose." Since being in the wilderness, I've had them more.

"It's like that but more intense when I'm around you. It's as if the universe is drawing me to you like a magnet." Within our little bubble, he reaches out and touches my cheek. "There's something special about you that both Gray and I feel. Bastian and Evie do their best to block it, but in the end, it's not something they can deny either." His finger trails along my skin as if I'm fragile—a priceless treasure. "You will fulfill the prophecy. I know it with everything inside me."

"And what if I don't?" If Avren taught me one thing, it's that I'm not special. Only another cog in the machine, making it work like a well-oiled operation. If any of the members clog up the mechanics, the Council sends them to the wilderness. It happened to my father, to Arazian, to Levi's parents, to me.

Levi drops his hand, lays his head on my pillow, and opens his arms. "Come here."

I snuggle into his arms, feeling safer than I have in years with a man I only met less than a week ago. He opened his heart to me. Something I only felt with my father.

His fingers trail along my hairline. "Block out all the lies they've fed you over the years about your value to society. The Kindred Few wasn't complete until you came along. You're an integral piece, not only to our plan but to our family. Never discount your worth."

Knowing he can't hear me without seeing my lips, I whisper, "I love you." They are words my dad used with me, but it's been a long time since I uttered such a powerful expression of my feelings. And I mean it. Prophecy or not, I will fight through Avren and the First City to defend my brother.

WHEN I WAKE, I look over at Levi, cocooned snugly in blankets. Shivering and hungry, I snatch his coat from a nearby chair, pick up my boots, and go out to the hallway, closing the door as quietly as I can.

Soft voices drift through the stairwell from the room below, so I pull on my boots and head out to see if I can scrounge a piece of fruit or bread.

Images from the night before come to the forefront as I find the table we sat at for dinner. My heart races just thinking about Quinn Malum—his long silver hair, hypnotic amber eyes, electrifying touch, and promise to meet again. Did he feel the same spiritual connection the others sense in me? I shake my head to break free from his hold. Without him here, it's manageable. And currently, my stomach says it could give a rat's ass about Quinn Malum.

"Good morning, sweetie." The same woman stands behind the bar, serving up a plate of eggs and bacon to an older man. "Can I get you something to eat?"

"Yes, please," I say, leaving a stool between me and the man. "An apple?"

The woman furrows her brows and pouts. "No wonder you're so skinny. I'll fix you a plate of eggs and bacon, along with a serving of porridge to start."

Before I can protest, she's gone.

The man beside me clears his throat. He sets down his fork and looks at me. "You're clearly human. Were ya born in the wilderness?"

"No," I say, wondering how much I should tell a stranger.

With his gray beard and tattered clothes, he seems harmless enough. "My parents raised me in Avren."

He turns back to his breakfast, filling his mouth with eggs. "A *Citizen*."

Both as an Undesirable and as a Citizen, the evicted face persecution. I felt it from Guy and Flynn's friends in the city. And it's rampant here. "No longer, sir. My mother died before my eighteenth birthday."

"And your father?" The man keeps his focus on his eggs, continuing his intrusive questions.

"He left for the wilderness when I was younger. Decided his job on the Council was too much." I smile at the cook as she delivers my steaming plate of food. I devour a piece of bacon.

The man picks up a saltshaker, adding a healthy dose to his eggs. "Mildred never seasons a single thing around here." Instead of diving back into his breakfast, he taps his fork on the side of his plate. "What's ya father's name?"

"Daxson Barellis, but his good friends and my mom called him Dax." I take a sip of water, hoping this man has heard of him before. Not that I'd want to see the man who left me in favor of a life of adventure.

The man mumbles an indecipherable string of words as he wads up his napkin. "Can I get my bill?"

"What was that?" I ask, desperate to hear more from this man who obviously knows something.

"If you know what's good for ya, stay away from your father and his whole lot. The Northern Duke's not to be trifled with on a good day." He mutters a few curse words, counts coins from his pocket, and drops them on the counter. "No worries, Mildred," he calls. "I overpaid ya."

I grab the man's sleeve as he slips from his stool. "Please, tell me more."

"The only other thing I'll tell ya is the man's crazy. Same goal as the rest of the Redeemed, but he thinks working with the

Supes is the way to accomplish it." He rakes his eyes over me. "Scrawny little thing, aren't ya? The Northern Duke will eat you up and spit you out. Doesn't matter you're his spawn."

I sit back down on the stool to steady myself. Dax Barellis is alive and well. Did he know about my mother's death and my expulsion? And if he did, why didn't he send someone for me? The Northern Duke does not sound like the man I knew. The man who bought me a music box, and who my little heart loved until he broke it.

"Do you want to take breakfast up to your husband?" Mildred breaks into my thoughts. "He says you have a bit of traveling out to your sister's farm." She leans over the counter, closer to me. "They say the way to a man's heart is through his stomach."

"Thanks for the advice." I give her a quick smile, not having the strength to smash her illusion of my relationship with Levi. "Can you pack him something to go?"

"No problem. I'll have it ready when the two of you check out."

I climb the stairs to our room in a daze, chewing on the old man's words. When I enter our room, Levi's awake and dressed, sitting in a chair and reading a book beside the oil lamp. The world outside is still gray with the early morning light. He looks up.

"Good morning." I close the door and lift my pack to the bed to organize it. "Did you sleep well?"

Signing, he says, "Surprisingly well. How about you?"

"Fine." I remove a sweater to throw over my tunic. There's a chill in the air. "What do you know about the Northern Duke?"

His eyes widen. "Where did you hear about him?"

"At breakfast." I don't want to reveal how I know the duke. A lot of emotions swirl through me regarding my father and abandonment. "An older man mentioned the faction of the Redeemed who work with Supes."

"Supes… wayward Miscretes." Levi sets his book on the table beside the oil lamp. "The guy's missing a few screws in the head."

Though I want to know more about my father, I drop it for now. As soon as the first rays of the sun hit, I want to be on the road so we can get back to Rumsford before dark. "Sounds like a real piece of work. Are you ready to head downstairs?"

He stuffs his book in his pack, shrugs on his coat, and throws his bag on his shoulder. "Are you sure you want to go to Mafekadi? That's where that fairy's headed. What happened last night made me nervous, and I'm part fae."

"You said most of the fae in the town are harmless, right?"

"Yes," he says.

I remove a dagger from my cloak. "And you said this is made of iron, correct?"

"Yes… but…"

"Then I have confidence in our ability to defend ourselves if needed." I throw on my cloak and open the door. "You coming?"

NESTLED in a valley between the sloping foothills of the massive mountain, about a two-hour hike from Rumsford is the settlement of Mafekadi. Along the way, Levi and I discuss the prophecy and Avo, his closest friend among the fae.

When we finally crest the hillside, the air is thick with enchantment, tingling my skin. Looking down at the village, I see it holds a blend of organic architecture and natural formations. Giant mushroom caps serve as rooftops, while intricate carvings depicting scenes from fae folklore, cover the walls of the homes. Elaborate treehouses constructed from intertwined branches and vines sway gently in the breeze, creating a seamless connection between the structures and the surrounding forest. Wind chimes hanging from the same trees emit haunting tunes throughout the valley.

A brook meanders through the center of the village, providing a mirrored surface to reflect the deep greens and vibrant colors of the surrounding foliage. Stone bridges arch over the water, connecting different parts of the village and leading to communal gathering spaces.

My mouth hangs open. Never in my life have I witnessed the antithesis of Avren. The city is the pinnacle of human innovation and progress, creating imitations of the natural world with metal, stone, and plastics. Mafekadi embodies what it looks like when creatures and the natural world work together. "I'm speechless."

"It's pretty amazing, right?" Levi loops his arm in mine and drags me along the moss-covered path.

As much as I want to delve into the intricacies of the village's beauty, standing on the hillside and admiring it from afar is almost as tempting. It's a dream. At any moment, someone will pinch me, and I'll wake up. "How does it make you feel to be here?"

"Like I'm home." The corner of Levi's mouth tilts upward. "As much as the four of you are my family, Mafekadi stirs the part of me I try to hide."

"I like that part of you." I adjust my hold on his arm, drawing him in closer so he knows I'm here for him no matter what happens. "Don't hide it."

In the heart of the village, there's a communal square I assume is used for celebrations and gatherings. I can only imagine the breathtaking nature of a fae wedding. Ancient standing stones, each engraved with symbols, surround the square.

Many eyes are on us as we walk through the village. Although Levi is part fae and visits Mafekadi, he is still clearly human. The looks are more curious than menacing, and the overall calming magic in the air makes me feel at ease.

"Avo lives about two blocks from here." He leads me between two homes, through a garden, and into another patch of dwellings. Bright swatches of flowers adorn the cobblestone walkways to the homes.

While I want to visit Levi's friend, I haven't forgotten about the material I hope to purchase for the new clothes. But looking at Mafekadi, I don't see a single store. I might find a tailor in Rumsford on the way back.

Levi knocks on the door of a home with thousands of daisies growing up to our waists beside the front walk. The smell of the entire valley is intoxicating, and I'm not sure if it's the scent of the flowers or the magical nature making me want to find a patch of grass to take a nap in.

Standing outside the door, my eyes start to close before I'm startled awake by its opening. A man, about a head taller than Levi with long, golden hair, stands on the threshold for a second before embracing my friend.

"Levi Crassus! It's been months." He sways back and forth with his arms still wrapped tightly around the smaller man. There's no smile on his face. "I almost thought you'd joined the First City."

Levi pats him on the back, probably not hearing a word he's saying. He moves away from his friend and holds a hand out to me before signing, "This is Maribel Windsong. The woman I told you about in the letter I sent with Wix."

"Ah… the Citizen gone rogue." Avo pulls me into a hug, but it's not as tight as I expect it to be. "Levi's told me all about you. Didn't think that exclusive little group would ever let another one in. You must be something special."

"If you count a woman who's never cooked, cleaned, or shot an arrow straight regularly as special, then you're a genius in your assessment." I still don't understand the magnetic pull Levi feels around me. "Unless my personality draws you in." Smiling, I follow Avo into the house.

"Have a seat," he says, ushering us to a bench formed by the giant roots of a tree. Entanglements of herbs and plants hang from the ceiling, giving the room a thick smell. Earthen-colored pillows cover the seating area. Bringing us each a cup of tea, he sits on the floor by our feet, his legs crisscrossed. "The prophecy's clear. One savior will come from Avren." Moving to his knees, he lights a long stick in the fireplace before bringing it back to me.

"What is that?" In the wilderness, there are many things I've witnessed not present in the city. Most have to do with the spiritual realm or necessities not needed in a progressive community.

"It reveals the hidden." Avo moves the smoking stick slowly around my body. It has a sweet, woody aroma which calms my nerves.

I close my eyes, giving in to the fae's magic. Though I don't know Avo enough to trust him, I trust Levi. If this creature can decipher the puzzle of who I am, I have no problem with him waving his smoky wand.

"It is written." Avo's voice echoes through my head. "So shall it be."

I open my eyes and look from Avo to Levi. "What's that supposed to mean?"

"Your presence, your aura, and the clear attraction you emit tell me you are the first half of the prophecy." He brushes his long hair over his shoulder and tosses the smoking stick into the fire. It releases a purplish hue in the flames. "I'm but a simple fae, but my instincts hold the same clarity as the greatest among us."

"Do you know anything about the missing piece of the prophecy?" Levi signs out his words.

"If you didn't have luck with your uncle in Frostacre, I'm afraid you won't find an answer here. The Unseelie Court stole the prophecy from us years ago. They are the ones to ask." He stands and leans against a door, probably leading to a bedroom.

"Bracken won't tell me anything. It's like asking a wall for help." Levi draws in a sharp breath, places his elbows on his knees, and buries his fingers in his hair.

"Do you think the fae from the Unseelie Court will listen to me?" I place a hand on his back, trying to find some way to be useful. "If Avo can see I'm a so-called savior, won't they sense the same thing? I need to know who I'm working with if I'm supposed to take down two cities."

Levi sits up straight, interlocking his fingers with mine. "You're never to go to Frostacre. It isn't safe for a human."

The door to the bedroom opens, revealing a fae with silver hair. Quinn Malum. "She doesn't have to travel to Frostacre alone. The king sent me to be her personal escort.

CHAPTER FIFTEEN

*L*evi draws an iron dagger from the inside of his coat, leaps to his feet, and holds it in a shaking hand pointed at Quinn. "Over my dead body."

With a bored expression, Quinn holds a palm to Levi's forehead. "Fine with me."

My heart pounds, and I watch in horror as my friend crumples to the ground. Without a second thought, I drop to my knees beside his lifeless body, my hands trembling as I try to shake him awake, the weight of fear and helplessness settling in my stomach.

Wake up, Levi.

"You said no one would get hurt." Avo's voice sounds miles away as I gather Levi into my arms.

A hand grips the back of my cloak, and I'm ripped away from him. He falls back to the floor. "He's not dead, only in a deep sleep. Should give us enough time to get halfway to Frostacre."

A coal of hatred ignites deep inside my chest, ready to burst out and show this evil fae exactly what I'm made of. With two swift strokes, I jab him in the face with my elbow and execute a perfect round kick, knocking him on his ass.

Bastian would be proud.

I race to the front door and throw it open, only to find two enormous wolves waiting for me outside. Saliva drips from their mouths as they claw at the ground with paws the size of my head. My beleaguered heart races with adrenaline, which is rapidly dropping with the loss of my escape.

"You don't think I travel alone, do you, Miss Windsong?" Standing, Quinn crosses the floor in two long strides, snatches my arm, and pulls me tight against him. "When the king of Frostacre delegates a task to me, I don't disappoint."

The same icy chill I felt the night before rushes through me in a shiver.

Quinn muscles me out the door, practically throwing me on top of a wolf. To my surprise, I'm resting belly-down on top of a saddle. "Sit up, or it will be a very uncomfortable two-day ride."

Besides the stupid prophecy, what does the king of Frostacre want with a "useless woman from Avren" as the commander puts it? I struggle into a seated position, finding the rancid, steaming breath of the creature beneath me almost too much to take. The wolves seem so out of place in the peaceful valley of Mafekadi.

Avo clutches the doorframe, his face sheet white and tears streaming down his face. "I'm so sorry, Maribel. You're such a pleasant girl, but he threatened to kill Levi." He looks back into the room behind him. "I'll make sure he recovers, if he doesn't stab me with his iron dagger when he wakes. I'm afraid he'll never forgive me for this one." The fae closes the door, leaving me alone with Quinn and his monster wolves.

"Why did you manipulate him?" I clutch the saddle, afraid I might fall from my mount. I glance over the side at the dizzying height.

Quinn adjusts his saddle, places a foot in the stirrup, and with one lithe movement, sits atop his wolf. "It's the only way to get what you want." A wicked smile spreads over his lips. "Besides, he won't have to worry about it for too long. I dropped a healthy dose of ground Sneed Root into his tea. Deadly to fairies."

With that, Quinn's wolf takes off, with mine right behind it. I don't have a chance to process what he said because I'm clinging to the saddle for dear life. The wind howls around us as the wolf's powerful muscles surge beneath me, propelling us forward through the forest. The rhythmic pounding of its paws against the earth echoes in my ears along with a voice somewhere in the back of my mind screaming that I need to turn back. But it is impossible.

The world blurs around us, trees becoming a kaleidoscope of greens and browns as we speed through the dense forest. As it navigates the wild terrain, the wolf maneuvers around obstacles, leaping over fallen logs and weaving through the underbrush. My hands ache from holding on because half the time, it feels as if I'm about to fall to my death.

And yet, like Mafekadi, there's an untamed magic in the journey somehow keeping me from slipping. When I entered the fae village, I felt alive for the first time in my life, making my mundane existence within Avren's walls feel lifeless. Although Quinn is taking me to a place that turns my skin cold just thinking about it, this journey is what the wilderness is all about.

We finally slow to a halt outside of Rumsford. Quinn dismounts his wolf but doesn't make any kind of move to help me get down.

"I need to pick up something I left behind." He crosses his arms, giving me a smug expression. "My wolves will babysit you while I'm gone."

As he strides away, the arrogant straightness of his back, along with his confidence, makes him even more attractive. I shake my head, trying to clear it of his glamour.

"Oh, and Maribel, darling." He turns, looking a hundred times better than any of the models in the city. "If you try to escape, we'll ride together for the rest of the journey, and Brutus will go back to Mafekadi and tear your friend to shreds." He pets his wolf on the muzzle.

When Quinn is nowhere in sight, I test the waters by slipping slightly to the right in the saddle. It garners a low growl from my wolf. A warning. Even if I manage to drop to the ground, I believe the fae's word about killing Levi. What's the worst that can happen if he takes me to Frostacre? The king wants me for a reason, which I assume involves keeping me alive. He sent a bounty hunter after me. I play out different scenarios: he keeps me in prison, he sends me to a laboratory to test my abilities, or he wants me as his queen. Ok, my mind is wandering a bit too much. I give into my furry prison, pitching forward and laying my head on its neck.

The absolute worst scenario would be if the Kindred Few come to rescue me. Grayson and Levi won't hesitate. They were in Frostacre days before. Bastian and Evie will grumble about wasting time and resources on me, but in the end, they'll give in to their brothers because they're family.

I close my eyes, succumbing to the gentle rhythm of the wolf's breaths.

"Wake up, Maribel," a voice tickles my ear. "We need to get to the Gretis Expanse by nightfall. Word of your existence has spread, and I have little doubt the vampire queen wants in on this action."

"But why?" I sit up, my back aching from lying in a strange position for so long. If I fulfill this damn prophecy and take down two cities with my bare hands with a mystery person by my side, who's saying I won't dismantle the Supe kingdoms too? Apparently, I have kickass, untapped skills I have no knowledge of.

Quinn mounts his wolf, then circles around me as easily as if he were guiding a horse. His silver hair flows over his shoulders as if painted by an artist's brush. "I am the simple retriever. Those are questions for King Cirrus, if he chooses to answer."

"If I'm so powerful, Mr. Malum, why aren't you shaking in your boots?" I wish I had the power to call lightning down and blast him into oblivion for what he did to Levi and Avo.

In a slow, methodical motion, Quinn sidles up beside my wolf and leans in close. His breath has the power to freeze me from the inside out. I shudder as the pad of his lip touches my earlobe, but I can't seem to move away. "Because you haven't had your awakening. When we reach the expanse, I can lay you down in the grass and show you all kinds of things."

I lean away from him, almost falling from my wolf. "In your dreams, fairy boy." The real power coursing through me is the ability to resist his glamour in brief spurts. If I can push the edges out for longer periods, I might see the bloodthirsty, disgusting creature hiding behind his pretty face.

He frowns. "Methinks, you have a too much freedom for such a smartass little girl." With a wave of his hand, golden rings encircle my hands, keeping them in place on my wolf's saddle. A shimmering material floats through the air and covers my mouth.

What the hell? I try to say the words out loud, but nothing comes out.

"Behave yourself, and I might remove them tonight." And with that, Quinn takes off again, my wolf following closely behind.

We ride along a less-travelled path, circling the Lake of Glass. The day before, when Levi and I walked the shore, my heart was full, basking in the opportunity to get out of the cabin and explore. Today, going to a new place fills me with dread. The bindings make me feel more helpless than I did before, and I still don't know what the king of the Unseelie Court wants with me.

Beyond the lake, the landscape thickens with pine forests, farther to the south of the Grove. As Quinn slows his wolf near a stream, I gaze into the valley below. How far away are Bastian, Grayson, and Evie? What will they do when they return and Levi and I are gone?

Quinn dismounts, leading his wolf to the water. With a flick of his wrist, my bindings disappear, and he holds a hand to me. "Get down. Humans have so many needs to attend to."

I twist onto my stomach, placing a foot in the stirrup, and hop down, stumbling and landing on my bottom.

"So graceful, my dear." He takes the reins of my wolf and leads it to the stream, where the creature greedily laps up the water. "The king prefers curtsies."

"Remind me to practice after I use the little girl's room." I inch toward a tree and motion with my thumb. "Do you mind?"

He removes a pipe from a satchel slung over his shoulder, strikes a match, and lights it before slinking down and sitting against a tree. He closes his eyes. "Don't be gone for too long."

Behind the tree, I rest the back of my head on the bark and envision my next move. About ten minutes ago, we passed a stand of boulders I recognized as a place close to the Grove. And the Grove isn't more than ten minutes from the cabin. A mixture of fear and excitement stab at me. If I make a run for it, he will catch me—especially on a wolf. But there's a possibility I can make it back to the cabin within the safety of the wards before he knows I'm gone.

I need to try because the alternative is too horrific to imagine. Levi never told me about the king in Frostacre, only about his uncle.

Not wanting to think about it anymore, I creep along the leaf-littered path until I'm confident I'm out of earshot, and then I sprint. I can only pray to the wilderness's gods above—something I've never done before—that I'm headed in the right direction. After a minute or two of running, I'm out of breath. I want—no, I *need* to stop, but the fear keeps my legs pumping.

With the Grove in sight, I hurtle over a log, only to trip on my own feet and land flat on my face. A spray of loose dirt enters my mouth and I sputter. From the sting on my knee and elbow, I'm certain I have multiple scrapes. But I need to keep moving. Scrambling to my hands and knees, I pull myself to a standing position, though my body cries out to remain vertical.

The air is suddenly thick with magic. Unlike the magic in Mafekadi, this has a stranglehold on me. I struggle to free myself from my invisible bindings.

"If you take advantage of the freedoms I afford you, I'll have to keep you close." Quinn saunters toward me from beneath the shadow of a large tree. "And I have no option but to punish you. Which do you prefer—a rat's tail or a pig's snout?"

I pinch up my face, frustrated to have come so far yet fall just short of my goal. There's nothing I have to say to Malum.

Take me to your king. Let him do as he pleases. I hope you rot in hell for this, you piece of fairy shit.

"Where's my wolf?" I grumble. "You'll have to help me up."

Quinn's lips pull into his infamous, evil smirk. "Oh, no, my dear. You'll walk the rest of the way to the expanse. And if we don't make it by twilight, you'll suffer the consequences." He pats me on the cheek.

An invisible force tugs me along behind him through the forested path. It's when I'm looking down, counting the square-shaped stones, that I hear something whiz past me, and then the sickening smack of an arrow hitting flesh. I duck, unsure of who or what is attacking us, before looking at Quinn.

Lodged in his chest is a flaming arrow, his beautiful fae face melting away from the heat right before his entire body bursts into flames. My invisible bonds disappear, and I scramble on my hands and knees to the nearest bush, diving into the foliage. I struggle to control my staggered breathing as I try to picture the creature brave enough to take on a fairy. And what other kind of Supe wants me badly enough to risk its life?

Footfalls crunch on the path beside my hiding place. I bite

down on my lip, trying not to breathe. Through the leaves, I see heavy black boots. If it's a vampire or werewolf, I'm sure it can smell me from a mile away.

"Are you going to come out of there or continue your silly game of hide-and-seek?" The deep gravel of Bastian's voice lifts my spirit and mortifies me at the same time.

I stand, unsure if I should burst forward and hug him or remain in the safety of the bush. "You killed him." It's an obvious statement with the fae's burning carcass catching a nearby patch of grass on fire.

Bastian mumbles one of his favorite obscenities, removes his coat, and uses it to bat down the flames. "And I'll kill you and Levi once you tell me where he is. You scared the hell out of us."

"You weren't supposed to be back for a week," I say, hanging my head.

"And the two of you thought it might be a good idea to hand you over to the Unseelie Court on a silver plate?" He rakes his fingers through his hair. Bloodstains and jagged rips cover his clothing. A fresh scar runs from his right eye down to the corner of his lip.

Impulsively, I reach out and almost touch his cheek but pull back when he flinches. My heart drops. I repulse him. "What happened?"

"Failed mission," he grumbles, shrugging his coat back on. "Lost Lyden and could have damn well lost Mav if it wasn't for Evie's quick thinking." Impossible as it seems, his eyes darken, strands of hair falling over them like the first time we met. "And then when we get home, you're gone. We thought the Miscretes had you." He cocks his head to the side and crosses his arms. "But no, it was only a powerful fae bounty hunter, and your brother's still nowhere to be found."

I stare at my shoes, unable to look him in the eyes. They're icy fire, able to ignite me like the smoldering corpse on the ground. "Levi's safe. He's in Mafekadi."

"Mafekadi!" He grips my hand, yanking me from the safety of my mulberry bush. Despite the situation, I feel a charge of electricity with his calloused skin against mine. "He exposed you for an entire day. No wonder Cirrus's pansy sniffed you out. We have wards on the cabin for a reason."

"Well, maybe I'm tired of you confining me to the cabin. If I'm let out, I need a babysitter." I drop his hand, balling mine into fists. Yes, the Council controlled my life in Avren, but my situation here isn't much better.

"You don't understand." His eyes drill into mine as if begging me to see his side. "We don't know the complete prophecy yet, but if you fall into the hands of a Supe leader, they'll do anything to find the other piece of the puzzle, do away with Avren and the First City, and set up their own dominion. Do you want to see the humans who survive the attack subject to slavery?"

I bite into my lip, chewing on the hypothetical projections he's thrown at me. "And what's the alternative?"

He takes a step closer to me, making my hands shake slightly. His palms lightly grip my upper arms as I drown in his lakes of crystal blue. "Peace. No pillars of fear rising as sentinels in the north and the south. The prophecy promises balance once we defeat Avren and the First City."

With his fingers practically burning through the thin material of my sweater, I swallow, wondering if he feels the tight cord between us. "And your job is to keep me safe and get me in shape for the monumental task ahead of me."

He drops his hands, and I breathe again. "Exactly. And having you wandering miles to the south, unguarded, doesn't make my job any easier."

"Why don't you trust Levi to protect me?"

He glances at the pile of ashes lying on the ground, a testament to where trusting his brother got me, and I don't say another word.

CHAPTER SIXTEEN

*G*rayson and Evie suit up to travel to Mafekadi and collect Levi, loading their holsters with enough weapons to take down Avren on their own. My gut twists in knots when I realize this will leave Bastian and me alone together in the cabin. Images from my dream rush in from my subconscious, and it's everything I can do to keep from dropping the dish I'm scrubbing in the sink.

He's your brother, Mari.

"We'll be back in a couple of days. The two of you behave." Grayson winks at me before pulling me into a hug. "Sorry we're leaving him to babysit you, but he needs to continue your training."

"I understand." I really don't. Grayson took down a were-wolf, so he's capable of training me. Why does it have to be Bastian, a person who thinks I'm about as worthless as a slithering slug?

And as quickly as I lay a dish on the counter, they leave, and we're alone.

Bastian settles into the armchair by the fire, puts on his glasses, and picks up the book I was reading a few days ago. That he's more than his muscles and warrior mindset draws me to him.

He's your brother, Mari... with no blood relation.

There goes my heart, trying to justify the thoughts I should never have.

As a family, we are alike in our fierce protection of our brothers and sisters because we only have each other.

I rinse off a dish and place it on the counter to dry before wiping my hands on a towel. My heart races, threatening to break through my chest. He's given me no sign that he wants more from me than a sibling relationship. But he must feel it.

With slow steps, so as not to disturb his reading, I round the armchair and sit on the ottoman beside his feet. He doesn't look up, totally engrossed in his book.

It feels like hours pass before I finally work up the courage to place a gentle hand on his ankle. "Bastian?"

He looks up at me, one eyebrow raising slightly, then at my hand on his ankle. Without responding, he reaches into his pocket and removes the glowing blue anklet he hid while he was away. "I don't want soldiers sniffing around here." He tosses me the ring. "Put this on. You'll go to work tonight."

My heart plummets. I thought we'd have alone time. Time to work out the confusing feelings I have for this man. "Don't you want company when the others are away?"

He lifts his shoulder as the corner of his lip rises into a slight smirk. "I like my alone time. And if I get lonely, I can ask Susan to spend the night." But the glimmer in his eyes tells me something different, like he's begging me to stand up to him—to push past the wall between us.

But I can't.

I'm not strong enough yet. Too many years under Avren's rules regarding relationships have left their mark on me. In my brokenness, I can't make the first move, no matter how hard it was for me to touch his ankle without permission.

My throat is so dry, it feels as if it's stuffed with cotton balls as I work up the courage to ask my next question. "What happened with Lyden?"

He shifts in the armchair and frowns, keeping his gaze on his book as he traces the embossed title with his finger. "I let him down." There's an unfamiliar crack in his voice, one I'm sure he keeps hidden from most. "I let Mav and Carl down."

His vulnerability makes my palms sweat in my lap. There's so much I want to say to him: *You could never let them down... I'm sure you tried your best... You're the commander.* But the words stay trapped behind my lips. They're trivial to him.

"I told the others not to follow me into their stronghold. To protect them." Red rims his eyes as he holds back his dark hair, fingers buried in his long bangs. "In my fucking vanity, I thought I could go it alone." His chest heaves, and I can tell he's fighting back the tears. "It was me and Lyden alone in the cave, and I should've known it was a trap. The second they swarmed, he screamed out for me, but there was nothing I could do as I fought the bastards off with my sword."

"What happened to him?" I've inched closer, my knees now touching the chair.

"When I finally broke free, there was nothing left." His sobs finally come as he reaches out and pulls me into his arms.

I stiffen, unsure what to do in the embrace of a man who lives his life to confuse me. But he doesn't let go, so I slip my arms around his back and rest my head on his chest. The heaves come at regular intervals. He needs the comfort of someone in his arms, and my infatuated heart will play that role despite the damage it might bring.

His chin rests on top of my head. Fingers trail along my back. I know he's thinking. But I'm not sure if he's reliving the experience or trying to determine how much he wants to divulge. From the awkward embrace, it's obvious he doesn't spill his heart out very often.

"What if they see me as weak?" His words hang between us, spoken so softly, I don't know if I hear him correctly.

I lift my head to look at him. There's an unfamiliar vulnerability in his expression. His eyes search mine, and they don't hold the confident steel of the commander. They're softer, seeking advice from an equal.

"No one in this entire world sees you as weak, especially me." Heat rushes to my cheeks, so I quickly add, "You're Commander Bastian Hale."

With a brush of his hand, his fingers linger along my neckline as he raises the silver locket Levi gave me in his palm. "Filled it with yarrow, didn't he?"

"Yes." A smile crosses my lips, thinking about Levi's return.

Bastian holds the locket between his thumb and forefinger. "Probably told you it would protect you from the fairies in Mafekadi. Lot of good that did you. From now on, I'll be your fae repellant, and your vampire repellant, and your werewolf repellant."

Does that mean he plans to keep me close?

"Didn't tell you it's one of his top ten major allergies, did he?" He rolls his head to the side, appraising me again.

"That makes sense." I take back the locket, our fingers briefly touching. I shiver. "He's part fae."

His eyes widen. "How do you know that?"

"There's a lot you get to know about someone when you're left alone together." Gathering a bit of courage, I touch his shirt with my fingertips. "What secrets are you holding?"

He doesn't reward me for my bravado, instead moving me to the side so he can stand. "Better change into your work clothes. They'll expect you before the sun sets and, like I said, I don't want them snooping around here."

My shoulders slump. I thought I'd broken through to him, but the grumpy side of Bastian has resurfaced. The thought of facing the guards at the cave into the city and my boorish boss again has me reeling. "Can't we hide my anklet? If I stay here, I can repair your fighting gear."

"They'll find out." He clomps to the doorway, removes his cloak, and throws it over his shoulders. "They always do."

"Sounds like you have experience," I grumble, disliking the idea of giving up on the fight.

"I said, get your work clothes." He tosses a rope, an apple, and a book into a sack. Strange combination. "I don't want to get home too late."

We trek through the forest in silence as I chew on my inner lip and wonder what my punishment will be for missing work the past couple of days. Probably an extra hour here and there. Maybe putting me on public bathroom duty for a day or two. Bastian will make up an excuse for me.

To my surprise, he walks beside me as opposed to our usual commander-and-subservient position. In the silence, every nerve in my body picks up on the occasional brush of his sleeve against mine, noting how he quickly moves away.

A cool breeze rustles the tops of the trees. It masks the usual noises in the woods that have me on edge. Bastian's presence also has me much more at ease in a place that haunts my nightmares. Even the glow of the luminescent forest doesn't calm me in the same way. He can single-handedly relax and ravage me in the same breath without knowing his effect.

When we reach the top of the hill, he removes a dagger from beneath his cloak and holds it in his left hand. With his right, he takes mine, surprising me. "If the guards think we're together, they're more likely to leave you alone. Bunch of dirty lowlifes."

I don't argue. If I never have to encounter Grayson's school friends again, I'll die a happy woman. Besides, I enjoy having his hand in mine again. With my free hand, I lift the hood of my cloak. The less attention I draw, the better.

"Will you come to collect me?" The others are gone, so it is an obvious answer, but the silence is deafening.

"Be ready when the moon is at its highest in the sky." The lump in his throat bobs as he stares at the line of guards at the entrance. "I'll wait by that tree." He nods at a tall fir to the left of the soldiers.

My fingers grip his tighter. "I still don't see why I can't stay with you. We can hide the anklet far away from the cabin. They'll never find me."

With a quick tug, he has my shoulders in his hands, his eyes drilling into mine. "You don't know how to take no for an answer, do you? I've already said I can't be alone with you."

I study the lines of his face, trying to decipher every crease and angle. Desperation makes me want to touch the scar on his lip, but I tremble with the thought. "I'm still not sure why the tough commander can face a vampire or an army of Miscretes but he's afraid of me. I can't hit a tree with an arrow ninety percent of the time."

When I don't move away, he closes his eyes, his chest rising and falling. He massages my shoulders with his gentle touch. "I feel things toward you I shouldn't. There's a magnetic pull I'm desperately trying to fight, but whenever I think I'm gaining ground, I slip backward." He drops his hands, breaking the connection I crave whenever he touches me. "We'll continue training, but only in the Grove with the others around." He rakes his hand through his hair. "I can't believe Gray and Evie left me alone with you."

"They know?" I'm already reeling from his admission. No wonder he acts like such an asshole around me. Has he talked about his desires with them? Pinpricks of embarrassment prickle my skin. This is only a crush—one I can keep to myself in the privacy of my dreams.

He clears his throat, staring over my shoulder at the guards by the entrance. "I mentioned it to Gray. Thought he'd know a way to snap the connection, because I haven't found a way to break it myself."

My gut twists with nausea. "Sorry to inconvenience you." I whip around and march toward the guards, done with this conversation. He has a girlfriend. I get it. But he doesn't have to make me feel like I'm a wart on his thumb.

"If it isn't Grayson's little sister." The taller guard who gave me a hard time the other night walks up to me, appraising my outfit. He glances around and smirks. "Doesn't look like you have your bodyguard tonight." His smirk widens as he reaches out and touches my hair.

I smack his hand away, the uncomfortable twist in my gut transforming into bubbling anger. "Don't touch me."

He circles me, his eyes raking over my chest. Why did I wear Evie's blouse that clings a little too tightly to my breasts? Because I was thinking about spending time with Bastian, not coming to work in Avren.

"You haven't shown up for work the past two nights," he states, taking the clipboard from the metal box. "Supervisor moved you. Can't have workers not showing up for mission-critical positions."

"The Sweet Street Bakery is a mission-critical position?" I suppose if children aren't getting their sweets, there could be anarchy in the pristine streets.

"For some it is." Without warning, he swats me on the bottom with the clipboard. "But with a little persuasion on your part, I could move you back to your cushy job. Give me fifteen minutes behind the trees over there."

"Like hell. I'd rather clean toilets." I want to use the leg sweep on him but think better of it. "Take me to my job running the machines in the cavern. I know that's where you moved me." The idea of running the machines all night is soul-sucking. But losing my virginity to this man would kill me.

Instead of turning to lead me to the cavern, he grips my hair, making it obvious that he's made up his mind. The other guards keep their gazes away from us, and I know this practice is a regular occurrence for the women of the wilderness.

He drags me behind a stand of trees, their luminescent glow lighting the twisted grin on his face. This is all about power for him, and I need to stop it. As he lowers a hand to unzip his pants, I plant my left leg and swing out my right, knocking him to the ground. Before I can think about running, he reaches out and snatches my ankle, and I hear the crack as I fall to the ground. My face plants in the soil. Pain spreads up my leg, but a voice in my head tells me to run. I can hear him crawling toward me, his panting heavy. As I lift to a sprinter's position, my injury becomes too much to take. Seconds after he grabs hold of my injured ankle, twisting it in an unbearable grip, he releases, and I fall back to the ground, my face covered in dirt and tears.

Strong arms wrap around me, raising me from the ground. Gentle lips touch my ear and whisper, "You're a badass."

Right. The soldier was seconds away from raping and possibly murdering me, and I'm the poster child for tough women everywhere. I'm too tired to argue, nestling into his familiar scent—woodsy like a campfire. The pain of my ankle dulls in his presence. Bastian Hale makes me feel safer than my comforter in my bedroom in Avren. I keep my eyes closed, resting my head on his shoulder as I hear the snap of my ankle bracelet and the thud as it hits the ground. I let him carry me back to our cabin.

As he walks in silence, I want to ask him about the soldier. Is he dead? Not that I care. The Council allows guards to control the Undesirables however they see fit—to treat them like cattle, doing the dirty work to keep the people of Avren alive. For the first time, I see clearly why the Redeemed need to destroy the city.

"Susan will be angry. I told her we had the cabin to ourselves tonight." His hand moves back and forth on my arm, and I'm not sure if he's trying to comfort me or if he's doing it as he's thinking. "She's already jealous of you."

I open my eyes, letting them adjust to the lights above us. His face holds an unfamiliar look. His eyes appear softer as they search my face. His full lips lift into a slight smile.

"I've never studied your face before. You're the first person I've met with perfect skin. I'm afraid to touch it because you might break like a doll."

Is that a backhanded compliment?

"Before you came along, the soldier didn't have an issue with burying my *perfect* face in the ground, so it must not be that rare." I, along with the others in Avren, had ways to care for our skin using minerals from the caves. Exfoliating our skin in the mud baths of Galraith was a routine with my mother. My hand shaking slightly, I touch his cheek. "You should try a mud bath sometime."

He laughs, shaking me with the movement of his chest. "A bath in mud. That's a new one. I thought farmers reserved dirty baths for the pigs." He lifts an eyebrow and raises the corner of his lip. "But I have to admit, it sounds intriguing."

Silence falls between us, so I close my eyes to rest, nuzzling my face against his chest and taking advantage of the closeness—a luxury I'll probably never experience again.

About halfway to the cabin, he stops and sits by a tree, keeping me in his arms. I readjust so I'm sitting in his lap but don't move my head from his chest. "I never wanted to kill someone so badly in my life."

"If I hadn't twisted my ankle, I think I could have gotten away." I look down at my boot. My ankle pulsates beneath the tight leather.

Bastian lifts to his knees, turns, and sets me on the ground. He touches the laces on my boot. "May I?"

I nod. The heaviness of the sole of my boot pulled on my ankle during our trek through the woods, making it ache more.

He unlaces the boot all the way, then gently lifts my ankle to slip the shoe from my foot. When he rolls down my sock, I wince, feeling a shock of pain shoot up my leg. A black and purple swelling protrudes from my skin.

"It's more than likely broken." With my sock still off, he scoops me into his arms and carries me to the nearby stream, having me rest on the bank. "Put it in the water for a while."

Obeying my doctor's orders, I gingerly dip the lower part of my right leg into the water. It's ice-cold. "In the city, we have healers who care for the sick and injured. Are there any healers in the wilderness?"

"There's Ben Finch. Lives on the far side of the Lake of Glass in a hermit's hut. Guy's as crazy as they come, but he's helped me remove a stray arrow or two." He lowers his tunic from his shoulder, revealing a scar about the size of a small stone. "Hurt like hell."

"If my ankle's broken, what do you think he'll do?" Images of what I used to think people in the wilderness looked like come to mind.

"Keep it immobile, possibly reset it." He gives me a wicked grin, setting my heart racing.

"Can we do it without Ben?" All I want is to lie in my bed and fall asleep. Walking another hour past the cabin, even in Bastian's arms, sounds daunting. "It will heal eventually."

"We could, but we can't. If you're the so-called savior of the world, I need to get you back out on the training field. Having you in bed for a month won't work." He carries my boot over from the spot by the tree then yanks the hem of his shirt from his pants. Before I know it, he has his tunic completely removed and I'm staring at his chest.

Oh, help me.

Bastian is the most beautiful creature I've ever laid eyes on. Runes dance along his skin, over his pectoral muscles and circle his arms. One is of the four intertwined circles on my locket, a sign of his commitment to his brothers and sister. His hard chest muscles lead down to a trim waist where his pants hang low.

I swallow, ripping my gaze away before he catches me looking.

He drops to one knee beside me, lifting my leg from the water and using his tunic to dry it. His fingers move in a slow, soft pattern which feels more intimate than it should. "I'm not hurting you, am I?"

"No."

Only my heart.

This side of him is so different from the commander on the field, or the brother brooding around the others. His words from the morning in the field with the vampire come back. *Touch her and die.*

Three times he's killed someone or something that tried to harm me. He takes his familial bonds seriously. And that's how he sees me—his little sister. Sure, he has his weird, twisted magnetic fascination with me, but he's trying to break it.

Maybe I should try harder to break it.

"We'll keep your shoe off the rest of the way," he says, bending over to lift me and not bothering to put his shirt back on. He knows what he's doing.

I trace his Kindred Few tattoo with my pointer finger. "When do I get one of these?"

"When you earn it." He doesn't look down as I continue to trace the circles on his skin. "You're not there yet."

CHAPTER SEVENTEEN

a small fire smoldering in the hearth lights the cabin when we enter. The echo of the empty space needs the laughter and banter of the other three, but all I hear are Bastian's heavy footfalls and his breathing. Instead of heading for my bedroom at the rear of the cabin, he carries me to the stairs.

"You'll be more comfortable in my bed tonight." When I go rigid in his arms, he adds, "I'll sleep in Gray's room."

He lays me on the mattress and lights the oil lamp on the bedside table. I act curious, as if this is my first time in his room. Everything is in the same place—the papers on the desk, the drawings on the wall, his bookshelf. I skim my palm over his gray blanket. It's softer than I imagined.

I inspect a parchment nailed to the wall with the five intertwined circles. Each one has its own intricate personality, differentiating itself from the whole. Mine contains arrows, with an occasional heart sprinkled in. He's written my name in neat cursive script along the edge of my ring.

He follows my gaze, runs his hand nervously through his hair, and sits beside me on the bed. "Uh... yeah. As much as I don't like to admit it, you're one of us now. Like it or not."

I prop myself up on my elbows and wince. With this pain, I'm not sure I'll sleep tonight.

"Are you ok?" He reaches out, touching my arm.

I chew on my inner cheek, trying to work up the courage to ask him my next question. His current sympathy for my plight might make it easier. "Will you stay here tonight? I don't think I can sleep, and I could use something to distract me from the pain."

He appears to contemplate my words before saying, "Move over... slowly."

Using my good ankle, I shimmy closer to the wall as Bastian settles in beside me, his shoulder touching mine. "I didn't know you were an artist."

"I'm not." He frowns, appraising his work. "I doodle when things are bothering me."

"And I bother you?" The question opens up a world of possible answers, but I don't care. The only person I've ever had genuine conversations with was my dad. He questioned the very Council he was on, and though I was young, I understood him, unlike anyone else in my life.

His hands are in his lap. He twists a black ring on his pointer finger as he sits in silence. "You bother me more than anyone I've ever met in my life, Windsong."

I quirk my lip when he uses my last name. Is it a term of endearment? And I'm not sure what to make of his proclamation. Do I bother him in a good or bad way? I've already opened a new world between us. Why not continue pushing him? "How so?"

He shifts so he's facing me, close enough that I could reach up and cup his cheek, but I keep my hands firmly beneath my legs. "Ever since my parents died, the prophecy's words have provided the hope I've needed to get by. Someone more powerful than me is out there who will know how to take down the two cities and bring peace to the wilderness. My role was to be a pawn in the savior's army, and if I was lucky, a knight or a bishop. And then you show up with your stupid oversized canvas clothes and terrible aim. Gray insists you are the one. So, I continue to train you because he's my brother." He lifts a hand to my face. "The damn feeling won't go away. You've got me drowning so deep, I'm unsure how I'll ever come up for air. And I've tried to sort my obsession out. Is it attraction or purely a need for self-preservation? My heart knows you're the savior and it wants to protect you, so you can fulfill your role." His finger skims my cheek. "But is it something more?"

My breath catches, my body humming as he moves in closer, resting his forehead against mine. In the stillness, I can hear the pounding of my heart against my chest. Whatever is between us, it goes both ways.

His lips brush over my cheek, leaving a chilling trail to my ear. "As much as I want to, I can't stay away."

Like a forest fire, my body feels like it could go up in flames. In my few heated kisses with Flynn, I never felt the rush of liquid inferno Bastian ignites in me. It's fitting he smells like a campfire.

As he draws back my head, his lips continue to explore my neck, leaving both peppered kisses and lingering tugs as he sucks my skin between his lips. The touch of his mouth sends bolts of electricity to my core.

When he releases my hair, I move a hand along his cheek, running my thumb over his stubble, and he tilts his head into my palm. Hooded with desire, his eyes drop to my lips, and he leans forward to take my mouth with his. The feeling of his full lips on mine is exactly how I imagined it: gentle at first, taking time to savor the taste of each other. Then his teeth scrape my lip, and I open my mouth for his tongue to explore. I barely have time to enjoy the tangle of his tongue with mine before his hand slips down my side, gripping my waist. It slides beneath my shirt and rests on my stomach.

I pull back to catch my breath. "Bastian."

He doesn't respond but lays me farther back on the pillows,

placing a leg on either side of my hips. His long hair partially covers his face as he leans down to take my lips again. Acting purely on desire, I lift my hips to his, but an intense jolt of pain streaks through my leg. Tears fill my eyes, and I curse my injured ankle.

"Are you ok?" He's off me and kneeling beside the bed, his fingers running through my hair. "That was stupid."

Being an insecure idiot, I wonder if he means kissing me was stupid or climbing on top. "Other than the last part, I kind of liked it." My face warms from my vulnerable declaration.

He slips his hand into mine. "I'll get you to Ben tomorrow. For now, it's probably better if I sleep across the hall." There's an unfamiliar shyness in his expression.

I sit up straighter in the bed and place my hands in my lap, twisting the blanket. "It's probably also not the best idea to kiss me when you have a girlfriend."

With that, he's on the bed again, his hand on my thigh. "Susan's not my girlfriend. We spend time together, but we have a mutual agreement to keep feelings out of it."

"You better reiterate that to her. She made it clear that you belong to her. Suggested I spend more time with Rafe." I lean on my side, taking extra care with my ankle.

"Under no circumstances are you to be alone with Rafe." He frowns, his hand massaging my leg. "He's a werewolf in sheep's clothing and always looking for his next conquest."

I don't want to be anyone's conquest—even Bastian's.

"I'll remember that." I force out a weak smile, still sad our kiss kept him from staying. There are so many questions I have about the prophecy, the First City, and about what happened to his parents. They can wait until morning.

He leans forward, kissing me on the cheek and enveloping me in his warm aura. "Good night."

His scent lingers after he's left the room, so I wrap the blanket around me, imagining he's still here and trying to block out the pain of my ankle. I lie awake for a long time, first listening to the sounds across the hall, then the melody of crickets and other creatures outside the window before drifting to sleep.

A SOFT KNOCK on the door wakes me. I stretch my arms above my head. The sharp pain in my leg has blood pumping harder than usual through my veins. I groan loudly, fighting back the tears.

Bastian slams the door open and sits on the bed beside me, lifting the blankets as if they're made of lead, probably trying not to hurt me. He rolls up my pant leg to reveal an ugly mass of black and purple that used to be my ankle. "It's worse than I thought. I need to get you to Ben before you go into shock."

My stomach growls, taking priority over my ankle. "Is there an apple I could take on the road?"

"I made us sandwiches." He stands and walks to the door. "I'll come back to get you in a minute or two."

I shift in the bed so I can hang my legs over the edge and use my arms to prop myself up to a sitting position. It's terrible to feel useless. I balance on my good leg to stand, then hop over the floor to the desk chair, making it easier to manage. The letter Bastian wrote to his friend Xavier was still there the night before, but now it's gone. He didn't want me to read it.

"What are you doing out of bed?" He stands in the doorframe with his cloak and pack on. In his hand is what I assume is my sandwich wrapped in a napkin.

"Put yourself in my situation. You'd never lie around doing nothing." I sit down in the chair and lace on my left boot.

He quirks his lip, scratching his ear. "Yeah… well, at least I'd be smart about not following the doctor's orders. I'd use a crutch so I wouldn't fall."

I lift an eyebrow. "So, you're Doctor Hale now? Better not let that go to your head like the whole commander role." It's flirting, but the truth in my words settles like bricks between us.

"I didn't ask for it." He leans against the doorframe. This morning, he's tied his hair back, revealing his beautifully chiseled jawline. "It's a role I fell into. After my parents died, I wandered for a while, lost in my grief. When I found Levi again, the others assumed I was a rebellion fighter. More like I lifted one too many hay bales in my life. Gray taught me how to use weapons. Turns out, I'm a natural."

"I meant nothing by it." I brace my hand on the desk to stand. "You fit the role so well, I figured you relished in the attention."

"It's the complete opposite." He crosses the room to where I'm standing. "Put your arm around my neck." I comply, and he sweeps me up into his arms as if I weigh nothing. After our time together last night, his touch is magnified, searing my arm and thigh.

I rest my head on his chest as he carries me down the stairs to the living area and then out the back door by my bedroom. We take a different trail than the one we use to go to the training grounds. It's also much later. He let me sleep in.

"I was the youngest of three brothers." He breaks my concentration on the rhythm of his heartbeat. "Frank and Chilon always outshined me in everything—wrestling, farm work, attention from our parents, women. This pushed me inward, so I turned to books and learning to find my worth in a strength-dominated world. Muscles and physical prowess accomplished tasks around the farm, not knowledge of fairytales and enhanced vocabularies."

Still hesitant to touch him, even after our heated kisses the night before, I lay a hand on his chest. "But you have both."

He laughs. "I didn't always. Compared to my brothers, I was a scrawny child. It took years of working on the farm to build my strength. And years of having my butt kicked by them."

"What happened to your family?" I let the question hang

between us, knowing the same hurt all too well. Levi told me the story, but I want Bastian to open his heart to me.

His face darkens as he stares ahead of us. Strong hands clutch me tighter. "Miscretes. It wasn't random. It was almost like they were after something my parents had, and they didn't plan to leave a single living thing standing until they found it. Burnt down the farm, our home, and slaughtered my entire family."

I close my eyes as waves of his pain roll off him, drowning me in the intensity of his aura. The connection between us is palpable as I grip his arm asking, "How did you escape?"

The question threatens to pour more heaping piles of guilt on him, but there's something about him that makes me want to know everything.

A stream of air exits his nostrils. "We had a bunker for storms hidden behind the barn. When the creatures approached, my parents told my brothers, Levi and me to run for it. We dashed away to the deafening screams of my mother, my heart pounding in fear. When we rounded the barn, a gang of creatures waited for us. It was as if they knew we'd try to escape to the bunker." A stray tear rolls down his cheek, and I want to wipe it away, but I'm mesmerized by his story. "Frank told us to run for the bunker. He'd fight them off. I didn't want to leave him, but Chilon gripped my hand and pulled me away. He flung open the metal door, our chests heaving as we stared down into the pitch-black hole. That's when I turned around." His eyes squeeze shut as if he's trying to block out the memory.

"You don't have to tell me." I lift my hand to his face. The pain, now radiating through me as intense heat, is almost too much for me to take. "I can feel it."

His eyes flick open, their intense blue drilling into me. "You can feel my emotions?"

"I can." I don't understand what's happening between the two of us, but the invisible string has morphed into an iron rope. "You watched Frank die."

He swallows, and the lump in his throat bobs. "Yes. And I heard Chilon die. He forced me into the bunker and ordered me to lock it as the creatures attacked. For five days, Levi and I drowned in our misery in that earthen hole. Partly out of fear that the Miscretes were lurking above, and partly because I never wanted to come up to breathe fresh air my family would never breathe again."

Watching my mother succumb to the sickness seems like nothing after hearing Bastian and Levi's stories. They also fill my heart with fear. As the savior, I'm to lead the wilderness against the First City.

"I wanted to burn them to the ground when I heard they took Lyden to the Ringlet Forest. To make them pay for what they did to my family." He holds me so close I think I might suffocate, but I don't complain. "They were too much. We're not ready to face the First City yet."

"Then we prepare for Avren." A hollow feeling tells me I'm not ready to face the city I once loved. Where Flynn wants to be a soldier. To think of him as an enemy is ludicrous. "First we free the wilderness from bondage, then we free them from fear."

"We need to find the other part of the prophecy. Without the second savior, our hands are tied." He leans down and kisses my forehead. "Good thing I've got a lot more work to do with you."

My cheeks heat. "Good thing."

About midday, Bastian follows a trail up a hillside littered with the bones of animals. Slashed into the bark of the trees are symbols that appear to be warnings to the casual travelers. Most depict darkness—skulls, weapons, and beheaded creatures. Tin plates hanging from tree branches clang together in the breeze.

"Are you sure this is safe?" I lift my head and try to take more of a sitting position in his arms. Everything about this place has me on edge. There's energy in the air, but it's colder than the dancing electricity I felt when Levi and I entered Mafekadi.

"There are other nasty creatures around here we'll need to

avoid, but you don't have to worry about Ben. Evie's known him for a long time." He rounds a massive pile of bones, and we're suddenly surrounded by cottages.

People mill around campfires, hang laundry, and weave baskets using reeds from a nearby stream. Everything seems like a typical village except for their unusual obsession with animal bones. That, and that everyone is staring at us.

"Act normal." Bastian puts on a cheesy grin.

"Right. Having an enormous man carry me into a village where the people decorate with bones is a very normal occurrence for me."

He sets me down, but I keep an arm around him to balance as he proclaims to those nearby, "We're here to see Ben Finch."

An older woman with wiry gray hair hobbles toward us. Her cane is carved from the largest bone I've ever seen. "Ben heals the Mastria, not outsiders."

"Come closer." Bastian takes my hand and holds it out to the woman. "Touch her and you will see the truth."

My hand shakes as the woman approaches. She raises a skeptical bushy eyebrow before resting her palm on top of mine. Her eyes widen before she turns back to the rest of the onlookers. "She is a savior."

The more they use the word, the more uncomfortable I become. I'm a dressmaker from Avren. My father was on the Council, but other than that, there's nothing significant about me.

A man steps out from a cottage about halfway through the village. He's dressed in a tunic and cotton pants, nothing signifying him as a healer. "Bring the girl to me."

CHAPTER EIGHTEEN

*B*en ducks beneath the low threshold, followed by Bastian, who has me in his arms again. The first thing I notice about the cottage is the pungent, earthy smell of herbs and ointments. A low fire burns in the hearth, providing limited heat to the small space. Muffled daylight comes in through the windows, illuminating the shelf with glass containers of strange concoctions.

After Bastian sets me on the small bed, Ben comes over to embrace him. "Bastian Hale. It's good to see you."

"Sorry I haven't visited." Bastian pulls away. "Training members of an army is no simple task." He furrows his brow as he lifts a bone from the table to inspect it. "The days grow near, Benny."

Benny? He knows this man better than I thought he did.

"Miscrete attacks on the southern border are more numerous. My brothers and sisters in Cina say they can no longer protect all the civilians. The First City's building their army again." Ben is younger than I thought a healer would be—only a year or two older than Bastian. In Avren, the healers are older and wiser Citizens, capable of performing miracles of medicine. Except for healing the sickness that took my mother. "The Supes and Redeemed need to band together and stop fighting each other." He crouches and lifts my leg, resting my ankle on his knee. "And what do we have here?"

Bastian lowers himself to our level and holds a hand out to me. "Ben Finch, meet Maribel Windsong, the newest member of the Kindred Few."

Hearing Bastian identify me as a member of the family warms something deep inside. With Levi, and even Grayson, acceptance is easier. To have the commander come around bolsters my confidence.

Ben's brown eyes take me in, probing and seeking as if he can see into the very depths of my soul. He turns to Bastian. "Does she know?"

"I'm right here." I brush my hair over my shoulder in frustration. "If this is about the prophecy, then yes, I'm well aware."

"You can see why I brought her to you." Bastian sits on the bed beside me. "Can't save the world on a bum ankle."

"I can see that." Ben's gaze is on me again, his brow furrowing as if he's trying to figure out a complicated puzzle. "It's only that I thought you'd be bigger and more... male."

Of all the chauvinistic, pig-headed things to say. I can understand why an ordinary person from Avren might not make the perfect savior of the wilderness. But to say I can't fulfill the prophecy because I'm a woman? My hands ball into fists as I dig my fingernails into my palms. "You get what you get, *phaloc*."

Bastian covers his mouth to hide his smirk. From what I've garnered, the derogatory term is as about as welcome as the sound of a werewolf's howl.

"You have the spitfire." Ben touches my lower leg, and I wince. When he removes my sock, I see my ankle has grown to the size of a large rock. "With your mettle, this shouldn't hurt too bad.

But just in case." He opens a drawer and pulls out a stick. "Bite down on this. Don't want to lose that sharp tongue of yours."

I do as he says, but not before glaring at him. Their friendship makes sense to me in a weird, twisted way. Ben's not afraid to say what Bastian's thinking. It doesn't mean I have to like it.

Bastian takes my hand as my nerves ramp up. How will a magician healer set my broken ankle?

"What are you going to do?" It's a legitimate question. In the city, healers used salt baths, massages, and gentle creams. They used casts to set a broken bone and ordered you to rest in bed for weeks.

Ben purses his lips as his eyes flick to mine. "I'm going to meld the bone back together with magic. It will hurt like hell."

Pain wasn't something I ever really experienced in Avren. The intent of the city is to avoid adverse experiences—avoiding childbirth, matching your ideal partner to limit heartbreak, and outlawing dangerous pastimes. Avren didn't use sharp edges in its construction and made the roads and sidewalks with a cushioned material. The real pain in my life came from my father leaving and my mother's death.

"Are you ready, Maribel?" Ben's long fingers circle my ankle, causing a tingle of pain along my swollen skin.

I look at Bastian beside me. He gives me a slight nod, his hand gripping mine tighter. He won't leave me to face this alone. It's a rite of passage. If I can make it through this pain, I'm ready to move on to what the future has in store for me.

"Let's get this over with." I lean my head against Bastian's shoulder, place the stick between my teeth, and close my eyes, unsure of what to expect.

It begins as a gentle heat, moving along my skin and prickling the nerve endings. If this is all I need to endure, it won't be so hard. But then, it morphs into an ache deep within my ankle. I bite into my stick, closing my eyes tighter. At the sound of a *crack*, Bastian wraps his arms around me and holds me close to his chest. It's no longer an ache but an excruciating pain running up and down my leg. Tears stream down my cheeks as my head spins, so I concentrate on the feeling of Bastian's arms instead of the pain threatening to rip me apart. My whole body shakes with the magician's touch, but if I make him stop now, I'll never go through with it.

And as quickly as the intensity builds to an unbearable crescendo, it falls, and Ben's warm fingers soothe my skin again in a gentle massage.

"You did it, Mari." His voice floats outside of me somewhere as I come back down from the other place I took myself to endure the pain.

My skin is clammy, making me shiver. Bastian smooths back my hair and kisses the top of my head, my champion in the pits of hell.

The two men talk as I dwell in the space between this world and the one I inhabited to escape. I try to focus on their words— next steps, communication with the Seelie Court and reaching out to a vampire queen. It's all a blur. The plans involve me, so I should concentrate on it, but I can't. My body's trying desperately to recover from the trauma it just went through.

"And what about the Northern Duke?" Ben snaps me out of my dream state. "His relations with the Supes in the north will prove invaluable if we want to present a united front."

I bite into my lip, not ready to reveal anything to this man I met a half hour ago.

"It might prove beneficial if he'll listen to us." Bastian places his hands on his knees and stands before digging my other boot out of his bag. He kneels before me, placing it on my foot, and working the laces. The intentional swipe of his fingers over the bare skin above my sock has me squeezing my thighs together and hoping his friend doesn't notice. His constant reminders of our connection make me wonder if either of us can hold out much longer. He takes my hands in his and pulls me up from the bed. My weight settles on my broken ankle, but it is no longer painful. I wobble and stumble into his arms as if I had I bit too much to drink.

"Let's get you home," he says, holding onto my arm to steady me.

I turn around and hold my hand out to Ben, the closed-minded magician. "It was nice to meet you. Thanks for your help."

"And you." Ben takes my hand. "You're going to need all the magic of this world behind you." He smiles at me and then at Bastian. "Take care of this one."

"I will," I say with a lot more confidence than I feel inside. Bastian is more there for me than the other way around. I've already faced one of Avren's soldiers and come up short, relying on Bastian's dagger to finish the deed.

About a mile out of the village, I break out of my daze, finally feeling like my old self again. Bastian walks beside me in silence. It's a respectful way to honor my healing process.

"Do you think we could decorate with bones when we get back to the cabin?" I keep my mouth set in a straight line, looking up at him to catch his reaction.

He stares straight ahead. "Only if they're the bones of Avren's soldiers."

I shake my head, unsure if he's serious or joking like me until he sweeps me up in his arms, spins me around, and pins me against a tree.

He brings his mouth close to mine. "What you did back there —going through all that pain to fulfill your destiny..." His lips dance along my jawline like they had in his bedroom. "That made me want you even more."

"So, pain turns you on?" It's a warped mindset if it's true.

"You turn me on, Mari. The way you stood up to Ben's

narrow-mindedness. The way you endured pain to heal. The way your lip quirks slightly when you're ticked off." He leans in to tug on my lower lip with his teeth. "Everything about you has my world spinning, and I don't know how to slow it down." He rests his arm beside my head on the tree. "When Gray said the Council had two more orphans for him, I wasn't happy. The four of us were fine without you. But you got into my head, and I can't shake it. Whenever I'm around you, I feel like the universe has us together for a reason. And this magnetic attraction might kill me." His face is inches from mine as his gaze drops to my lips. "But I can't imagine my life without it now."

Several howls break out in the woods. Dusk is falling around us, and we still have an hour to the cabin. Fighting werewolves was not how I intended to spend my evening.

Bastian slips a dagger into my hand, the bone handle smooth though awkward. "Silver. We've got to keep moving. Based on their howls, they've smelled your Avrenian blood." He opens his sack, removes a tunic, and tosses it to me. "Put this on. It might mask a bit of the scent."

I pull his tunic over my head, trying not to get lost in its woodsy smell. The focus needs to be on survival, not him—though the two go together. If I survive the next hour, my reward is a night alone with him in the cabin. The idea invigorates me.

As we rush through the forest on a narrow trail, it takes all my concentration not to trip and injure my ankle again. The howls are closer, ringing through the canopy and sweeping over the pine-needle-carpeted floor.

Panic sets in as a warm breeze rustles the leaves and sets pinpricks dancing along my skin. It's as if a werewolf's breath is hot on the back of my neck, threatening to rip it out before devouring the rest of my body. I stop to catch my breath. Images of Tanner lying on the ground helpless fill my head.

That won't be my fate. Bastian won't allow it.

A low growl comes from behind me on the trail. I see the

wolf's yellow eyes reflected in the moonlight before I see the rest of its massive frame padding toward me. I hold my breath, daring to glance up the trail at Bastian. He's about a hundred yards away with his back to us, climbing over a wall of boulders.

"Looks like I'm closer, little one." It pads toward me as I back into a tree.

Never in my life have I taken the life of another being. My hand holding the dagger shakes because I know what I must do. "Do you know who my travel companion is?"

"Yes." Saliva drips from its mouth, anticipating the kill.

I grip the knife tighter and swallow back the bile rising in my throat. "Then you know if you kill me, he'll hunt you to the ends of this world, making you endure a slow and painful death."

"We do not fear the Kindred Few." There's defiance in the creature's voice. "One of yours killed one of ours. It's time to return the favor."

The time is imminent. I root my feet, ready for its attack. As the wolf lunges at me, I crouch so it can't knock me to the ground and drive the dagger into its chest. With the force of the wolf's hind legs hitting my shoulders, I still get barreled over and hit my head on the tree.

I lie there, my head spinning, ready for the wolf to finish me. With my skills, it couldn't have more than a flesh wound, enough to tick him off.

A deep voice says something above me, but I can't decipher it. Large, soft hands cradle my head and carefully lift my body. I'm in Bastian's lap.

"You did it" His voice is low, reverberating through his chest. "You killed your first monster."

I slowly open my eyes and look at him before resting them on the massive heap of hair about ten feet away. Blood covers my hands.

"It wanted revenge for the other wolf's death." I don't know why I say it. There's importance in its motives, but I'm too drained to think about it. "That's all."

"Supes are and will always be our enemies. The sooner you learn that the better." He doesn't expound any further, only picks me up and carries me down the trail once again. "We need to get out of here. There are other wolves in the area. I think I found us a quicker way home." He stops at the boulder field and sets me down. "Do you think you've recovered enough to climb?"

"I can do it." The wall of boulders stands like a bulwark before me, but I set my hand on the first rock, carefully placing each foot to make sure I don't slip. I've had enough falls for today.

"When you're almost at the top, wait for me." Bastian begins his climb. Although he can likely climb much faster than me, he stays behind, probably expecting me to fall.

It doesn't take too long to get there. I scoot to the side to let him pass. From the ledge, he reaches down and holds out a hand for me to clasp. I scramble to the top with his help and rest on my hands and knees. The smell is what I notice first—like a forest fire mixed with methane gas.

When I look up, a massive beast lies in the meadow, eyeing me. Without getting up, I wrap my arms around Bastian's leg. Glimmering blue, green, and brown scales cover the creature. It releases a burst of fire into the air from its mouth. "What the hell is that?"

"I believe *'dragon'* is the appropriate term." He smirks. "But I'm sure you could butter him up if you called him Oh, Great Caspian, Lord of the Sky."

"I thought you just told me all Supes are our enemies." I scale Bastian's body like a ladder, refusing to let go. "If he turns on me, I don't think I can kill him with a dagger."

"And why would you do that?" He wraps an arm around me and pulls me in close to his side. "Caspian's a beautiful creature."

"Maybe because he can incinerate an entire stand of trees in a single breath?" I relax a little. The dragon doesn't seem too interested in killing us.

Bastian laughs, releasing me and stomping through the tall grass toward the beast. "Now you're offending him." He pats the dragon on its side, garnering what appears to be a slight smile on the creature's mouth. "He can incinerate entire forests in a single breath. Get over here. Caspian says he'll take us home."

My legs shake thinking about getting on top of a dragon. Riding a wolf was too much for me. "How do you know that? Can you speak telepathically?"

Bastian shakes his head and raises an eyebrow at Caspian. "Humans and dragons can't speak telepathically. He's lowered his shoulder. That's how I know."

Silly me to assume in this new world of supernatural creatures, powers I don't understand exist.

I stand beside Bastian, looking up the massive wall of scales leading to the top of the dragon's back. "I don't think I can do this."

"Of course you can." He scrambles up Caspian's side to the top, firmly placing one leg on either side of the creature's enormous back. Leaning down, he holds a hand out to me. "Come on. At this rate, the sun will rise before we make it home."

I back up slightly to take a running start. When I reach the side of the dragon, I leap into the air and take hold of Bastian's hand, slamming into Caspian's scales. An annoyed grumbling comes from the creature. With Bastian's help, I struggle to the top. I sit in front of him, my legs barely reaching each side of the dragon's back, but the commander wraps an arm around me, using his other hand and his legs to hold on.

When Bastian gives the dragon the word, the creature lifts off, using its incredible wings to rise above the meadow into the night sky. We can see for miles. Glowing villages dot the landscape surrounded by vast swaths of darkened forest. I look to the north and see the glowing beacon of Avren rising like a guardian over the land. The lights of the luminescent forest appear dim next to the city's bright grandeur. Reluctantly, I rip my eyes away from my birthplace and gaze to the south. The dark spires of the First City glow in the moonlight—an antithesis to the brilliance of the city in the north. But most in the wilderness know better.

All places hold their dark secrets.

CHAPTER NINETEEN

*D*espite witnessing the beauty from a mile above, I've decided traveling by dragon is not my preferred method of transportation. My hands ache from gripping Caspian's scales, and throughout the ride, I think a gust of wind might blow me straight off his back. Only Bastian keeps me grounded, his arm tight around my waist.

I'm still high on the adrenaline when I slide to the ground, thankful I'm no longer worried about my ankle.

Bastian bows his chin slightly to Caspian. "Thank you, dear friend."

And with storm-force winds, the dragon lifts off, soaring into the night sky. Never in my life did I think I'd add a dragon ride to something I'd do before I died. It lifted my soul in ways I can't explain while terrifying me at the same time.

"Do you do that often?" I ask as we walk the short distance from the meadow to the cabin.

"What?" He cocks an eyebrow. "Thank a dragon?"

I slap him on the arm, shaking my head. "No. Ride on one. It was like free falling with a safety net." I clasp his upper arm. "Or dancing among the stars with a dangerous partner."

"And do you do that often?" He stops and steps closer to me.

"What? Ride a dragon? You know it was my first time." My pulse quickens with his nearness. Our bodies are now less than a foot apart.

"No. Dance with a dangerous partner?" The corner of his lip rises as his eyes drink me in.

"The others won't be back until morning, right?" I swallow, unsure of how I want to proceed yet knowing my words probably acknowledge consent.

He lifts a hand to a stray wisp of hair falling over my forehead and tucks it behind my ear. "I'm counting on it." A shy smile crosses his lips. "Are you sure your ankle's alright?"

"It better be after the pain Ben put me through." I lace my fingers through his and tug him toward the cabin. Fireflies dance among the trees and tall grasses, calling out to their mates. I want this man, but the tiny voice of Avren nags away in the back of my mind.

It is not right.

You are not of age.

You are not married.

Everything within me wants to plug my ears and sing at the top of my lungs to make them go away, but they won't. The voices threaten to ruin my time with Bastian.

He unlocks the front door with the key around his neck. This time, he doesn't bother with lighting an oil lamp. We head straight for the stairs, trusting in his navigational skills.

At the top of the stairs, he opens the door to his bedroom and releases my hand. He lights a candle on his small writing desk, the glow casting shadows throughout the space.

The voices grow louder when he wraps his arms around me and rests his hands on my lower back. "Mari, I don't want you to do anything you don't want to do. You mean more to me than that. In the beginning, I tied our connection to lust. The first time I saw you, I thought you were a mythical angel. How else could I explain my attraction to you?"

His assessment makes me smile. "I'm no angel." Lifting my head, I look him in the eyes. "I was attracted to you too, but I didn't know what to do with those feelings. I grew up in a place where people look down on physical attraction, unless formed with a Council-appointed spouse."

But I can't help myself.

Long strands of dark hair fall over his forehead in sharp contrast to his eyes. He lifts a hand to my face, cupping my cheek in his palm, a gentle finger running along my skin. "We've come so far with you. But there's still a lot of work to do. Avren's brainwashing runs deep." He closes his eyes. "I can't imagine what it's like. Gray tried to explain it to me." Looking at me again, his eyes swim with sympathy, making me feel like a charity case. "Spending time with a person you're attracted to is the most natural thing in the world."

I don't want someone to be with me out of pity or because I'm a weird sociological experiment. Can we break Maribel out of her hypnotic allegiance to Avren and its stringent rules?

I step back from him, breaking the magnetic field, at least on my part. "I think you should sleep in Gray's room tonight." Sitting on the edge of the bed, I unlace my shoes. It's not like he did anything wrong. But he must want me for me, not because I'm the prophesied savior.

"Mari..." He takes a step toward the bed. "I didn't mean..."

I keep my focus on my laces, which thankfully are extra knotted tonight. His heavy footfalls cross the room, and the door opens and closes. Tears well in my eyes as my fingers work the damn knots. I wanted him to stay more than anything in the world. But Avren's rules run through my head on replay. And the ache in my heart tells me he's acting on the magnetic attraction. What happens when it goes away?

I lay my head on the pillow and pull the blanket up to my face, covering my nose. It smells like him—that warm woodsy scent that makes my head spin so much I can't think straight. It tempts me to cross the hall and spend the night in his arms. But my logical side wins out, and I fall asleep dreaming of the juxtaposition between dark brown hair and crystal blue eyes.

WHEN I WAKE in the morning, sunlight from the window streams in, giving Bastian's room a gentle glow. I stretch my arms and legs, enjoying my last lazy morning in the commander's bed. Tonight, I'll move back to my mattress on the floor. I'm also in no hurry because of how we left things last night. I can only imagine the inevitable awkwardness of our morning conversations.

Then I hear voices. More than one.

I scramble out of bed, not bothering to put on my boots, and open the door. Gray's door is closed, but that doesn't mean Bastian's not awake. I listen from the top of the stairs and hear Grayson's distinctive laugh.

My family is back.

When I reach the bottom of the stairs, the four of them sit around the table eating breakfast. Levi appears tired as he passes the basket of biscuits to Bastian, whose eyes are on me.

"Mari!" Grayson hops up from the bench to embrace me. "Bastian told us what happened with the guard and the werewolf. We're glad you're both ok."

Ok. A bit of a mediocre word. Kind of like so-so. Yes, physically I'm fine, but after last night, my heart's a bit in shambles.

"Evie and I whipped up breakfast this morning." He ushers me to the table, seating me beside Levi. "You can imagine our surprise when we arrived in the middle of the night and found Bastian in my bed. But I understand. With your ankle, it probably wasn't best for you to get up from a mattress on the floor.

Although Ben is a miracle worker." He carries the frypan of scrambled eggs to the table and scoops a pile onto my plate.

Levi slips his hand into mine beneath the table and squeezes. It's his silent way of telling me he's happy to be home and together again. I lean my head on his shoulder, thankful Bastian is on the other side of him and not across the table.

"Mari will not go back to Avren." Bastian's voice startles me. It holds so much command compared to last night when it held uncertainty. "I've disposed of the anklet so the soldiers can't find her."

"And what about the plan to keep our toe on the pulse of the city?" Evie speaks for the first time. The one person who still mystifies me. "If we don't have an informer from within, we are flying blind."

"Mari will not go back to Avren," Bastian repeats slower, enunciating each word. "She will not work the machinery. She also needs more time to train for her role."

"Speaking of that." Grayson sits in his chair beside Evie. "I spoke with Wix when we were in Mafekadi. He gave me a verifiable lead into the whereabouts of the missing part of the prophecy."

"Why should we trust Wix?" Bastian curls up his face in distaste before scooping another helping of grits onto his plate. "The fae don't even trust him."

Grayson leans his elbows on the table and tents his hands. "Because it makes sense. When Levi and I went to Frostacre to speak with Bracken, it was obvious he was holding back something. Wix says Cirrus has the prophecy in safe keeping."

"But why would the king of Frostacre want to prevent the destruction of the two cities? He can only gain from it." Bastian spreads butter on his roll.

"Because the two cities keep the focus off Frostacre. The Unseelie Court loves to conduct its business without the people of the wilderness or the other Supes bothering them. The cities shield them." Grayson leans back in his chair, propping his arms behind his head as if he's just released a major truth bomb.

"And if Cirrus has the prophecy tucked away, how do you propose we get it from him?" Bastian asks.

It's a perfectly valid question. I've already seen the power of the Unseelie Court through Quinn. He rendered Levi unconscious, killed a fae, and kidnapped me on the back of a wolf.

"By using Mari as bait." Grayson lifts his chin as if daring anyone to oppose him.

"No!" both Bastian and Levi say in unison.

Grayson rolls his eyes and shakes his head at Evie. "Cirrus has already sent his best courtier after her. The guy's desperate to have control over a key piece in the prophecy beyond the piece of parchment he has stowed away. Levi and Mari will distract him while the rest of us find out where he's hiding it."

Bastian taps the side of his glass with his fork. It's obvious he's stewing. "She needs a lot more training first. The son of a bitch lured her away from Mafekadi, taking Levi out with a touch of his palm. She needs to understand their tricks."

Levi crosses his arms, frowning. His silence is deafening.

"What do you think?" I touch his arm. He's the expert in the fae.

He uncrosses his arms to sign. "We need to keep you safe, but I understand we must possess the other part of the prophecy for the other savior to be revealed. Uncle Bracken won't tell me anything." Pushing back in his chair, he places his plate on top of mine. "I need to be the one to teach her about the ways of the fae." He glances at Bastian. "You can train her in the mornings, but I'd like the afternoons."

"Deal." Bastian scoops another helping of grits. "We'll need a foolproof plan in place before stepping foot in Frostacre. Cirrus knows you exist and will expect us. As I see it, this is our first step in the long battle ahead."

BASTIAN WAITS for me by the whetting stone. We've had no opportunity to talk about what happened last night. Just the sight of him—hair tied back, blue eyes on me, weapons crisscrossing his chest—brings back the longings. He's right. I need to break free from the years of the Council telling me how to live my life. But it might be a slow process.

"Your quiver is over there," he says in a flat voice, clearly not feeling the same magnetism I am at the sight of him. My heart deflates.

"Will we train with the others?" I jog to keep up with him as he starts the trek on the wooded trail. I'm not sure if either of us can take Rafe's relentless flirting today.

He doesn't turn around. "No, we'll train alone."

Instead of engaging in small talk and skirting the actual conversation we need to have, I remain silent. On the strap across his back, he has multiple daggers of different materials—iron, silver, wood, and steel. Unlike the soldiers of Avren with their fancy uniforms and polished swords, it's clear Bastian knows how to fight. If I hadn't seen him kill Quinn, I'd still know he was one of the best around.

"We'll work on your bow skills first." He removes his weapons, letting them fall to the ground with a clang. "Then we'll practice your dagger accuracy and hand-to-hand combat skills."

I chew on my lip, disliking his impersonal assessment of our time together. "Bastian, I…"

He removes an arrow from the quiver I set by the tree and lifts the bow. "You don't have to explain." His focus isn't on me but on a grove of trees on the far side of the meadow. He lets the arrow fly, hitting his target with deadly accuracy.

"Can we at least talk about it?" I pull at an arrow in the quiver, but its head is stuck on the other shafts. I keep yanking at it, frustrated. When it finally breaks free, I plop onto my bottom, unable to control my emotions any longer. Hot tears well in my eyes as I look down at a broken arrow. A perfect metaphor for my heart.

Bastian sets down the bow and sits beside me. He clasps his hands between his knees. "Listen. I get it. Well, maybe I don't totally get it, but I'm trying to understand what you've been through. Gray explained it to me. It took him two full years before he'd touch a woman. Upbringing runs deep. It's amazing you've kissed a man who's not your husband." He sighs, digging a heel into the dirt. "I'm a patient person. You're worth waiting for. And I'll wait as long as it takes. Besides, I enjoy just being around you."

I watch my hand shake as I bridge the short expanse between us and rest it on his knee. "You don't understand how much I want to."

The corner of his lip lifts. "Oh, I think I do." He leans in close, cupping my cheek and bringing his lips to mine. Their gentleness melts me, turning my insides to molten lava. And almost as quickly as his lips touch mine, he pulls away. "We better get to taking down some of these killer trees."

CHAPTER TWENTY

The morning passes quickly with archery target practice. By the end of a couple of hours, I'm hitting a tree three out of four times. Bastian's an excellent teacher and proves his patience isn't only reserved for the bedroom.

It must be close to noon when we move to daggers. In a demonstration in throwing the weapon, he removes ten daggers from his weapons arsenal. Within a two minute time period, he flings and accurately hits a one-foot circle he drew with ash on a tree with each weapon.

I hold a dagger in my hand, conjuring memories of the were-wolf's feverish body above me in the woods. A slick of sweat forms on my forehead as I try to zone in on the target. It fluctuates in and out of focus as my body continues to heat with the memory of killing the creature. Taking my stance, I draw back my arm, then arch it forward, releasing the weapon. It falls to the right of the tree in what seems like miles away from the target.

"At least you have the distance." Bastian stuffs his hands in his pockets with his attention still on the tree. "You've got to see your dagger hitting the tree when you release. Channel that energy through your arm, wrist, and hand." With another knife in hand, he takes his stance beside me. "You need a steady wrist, or it will fly all over the place." He follows through with the motion and exaggerates his position.

"Are you going to drag out my training for days to keep me from going to Frostacre?" I let the question hang in the air between us. In my gut, I know he doesn't want me to go. I don't have the steel to stand up to the Unseelie Court.

He doesn't look up at me but sits on a nearby stump, his hands once again between his knees. "You're not even eighteen, and Gray wants you to act like a brave warrior."

"I'll be eighteen next week. Will you let me go then?" I lift my chin, not wanting him, more than anyone, to treat me like a baby.

He lets out a short laugh. "You can go. I'm not preventing you. But if you can hit a persuasive fae disillusioning you with glamour between the eyes with an iron dagger, it might serve you well."

"What if I'm not strong enough to see through it?" Images of Quinn fill my head. He was charming and drew me in like a fly to a spider's web.

"Levi will work with you on that this afternoon." He checks the sun's position in the sky. "He's probably waiting for you now. Let's go back and eat lunch."

I help him remove the daggers from the tree before strapping the quiver to my back. Its familiarity is surprising after such a short time wielding one.

He sheaths his last weapon, then assesses me. We're close, as if he might kiss me again, but he takes my hand, weaving his fingers through mine. Walking together through the woods is so different from staring at his back. It's as if he finally sees me as an equal, not an orphaned reject from Avren.

As we draw near to the cabin, he drops my hand and clears his throat. "I don't want the others to know about us yet. They'll be no end to Gray's teasing. Evie will think I betrayed her, and it will devastate Levi."

"Devastate Levi?" I'd think he'd be happy for us.

"Come on." He rolls his eyes. "The guy's had a mad crush on you since the moment you stepped through the door. It's going to hurt him."

"But we're friends." At least on my part. How did I not see how he felt about me? Levi feels like a close older brother—the one you stay up with for hours telling secrets to. And he's filled a gap of what I missed out on in Avren.

Bastian laughs and holds the door open, letting me pass by. "Yeah, right."

Inside, the others are cleaning up lunch. Two plates covered with dishtowels sit on the counter. Levi pauses his dish drying when we enter and frowns.

"How did the combat training go?" Evie sets a mug on the shelf of a cabinet. "You got her ready yet?" It's her usual mocking tone I've grown accustomed to.

Bastian ignores the sarcasm. "Great. We still have dagger and hand-to-hand combat to work on, but her archery skills are above average. There must be a warrior among her ancestors."

My cheeks heat slightly with the praise.

"We'll keep working on it this week." He lifts the towel, tosses it to the side, and carries his plate to the table. "I've let my Grove students know Mari is my top priority this week."

"How does Susan feel about that?" Evie leans against the counter. "Not seeing you for a week?"

"I didn't say I wouldn't see her." Bastian takes a drink of water before scratching the back of his neck, which I've discovered is his go-to action when he's nervous. "My afternoons and evenings are free."

Heavy lead sits in the depths of my stomach. He'd told me she didn't matter to him. I don't want to be jealous. He's told me how he feels, and I should trust that, not my insecurities.

Levi sits across the table from Bastian, the frown still firmly set on his face. "You said you'd be back before lunch. I have a long session planned for us this afternoon, and you've cut into it."

Bastian pushes his plate to the side, rests his crossed arms on the table, and leans forward. "Then shorten it, brother. I didn't want to interrupt our progress. I'll cut my session short tomorrow and give you extra time."

I carry my plate to the seat beside Levi and place a hand on his forearm. "Bastian told me you can help me resist the glamour of the fae."

Levi's entire demeanor changes with my touch. It's obvious he knows there's something going on between his brother and me. The others may be oblivious, but he's intuitive. Having imperfect hearing has heightened his other senses. "Eat your lunch. I'm going to take you to Nevil Falls when you're done."

Bastian purses his lips, trying to suppress a smile as he nods his head. "But most people only go there to…"

"Shut up!" Levi glares at him.

This is not what I want. My growing feelings for Bastian shouldn't impede my friendship with Levi. "I'm going to take my sandwich with me. Am I dressed ok?" My fighting gear now fits like a well-worn glove.

"Perfect," Levi signs.

"Take weapons with you." Grayson opens the cabinet to pull out an array of daggers. "Mari, do you prefer a cross-strap belt or a weapon's cloak?"

"Can I bring my bow and arrows?" I cross the room to pick up my quiver. "Besides, it's the middle of the day. We're not likely to run into anything too dangerous."

"The fae of the Unseelie Court are after you." Bastian pushes back in his chair. "Or did you forget I killed one of the king's top fairies?"

"I can sense them a mile away." Levi attaches the weapon belt over his chest. "I'll protect her if needed."

"What if I came along?" Bastian removes a second belt from the cabinet.

"No." I don't want him undermining Levi's capabilities. Each member of the Kindred Few has their own strengths. Bastian's are obvious. Grayson is the outgoing negotiator who can wield a weapon almost as well as his brother. Levi is the glue that holds the group together. His subtle ways make everyone feel like they belong. And Evie—well, it's comforting for me to have her female energy around. I hold up my bow. "How will I know if I'm any good with this thing if you're always there to take over?"

Bastian nods but doesn't protest. A small smirk crosses his lips.

Levi and I head out the front door and travel toward the river. A light breeze rustles the leaves in the canopy above, where sunlight pokes through and illuminates the forest floor. Birds hop along the ground looking for a noontime meal. In Avren, people described the wilderness as a terrifying place where monsters lurked around every corner—and at night, they do. But at this time of day, it holds a magic I never imagined, like if things were different, the world could be at peace.

With hands in his pockets, Levi remains quiet beside me, but I'm not sure if he's taking in the nature or working out what to say.

"I'm sorry about what happened in Mafekadi." As much as I'm enjoying the forest, I can't stand the silence between us. Levi's too important. "If I never talked with Quinn or realized he was a danger or listened to you when you tried to warn me..." I swallow, my heart heavy. "I'm sorry about your friend."

Levi stops to face me as he signs, "Avo's death was not your fault. The blame lies solely on the fae who killed him."

I wrap my arms around him, laying my head on his chest for a second before pulling back so he can read my lips. "When you fell to the ground, I thought you were dead. I can't imagine a world without you in it."

He brushes back a stray wisp of my hair with his fingers. "It goes both ways. Before you showed up, life was pretty boring. You've brought a new purpose into all our lives… even Evie's." His green eyes assess me behind his glasses, but he must not find what he's looking for. He drops his arms to release me. "We better get to the waterfall. Bastian cut into too much of my time."

It only takes us five more minutes to reach Nevil Falls, the majestic cascade rushing over a cliff and into a swirling pool below. Magic fills the air, widening my heart to all the possibilities this new life offers. It's no wonder lovers come here to pass the time. Did Levi pick this spot to train or for other reasons?

He lays a blanket on the ground, and we both sit as the mist from the waterfall sparkles in the sunlight, adding to the magic. "I thought we'd talk first, so I can tell you what I know, and you can ask questions. If we have time today, we'll practice."

Deep down, I'm nervous. Quinn's glamour was difficult to resist. No one prepared me. "Teach me everything you know."

His finger trails along the rudimentary pattern in the blanket. "This isn't easy for me—giving away the secrets of my people. But I'm only a quarter fae, so that means I'm three-quarters human. And the Kindred Few holds my allegiance." His forehead wrinkles as his eyebrows draw in. "I didn't tell you the truth before. I have told no one the truth. My parents never lived in Avren. I only use that story to drum up anger against the city's rejection of people living with disabilities. The truth is, my mother lived in Frostacre until she met my father. Because she took him as a husband and not a lover, the Unseelie Court cursed both of them. They were not only forced to leave but Cirrus took away their ability to hear, along with their entire lineage." He lifts his hands and pats the air at his waist three times. "If I have children, they'll have the same fate."

"That's terrible." I put my thumb and index finger together and flick up my hands in a sign I've seen the others perform. "But wonderful at the same time. Not only will they inherit your green eyes, but they'll also see the world from your perspective."

A wide smile crosses his lips at my efforts. "It is. I know you've wondered how I accepted you with open arms when you first arrived. Gray naturally accepts you because he identifies with your plight. For me, accepting orphans into the Kindred Few is my charge. Although we're only two years apart, I can treat you with the kindness of a father or an uncle. The pain of losing Tanner hit me hard."

"I never knew that." I lift a small stick from the ground beside the blanket, running my fingers along the bark. "You didn't know him."

"It was clear when you arrived that you fulfilled the prophecy, but I planned to take you both under my wing. Evie and Bastian didn't want more than four in the Kindred Few, but I'd take forty and change our name if needed. This is my purpose. *You* are my purpose, Mari." He takes the stick from my hand, drawing my eyes up to his. All along, our connection was a brotherly or even fatherly one.

"You'd make an amazing father." I don't want to hurt him, but he needs to know how much his acceptance has meant to me. "And someday, you'll make the best uncle. Surely Grayson and Evie want children."

"Not in this world as it stands." He snaps the stick in half, startling me. "Until the First City and Avren's chokehold on the wilderness are broken, bringing new life into this world is dangerous."

"And the first step is to find the other *savior*." I hate the sound of the word. A pampered seamstress from Avren has no right walking around the wilderness declaring herself as their savior.

"Exactly. We need the other part of the prophecy." Levi rests his back against a nearby tree, ready to set in for the long haul. "And to do that, we need to travel to Frostacre. Uncle Bracken is my mother's half-brother—the one not born to a human father. They grew up together because my grandfather had plenty of his own human lovers. Bracken's father took my mother in as his own child, so she grew up in Frostacre."

"Until she met your father." The story is romantic and tragic at the same time. I can't help being drawn in. His mother was torn between her two natures, similar to how I am torn between Avren and the wilderness. "Was it love at first sight?"

He laughs. "Not at all. The fae wanted to expand their realm into the land where my father's family farm was located. Because of her humanness, the king sent my mother as a liaison, using her fae nature to trick his parents. With no land to work, my father was essentially homeless, and my mother took pity on him. She had a cabin built on a new piece of land for his family and paid regular visits. It was a slow-burn romance."

"The same cabin you grew up in?" Violent images of his parents' deaths and Levi hiding beneath the bed from the Miscretes resurface.

"Same one." He gazes over my shoulder, lost in thought.

The sound of voices fills the woods behind us. I scramble to my feet and mouth, "Get off."

Levi snatches the blanket and follows me into a stand of bushes, crouching beside me. The mingling of our heavy breaths rages in my ears as I strain to hear.

Without a word, I poke my head out. Three soldiers of Avren stroll along the trail, appearing to be more on a wayward adventure than official business. They laugh and joke with each other, one puffing on a rolled-up paper before handing it to his friend. The third is all too familiar to me.

Flynn Baxter.

The last time I saw him, he admitted that he still loved me. And he's a soldier now, tasked with killing Undesirables or dragging them back to their work duties. My heart is in my throat. I sink back into the bush and take Levi's hand in mine before mouthing, "Soldiers."

As the savior of the wilderness, I don't think this will be the last time we cross paths, but I desperately hope it is.

CHAPTER TWENTY-ONE

*W*e wait in our hiding spot until the voices are long gone. The sun's angle tells us it's not safe to stay any longer, so Levi holds the blanket over his arm and takes my hand.

"Were those soldiers familiar to you?" he asks, as if he intuitively knows the answer.

I draw in a breath, letting my chest rise and fall. "Flynn and I were close. He was the first boy I kissed. It started about a year ago. He recently earned his ranking as a soldier."

"Isn't it illegal to kiss someone who isn't your spouse in Avren?" He raises an eyebrow.

I grip his hand tighter, remembering the nerves I felt when Flynn stole me away to hidden places beyond the watchful eye of the Council. I loved and hated the rush of passion as his lips pressed against mine, his wandering hand moving from my hip to my breast. The only thing I wanted was for the Council to pick him as my husband so we could legitimize our need for each other. I loved him.

But as a soldier, he stands for everything the Kindred Few are fighting against—oppression, dictatorship, uniformity.

Unless he became a soldier to look for me.

Our heated times in secret places tell me he has a rebellious nature. Maybe I can save him.

"If caught, the Council would have expelled us from the city or made us a spectacle by hanging us side by side in the city square. Unmarried lovers are strictly forbidden." I touch my lip with my free hand, recalling a much different kiss—Bastian's. His kisses were my first without guilt attached. But when I thought about taking it further, I made up excuses and let the voices in my head cloud my judgment.

"That's terrible." He uses the same sign I used earlier to describe the curse brought on his family. "Don't let your upbringing hold you back. You have a choice. It's all in your head. With me, it's physiological. Because of the fae, any children I choose to have will be born deaf." He leads me onto a path meandering through the woods to the left. "Most of the fae rules won't apply to you when we travel to the Unseelie Court. King Cirrus wants you there, so you won't need to bring gifts to gain an audience with him. The issue will come when you want to leave. Once the others find the prophecy, we'll need a plan in place to free you."

"And what's the best way to distract him?" An audience with the king who sent a bounty hunter after me doesn't fill me with excitement.

"Your mere presence will enthrall him. He's waited centuries for you to appear, watching Avren and the First City grow in power. Neither want anything to do with the fae. But they hold the humans in the wilderness in check, so this makes Cirrus happy." He releases my hand, picks up a stick, and tosses it into the trees. "I'm still not sure how he thinks he'll prevent the prophecy from happening. It's the tome of his own people, so it's written in stone."

"Sometimes the inevitable is difficult to take. I felt the same way when I faced the Council a few weeks ago—like maybe I'd be immune from their age rule. We all know how that went." We pass through a meadow that looks familiar to me, and I stop him, wanting to learn something from our time together. "What do I need to know about the fae?"

"They don't lie. Cirrus will tell you like it is if you ask him." He signs as he talks. "The longer you and I can keep the king busy, the more time the others have to find the prophecy."

"If he doesn't lie, can't we ask where it is?" It seems logical to me, but I also know it means we're laying our intentions bare.

He raises his eyes to the darkening canopy. "Just because they don't lie doesn't mean they don't skirt around the truth and manipulate it. Cirrus intends to keep you, and he won't let you leave without a fight. The prophecy holds the most precious secret in the land. He clutches it in his iron grip."

I reflect on his words as we journey the rest of the way to the cabin, where Bastian greets us at the door. He wears his white tunic and linen pants and holds a beer stein in his hand. He's surprisingly relaxed. After his comment about Nevil Falls, I thought he'd be nervous about me going there alone with Levi.

"And look who's back from their lovers' tryst by the falls." He leans his free elbow on the doorframe. "You've got to tell me, Levi. Is she as good as she promises?"

I glare at Bastian. *What a jerk.*

Beyond annoyed, I shove past him, not wanting to relay any information. I had looked forward to an evening of talking through strategy with the other three, but unfortunately, it seems Bastian has had one too many. I storm past Grayson and Evie in the kitchen and slam the door to my room, flopping down on my mattress, tears stinging my eyes.

The door opens a few minutes later, then closes softly. A hand touches my back.

"Bastian's stupid when he's drunk," Evie says.

HEATHER KINDT

I spin around to face her, shocked to see her sitting on the floor beside my mattress.

"I thought you could use a big sister right now." She gives me a rare smile, then pulls her knees to her chest. "The moment you left with Levi, he started drinking. After a few, his lips loosened, and he couldn't stop talking about you. When did you enchant my brother?" She shakes her head, red curls hanging loose from a tie behind her neck. "Bastian doesn't fall for women. They fall for him."

I lay my head on my arm and let out a stream of air. "It's our stupid magnetic connection. If we didn't have that, I think we'd kill each other." I hate not being able to control my feelings for him. It's something I've mulled over asking the fae king about. Does it pertain to the prophecy? Despite my desire to break our connection, curiosity takes over. "What did he say about me?"

"What didn't he say about you?" She clasps her hands in front of her and flutters her eyelashes. "'Mari has the most beautiful hair. Have you seen how the light catches the golden flecks in her eyes? She's a natural with a bow and arrow.' You've got him wrapped around your finger."

I wipe my eyes on my quilt, unsure of how much I want to share with my *big sister*. She hasn't given me a reason to trust her. "Like I said, there's a weird mojo going on between the two of us. We can't explain or stop it. When we figure it out, I'm sure he'll be the first to snap out of it."

She reaches out, lifts my braid, setting it over my shoulder, and examines me. "Since his family died, happy moments have been few and far between for Bastian. Why fight it so hard? I don't want to see him miserable again."

I drag my teeth over my lip. My experience with men is extremely limited, and other than Flynn, I'm not sure how it's supposed to feel. That relationship was secretive. If someone caught us, they'd turn us in, which made the act so much more

192

exciting. But Bastian isn't seeking a rush. "Because I want it to be real."

"Then give him a chance." She taps my leg, stands, and stretches her arms over her head. "And if you don't, I get that too. It took Gray nineteen rejections before he got a yes from me. These men are in it for the long haul. If Bastian didn't see a future with you, he wouldn't risk our family dynamics over a fling."

"But what about his other flings?" Susan comes immediately to my mind. Does Bastian want an open relationship where he's free to see whoever he wants? My stomach twists at the thought.

Evie lifts a book from the shelf and examines it before tossing it onto Levi's bed. "If you're committed to each other, they won't happen anymore. We'll all see to that." She walks over to the door and pauses. "You coming?"

"I think I'll stay here for a while." I snatch a book from the shelf to show her I'm serious about my alone time. "Been meaning to read this one." I glance at the cover: *Hiking the Elmridden Range*. "It looks riveting."

Evie smiles and motions to the living room. "I'll be in here if you need anything."

"Ok," I say, opening the book. "And, Evie?"

She turns back to me. "Yes?"

"Thanks."

After the door is closed, I place the book back on the shelf and fold my hands behind my head, staring up at the ceiling. Despite Bastian's comments when we arrived at the cabin, tonight is the first time I feel like I belong. I draw in a deep breath, hold it for several seconds, and release it.

Twenty minutes pass before the door opens again and Levi enters carrying a tray of food. He places it on the ground beside my bed and sits next to me.

"He feels bad." There's a slight frown on his face as he signs the words. "It was as much a dig at me as it was at you. I think he's jealous of my good looks and massive form." He holds up his arm and flexes his bicep.

I smile before tossing my pillow, hitting him square in the face. Rather than retaliating, he hugs it to his chest, lunges for his mattress, and places it behind his head.

"Come on, Levi." I pout and cross my arms.

He flings it back to me, reclines on his own pillow, and crosses his legs. "I wish things could stay like this forever." Tears glisten behind his glasses, making me want to bridge the short expanse and comfort him, but I stay put. "There's a lot of talk about taking down the cities with the saviors and freeing the wilderness, but the idea of doing it and the actual task are two totally different things. I'm worried about putting you in danger with Cirrus. I can't imagine what going against Avren and the First City forces will be like."

"We can only tackle one thing at a time." I snuggle into my pillow but keep facing him so he can read my lips. "If we think about the big picture, we'll all go crazy from the magnitude of the task."

"For being so young, you're an amazing woman." He rubs his eyes. "Now, eat your dinner so we can both go to bed."

BY SIX THE NEXT MORNING, Bastian has me in the meadow, aiming my arrow at a yarn doll he's propped on a fencepost. Our walk from the cabin was silent, and we avoided eye contact. With my arrow pointed at the chest of the doll, I feel his stare, and how, more than anything he wants to apologize, but his pride holds him back.

The bowstring shakes between my thumb and forefinger as I spend too long trying to hit my target. With a choice curse word, I send my arrow flying into the leaves of a tree high above the fencepost.

"Concentrate, Mari." He goes to retrieve my arrow. "I can't take you to Cirrus if you can't defend yourself."

"Like they'd let me waltz into the Unseelie Court with a quiver full of iron-tipped arrows on my back." I retrieve another arrow, this time focusing on a tree on the other side of the meadow from Bastian. I draw back and hit my target. "Knowledge of the fae is much more valuable. If I know what to expect... how Cirrus might trick me..."

"You're leaving with us." He grips the arrow in his hand, his knuckles turning so white, I'm afraid he might snap the shaft in half. "I'll burn the place down before I let them have you."

I lay the bow on the ground and place a hand on his chest. "You've got to trust me. You've got to trust Levi." I slide my hand to his cheek, running my thumb along his stubble. "He's your brother."

He closes his eyes, his lashes impossibly long as he leans into my palm. "This is new for me. I'm afraid if you fulfill your purpose written within the prophecy, I'll lose you. Control's important to me. Having my battle plans laid out on the table, each scenario thought through using stratagem, pieces on a map." He pitches forward and touches his lips to mine. "I don't want to reduce your significance to a wooden token on my map."

"It's not your job to protect me." I could get lost in those eyes —in his pain. "We're a team. All of us. We go in together and come out together. And as far as Levi is concerned..." I trace his lip with my pointer finger. "Besides Gray, he's the only one who accepted me when I first arrived."

He winces.

"I understand the reservations you had, but it doesn't change that he's become my best friend." The truth must hurt him. In Avren, they teach us to always portray everything with honesty, not the deceit the Council uses regularly. "It's easy to love Levi."

He averts his eyes, staring intently at his boots. "It is. I won't pretend that I don't want to be the one you trust the most. I also know I need to earn it." His attention draws back to me as he takes my free hand. "It doesn't help if I act the way I did last night. I'm sorry about what I said. I'll make it up to both of you by having you home early for Levi's training today."

I smile, peck him on the cheek, and release his hand to pick up my bow. "I'm sure he'd like that. He'd like you to acknowledge that his time with me is just as important as what you're teaching me."

The morning wears on. I shoot so many arrows, my arm shakes when I hold up my bow again, but Bastian is insistent. Competency isn't the goal. It's perfection. My body's exhausted, and the commander's demands are impossible.

"Again," he says, arms crossed, feet spread. "I need you to hit the bullseye every single time."

"Why?" I slump my shoulders and let the bow fall beside me. "So I can hit a Miscrete in the left eye instead of the right?" I sit on a stump and rest my elbows on my knees, face in my hands. He might get me back to Levi early, but my mind's too jumbled to learn a thing.

"Because you're the savior." Unlike other times, he says it without a smirk on his face as he sits on the stump beside me. "And I'm your trainer. Your performance reflects on me. I've got a reputation to uphold."

With my hand still unsteady from exhaustion, I rest it on his leg. "What are you really afraid of?"

His gaze is on the forest. With his hair tied back in a knot, I can admire his chiseled jawline and the way the sunlight catches free tendrils of his hair, illuminating them to a warm chocolate brown. "I'm afraid of the unknown. What the rest of the prophecy holds. The other savior comes from the First City, a place brimming with torture and darkness. The thought of you working with a demon drives me mad."

I squeeze his leg, trying to reassure him. "And you'll be with us. I can't imagine fighting the soldiers of Avren or the Miscretes without you by my side."

He forces a smile, still looking straight ahead. He clasps his hands between his knees, lost in a different world. "Yes, of course."

CHAPTER TWENTY-TWO

That evening, we all sit around the common room, lost in our own pursuits. Levi and Bastian play a game of dice at the table, Evie provides a sullen ambience with the melancholy tune coming from her fiddle, Grayson reads, and I am on the floor by the fire, sketching out my ideas for the Kindred Few's new fighting gear. In my plans, it's sleek, breathable, and reflects each of our personalities, while brandishing our common symbol of five interlocking circles on the sleeve.

Grayson perches reading glasses on the edge of his nose and sets his book to the side. He clears his throat to make his big announcement. "We leave tomorrow." As if expecting protests, he adds, "We'll continue Mari's training along the way."

The tune from Evie's fiddle stops abruptly, with a squeal of the bow against the strings. It's clear our tactical leader didn't bother to inform his girlfriend of his plans.

Levi jumps up from his bench at the table. He signs wildly, "Impossible. She's not ready to stand before Cirrus."

Grayson buries his fingers in his hair and leans his head to the side. "I spoke with Matthias today. The Council knows. They've ordered a group of twenty soldiers to move in on the cabin tomorrow."

"They know what?" I close my sketchbook. Icy tendrils of fear creep through my veins.

Grayson leans forward, tenting his hands. "Matthias is my informant among the soldiers. One of the few friends I have left in the city. Somehow, they know you're the one the prophecy speaks of. This was their worry about releasing more Undesirables into the wilderness. They sit on their high thrones, sentencing their own people to a life outside the city, trying to control them with the anklets so they can watch for the rise of the savior." He slips down from the chair onto the floor beside me. "You know what they're like now. How Lady Raven and her lackeys don't care about the people. Our whole lives, we've grown up thinking they're gods, incapable of fallacy, because they hide the truth in a neatly wrapped package of Avren's beauty. Anything and anyone outside of this is discarded without a second thought."

"We can take twenty soldiers." Bastian opens the weapons cabinet. "Bunch of weak, pretty boys."

"If we can avoid conflict and attention when they show up and Mari's not there, they might leave us alone for a while." Grayson pulls a piece of paper from his pocket and unfolds it. "We'll spend a couple of nights in Tenny Rocks to prepare. It's the Equinox Festival, so the streets will be crowded with visitors." He holds up an advertisement for the festival.

Evie sets her fiddle on the table with a bang. Her gray eyes are ablaze in the firelight. "And why am I finding out about this with everyone else?"

Grayson rakes his fingers through his hair again as worry lines crease his forehead. Making decisions where four other lives are at risk can't be easy on him. "I only found out this afternoon. I've spent the last hour thinking it through. If we could stay, I'd keep us here, but the wards only protect against Supes."

"And what if the soldiers follow our trail?" Bastian straps two daggers into his cloak and reaches into the cabinet for more. "Can we kill them then?"

"We've got to be careful with our trail. Word will get back to Avren if we kill a bunch of their soldiers." Grayson looks to Levi. "Maybe a bit of fae glamour?"

Levi can use glamour?

"I think I can arrange something." He shoots me a guilty grin. "We've got to protect the savior at all costs."

What will it cost Levi to use the magic of his people? I don't have time to ask. Everyone gets up and heads to their rooms, probably to pack for our trip.

When I enter our room, Levi has a sack open. He stuffs in his green cable-knit sweater. He appears different from this afternoon, during our training session by the falls. Despite Bastian's comments from the day before, Levi was relaxed and provided me with a wealth of information about fae customs and traditions. It was as if we had all the time in the world, so we took a break to swim in the pool beneath the falls, laughing as we splashed each other with water. Now, his face is drawn, his lips set in a firm line as he places two candles in the sack.

I close the creaking door, which doesn't alert him to my presence. It's only when I step into the space near his bag that he looks up. "Do you think this is a mistake? Do you think we should stay and fight so we have more time to prepare?"

Having faced Quinn Malum and the soldier in the woods near the entrance to Avren, I don't want to fight the fae or the humans.

Levi rolls a long-sleeve shirt, stuffing it in beside the sweater. "We need to trust Gray's connections. He wouldn't ask us to leave unless it was necessary."

That night, I lie in bed staring up at the ceiling and wondering if this will be my last night in the cabin. As much as this entire experience has felt like someone has thrown a whole bucket of ice water in my face, I've begun the process of acceptance. These people are my family, and this place is my home. In the three weeks I've spent in the wilderness, I've experienced more than I ever did in my eighteen years in Avren.

Three weeks.

I must be eighteen now.

Happy birthday, Maribel Nexis Windsong-Barellis.

A silent nod to the long-lost father keeping me from being a true orphan.

BOOTS STOMPING down the stairs wake me in the morning. Levi's bed is empty when I lift my head from my pillow. Tenny Rocks is northeast of the cabin along the way to Frostacre. My heart skips a beat. My father lives somewhere in the north. But as a man who works with Supes, strikes fear in others, and bears the nickname the "Northern Duke," I don't think he lives in a village where they hold dances and partake in afternoon teas.

Levi told me more about Tenny Rocks the night before. It's the human outpost where they mostly reject the resistance. A majority of the former Avrenians go to work in the fields to grow the city's food, and those born to the wilderness support them. They hold onto the façade of peace for dear life, even if it means a life of slavery to the Citizens. Roughly a quarter of Tenny Rocks succumbed to the sickness when it ripped through the wilderness, taking many human lives with it. They'd rather hold festivals and spend time at the tavern than deal with the realities of losing loved ones and being relentlessly oppressed.

Maybe I'd still hold onto my former beliefs about Avren if Gray had brought me there instead of to the Kindred Few.

I dress in traveling clothes—a tunic and linen pants—and plan to wear a cloak with several daggers. I'll carry my quiver and bow.

The others are in the common room gathering supplies and weapons.

"Good morning, Mari." Levi shrugs on his cloak after signing his greeting. "Gray says we need to be long gone by eight. We'll shut the cabin up tight to keep the soldiers out."

If the soldiers are anything like the ones I ran across at the cave entrance, they'll burn our home to the ground. My heart aches knowing this might be the last time I see the cabin.

Grayson smiles and hands me a sack. "Breakfast to take with you."

"Thank you." I lift my cloak from a peg and pull it on over my traveling clothes before picking up my quiver. "How long will it take to get to Tenny Rocks?"

"About five hours." Bastian closes the weapons cabinet. A pile of swords, bows, and daggers lie at his feet. "Evie... Levi... give me a hand."

The three of them gather the weapons and carry them to the back door.

"What are they doing?" I ask Grayson.

He finishes packing the last of the breakfast sacks. "Hiding the weapons from the Avrenians. We have an underground bunker hidden in the yard."

"Then why don't we just go there and wait out the soldiers?" The thought of facing King Cirrus so soon seems absurd to me.

Instead of answering right away, Grayson crosses the room. His sandy-brown hair hangs loose over his forehead, and a warm feeling fills me as a dimple forms on his right cheek when he smiles. I've really come to trust my older brother. "I know you're scared. On our walk back from Mafekadi, Levi told me all about your encounter with Quinn Malum." He touches my cheek with his palm. "No one else understands how overwhelming all of this is—to go from your safe apartment with your future planned out into this cold world." He drops his hand, his eyes delving deep into mine, probably trying to assess my level of fear. "Cirrus

won't harm you. He's too superstitious for that. Dire consequences could come from killing a prophesied savior."

"But what about the rest of you?" I won't be able to leave
Frostacre without their help, but I realize the danger it poses.

"We've dealt with our share of the fae." He looks to the back
door as the others return from the yard. "Your primary role is to
distract while we find the prophecy. Piece of cake."

"You always make everything seem as if we're making a trip to
the Sweet Street Bakery for a cocoa and a sticky bun." I need
Grayson's calming presence to help offset Bastian's intensity.

Evie pinches Grayson's cheek and then his ass. "That's
because he's sweeter than a sticky bun."

"Is everyone ready?" Bastian stands by the front door. He
wears his long cloak, which is filled to the brim with weapons. "I
want to reach Tenny Rocks by noon and settle in so we can talk
through our plan in Frostacre. Levi, bring up the rear so you can
cover our tracks."

Our trek through the woods differs from the ones we've taken
to the Grove or the falls. No one speaks. The threat the incoming
soldiers pose is real. Part of me wonders if Flynn will be among
the ones tasked with rooting out the rebellion. If he is, I left
nothing behind to identify my ties to the Kindred Few.

I watch as Levi leaves a trail of iridescent dust behind us. Our
footprints disappear, every bent blade of grass straightens, and
snapped sticks reform. It is as if we were never there. My friend
holds secrets I've not even begun to uncover.

"Only about three more hours," he finally says as we pass
through a meadow still holding dew on the shorter grasses and
drenching my boots.

"Will the people in Tenny Rocks turn us in?" It's a question
I've held inside, not wanting to speak badly about the Redeemed.

"They're rule followers, mostly." He sprinkles another layer of
dust behind us. "They do what Avren says, but they won't betray
a fellow member of the Redeemed. Peace is more important to

them than anything. If they don't stir up trouble, the Council leaves them alone."

A gust of wind whips through the meadow, bending the grasses to the earth. I cling to Levi to keep from falling over as the other three duck low to the ground. Bastian looks back to make sure I'm alright. And then, after clearing the meadow of every insect and bird, the wind stops.

"What the hell was that?" I run my fingers through my hair, which is now a knotted mess.

"The fae." Levi scans the woods as if expecting to see something. "Cirrus is making it clear that he knows we're coming."

"Great," I mutter. "So much for a surprise visit."

"It's not impossible." Levi picks up the contents of his sack, which fell during the gust, stuffing them back inside. "My limited magic is magnified when I'm in Frostacre. There's a chance I can shield the others from Cirrus's watchful eye, especially if we're distracting him."

"You're coming with me?" My spirits lift. The idea of facing the fae king alone made me shudder. Levi understands the people of Frostacre better than anyone in the family.

He loops his arm through mine as we follow the others back into the forest. "Do you really think I'd leave you to face him alone? He cursed my family. The guy's a major dick."

I smile at his assessment, never expecting those words out of my mild-mannered friend's mouth.

The surrounding forest differs from the ones near the cabin. Tall pines stand close together, while shorter bushes pepper the floor, making it difficult to see too far ahead. Animals and birds alert us to their presence with squeals and the occasional flutters from the bushes. Darkness creeps along the ground, providing perfect shadows for a predator in hiding. Every noise has me on edge as my fingers grip a dagger in my pocket, ready for an attack.

"Chill, Mari." Bastian falls back to walk beside me as Levi

walks with Grayson, but I can't help but notice his attention remains on the woods. "The Supes won't bother us at this time of day."

"And what about the beasts?" I hold my dagger in front of me. When I was a child, my father told me stories about giant cats and wolves roaming the forests of the wilderness.

"You mean the ones I eat for breakfast?" The corner of his lip lifts as he looks at me to gage my reaction.

I stick my tongue out at him. He should know better than to mock my fear. In my short stint in the wilderness, a werewolf killed someone right in front of me, a vampire tried to attack me, and a fairy kidnapped me and poisoned an innocent fae.

Out of view of the others, he slides a hand along my lower back, reassuring me.

"I'm more concerned about Cirrus. What if I'm not able to distract him, and he senses the three of you?" Flashbacks of Quinn flattening Levi with the touch of his hand still rattle me.

His hand slips from my lower back to my hip, squeezing before he releases me. "You worry too much. There's what…" He holds up his hand and counts out each finger. "Five of us and like hundreds of them? No problem."

Bastian's lighthearted approach to my upcoming appointment with the king of the Unseelie Court does nothing to ease my worries. Without a miracle, there's no way the five of us will make it out alive.

CHAPTER TWENTY-THREE

A little past noon, stone cottages pop up with a canopy of trees still shading the road from high above. A man watches us as he adjusts his horse's saddle. Two children squeal, chasing one another and crossing the path a hundred yards ahead of us. Chickens peck at feed in the grass. They ignore the five strangers walking past them.

We cross over a bridge with a babbling brook beneath it, leading into a town made completely of stone. Small cottages and two-story buildings make up Tenny Rocks. A wooden sign creaks on a storefront, hanging by a nail and squeaking every time the breeze blows. Unlike the man with his horse, the people in the town don't appear bothered by us, going about their everyday lives.

Grayson leads us to a building with a sign reading "Tenny Rocks Inn." Light blue shutters line each window, giving it a homey feel. A fenced-in courtyard stands to the right where customers sit at tables talking, eating, and drinking. Fiddle music drifts from somewhere behind the structure, playing a familiar tune I heard once-upon-a-lifetime ago.

I follow Bastian into the inn, grateful to interact with humans who aren't Avrenians or my family. Their life in the wilderness reminds me more of the way I grew up: each person has an assigned task and carries it out so the society can continue.

"Say nothing about where we're going," Bastian says so quietly, I almost don't hear him, before greeting the innkeeper. "Good afternoon, Katiana."

She scowls at him, empties the bag of credits Grayson sets on the counter, and pushes one at a time to the side with her finger as she counts. Katiana is a woman almost as large as Bastian. She wears a white apron over her flowered dress, her dark hair tied back beneath a kerchief, and sports a bit of a mustache on her upper lip. I never want to meet her alone in a narrow alley.

Without looking up, she scoops the credits into the bag and mutters, "I should take this money and throw you out on your ass, Bastian Hale." She draws phlegm up her throat and spits it onto the floor by his feet.

"You stupid wench." Bastian draws a dagger and dives at the counter. "These are new boots."

Grayson and Evie pull him back as Levi plucks the dagger out of his hand.

"You know how he is, Kat." Grayson shoves Bastian's arm to the side. "All brawn and no brain. Pay no mind to him. We'd like your penthouse suite." He leans over the counter and pecks the monster of a woman on the cheek, then puckers his lips in an irresistible pout.

Cheeks flushed, Katiana fumbles for an iron key on the wall, unable to resist Grayson's charms. "One of you will have to sleep on the floor. Two beds are all I've got."

"You're a gem." Grayson pats her on the cheek after taking the key from her. "Remind me to save you a dance at the River Walk tonight."

The unhealthy shade of red continues to flame over the

innkeeper's cheeks. She places the bag of credits below the counter. "You're... you're going to be there?"

Evie shakes her head, turns, and climbs the stairs.

"Wouldn't miss it, darling." Grayson gives her one last look at his pearly whites before following his girlfriend upstairs.

The *penthouse suite* is quite cramped for three grown men and two women. Besides the beds, there's a rocking chair, a small cabinet with a washbasin, two bedside tables, and a tiny window letting in a sliver of light.

Levi strikes a match from his pack to light an oil lamp. "I can take the bed on the floor." He kneels to unroll a thin mattress resting against the wall. A cloud of dust lifts from the ancient material as he beats his hand against it.

"Nonsense." Bastian throws his cloak onto the chair, setting it rocking. "You and Mari are used to sharing a room. Just think of it as scooting your mattresses together."

In his drunken stupor a few nights before, he'd proclaimed his feelings for me to the others, but now he's acting like it's a big secret. I'll never understand the male species.

"If we hang around here too long, I'll fall into a serious depression." Grayson unfolds a piece of paper from his pocket. "I snatched this on the way in."

It's too dark in the room for me to read what he's holding up.

"You're not seriously thinking about going to a dance?" Evie wrinkles her nose, falls onto her bed, and spreads out her arms. "We've got to stay here and talk strategy."

"That's what tomorrow's for." Grayson walks over to a broken mirror on the wall and combs his fingers through his hair. "Tonight, we have fun."

As a teenager in Avren, I'd attend Council-sponsored dances. Chaperones measured the distance between dancers with a bejeweled stick. Rumors flew about how Lady Raven spied on us to determine matches. I always saw it as a chance to show off my latest creation. At the last dance I attended, I wore a deep-blue satin dress, cinched at the waist with a skirt that flowed to the floor. Black lace accented the skirt and the top of the bodice. My dance card was full, mostly with Flynn. There was no doubt in my mind that the Council would match such a handsome couple.

Until one became an orphan before her eighteenth birthday.

"It might give us a chance to blow off some steam." Bastian lounges on the rolled-out mattress, propped up on his elbows with his ankles crossed.

From her place on the mattress, Evie raises a hand, then drops it to her thigh as she considers Bastian through narrowed eyes. "You're supposed to be on my side."

Levi sits down on our bed, drawing his lip between his teeth before signing, "The people of Tenny Rocks always throw the best parties."

Evie scowls, sits up, and goes to the door. "And the three of you *always* gang up on me. Come on, Mari."

Without a word, I look at the men, each nodding their approval as I follow Evie out the door.

She's already at the bottom of the stairs, removing a small pouch from her cloak. It's beaded with the image of a single red rose. "I should have enough credits saved up from my job to do this whole dance thing properly."

I look up the stairs and back at Evie. "But I thought..."

"That we were going to take a walk and talk shit about the boys?" She shoves her pouch back into her pocket and tosses her hair over her shoulder. "We can still do that, but you're also going to need a dress for tonight."

The relationship between Evie and Grayson is stranger than mine with Bastian. I follow her out the front door of the inn, taking two steps to each of her long strides. She's a woman on a mission.

There's an excitement in the air that's palpable as we walk to the dress shop. The River Walk must be a big deal around here. Men and women intermingle in the streets, talking and flirting. Joyful music weaves throughout the square as workers hang brightly colored decorations above. It is nothing like the stiff-backed, high-collared, classical dances in Avren.

We enter a shop bursting at the seams with women. Colorful dresses line the aisles, where patrons of every shape and size hold them up for their friends to appraise. The claustrophobic atmosphere, along with the vast array of merchandise, makes me dizzy. It's so different from spending months selecting material, designing, and creating my own dress.

Evie rifles through a rack of dresses, occasionally pulling one out and scrunching her nose at it. When she holds a shorter cream-colored dress with no sleeves up, a slow smile crosses her lips. "Bastian will love it." She fingers the loose brown belt and turns the dress around. The material hangs so low, there might as well be no back to it at all. "It has the whole 'elven warrior' vibe."

My eyes widen. "That's for me?"

"Who else is dressing to impress Bastian?" She rolls her eyes in typical Evie fashion. "If we can find boots to match..." Her eyes dart to the shoe portion of the shop.

"What are you going to wear?" I push the dresses to the side to look at a lovely deep-green, full-length velvet dress, perfect for her. "What do you think of this one?"

"Really, Mari?" She checks the price tag on the cream dress. "We'll have to go to another store to find the boots."

"Aren't you going to get a dress?" I tug on her sleeve, slightly put out that our bonding time has turned into a setup. "There's a lot of dresses here that will look great on you."

Giving a curt smile to the woman at the counter, Evie lays my dress down. "I don't do dresses. Gray knows this."

My skin flushes with a rush of heat. At the dance, I won't be the only woman in a dress, but I will be the only one among the Kindred Few—a dress that reveals almost my entire back down to my bottom. The thought of being the center of attention for Bastian, Levi, and even Grayson is mortifying.

I remain silent as we walk through the streets of Tenny Rocks, looking for a shoe shop. Evie stops to ask for directions from the owner of a bookstore. Then we're on our way again, taking a stone staircase down to the riverfront.

A wooden platform spans the water. Workers hang similar decorations to the ones in the square above the dance floor, attaching them to trees on either side of the river. Unlit torches line the banks, ready to add a romantic ambience to the festive event.

"She said the shoe store is to the right about a block." Evie doesn't look twice at the River Walk setup, but I can't look away. It's so different from Avren's stuffy events and stirs something deep inside of me.

Not wanting to be left behind, I jog to catch up to Evie but chance an occasional glance behind me. "Do you think Bastian really wants to go to a dance with me?"

Evie continues to read the swinging wooden signs as we pass them. "I think Bastian would go to high tea with the wood nymphs if he knew you'd be there."

My stomach twists in knots, knowing the others see his fascination with me. But it's not real. Once we break the magnetic attraction, we'll have nothing left.

Inside the shoe shop, Evie finds a pair of thigh-high brown leather boots and makes me try them on. They're like nothing I've ever worn before. In the city, I wore comfortable flats and, in the wilderness, combat-style boots. The material hugs my legs dangerously, and suddenly I'm determined to make Bastian feel things beyond our unnatural connection.

After Evie purchases the boots, she places them in the bag with my dress.

"You're really going to wear that to the dance?" I rake my eyes down Evie's fighting gear. "From the way women were snatching up dresses in the shop, you're going to stand out."

"Precisely." She taps the end of my nose with her finger. "Why dress like everyone else?"

"To impress Grayson?" Even I can see how other women look at Evie's boyfriend.

She gathers the bag under her arm, turning up her nose. "I don't need a dress to impress Gray. He loves me this way." She exits the shop, looking both ways down the river. "He has to, or I'm walking."

"Then why are you making me wear a dress?" I follow her to the right along the river, where people in boats use long sticks to hang strings of decorations in the trees.

"Because you're a woman from the city. You live for this type of thing. Bastian knows this. He'd rather storm the First City than go to a dance, so enjoy him while he's soft." She twists her lips. "Never seen him this way before."

"But shouldn't we strategize for tomorrow?" The thought of facing King Cirrus sets my heart racing almost as much as the thought of standing in front of Bastian in the dress Evie bought.

"The less you know, the better. That way, he can't torture it out of you." She adjusts the bag under her arm as we turn a corner to climb the stone stairs. "Besides, the more relaxed you are, the more likely he is to believe your story."

"And what is my story?" Why would I walk up to the Unseelie Court's front door and request an audience with the person who tried to kidnap me? I scratch my head. Cirrus will see it for what it is—a distraction.

"Levi wants to mend things with the fae. Although a product of the sin, he had nothing to do with his mother's betrayal of her kind with his father. As a token of goodwill, he's offering you, the savior, on a silver platter." She rounds a corner into the busy town square.

"And if he doesn't buy it?" I watch a man on a ladder hang flowering vines from the ropes crisscrossing the square.

"He will." Her confidence is infectious but still bewildering to me. "Levi's a very good actor."

We enter the inn, and Evie hands me the bag. "Go get dressed. I'll be up in a bit to help you with your hair." She walks away and joins a man at the bar drinking a beer.

CHAPTER TWENTY-FOUR

A cool breeze hits my bare back from the open window, sending a chill through me to rival my nerves. The mixture of going to the dance with Bastian and facing King Cirrus has me on edge. Never in my life have I worn a dress that only falls to my mid-thigh. The belt, snug around my waist, shows my hourglass figure.

And the boots.

Trying them on in the store was nothing like wearing them with this dress. The bottom of the skirt falls about two inches above the top of the boots, making me feel like the elven warrior Evie said I'd resemble. I've never seen one, but I can only imagine. All I need is my bow and quiver.

Evie uses a heated iron rod to add curls to my hair, letting them fall in a cascade over my shoulders and bosom. And in this dress, my cleavage is on full display, and there's nothing I can do to hide it. While my sister isn't looking, I yank at the bodice of the dress, trying to cover the top part of my body, but it slips back down into its natural cut.

When she finishes my hair, she lays her hands on my shoulders, having me turn in a circle. "You'll do." It's a high compliment from my sister.

When I descend the stairs, Bastian, Grayson, and Levi are sitting at a table in the dining area of the inn. They're laughing over a round of drinks until they see us. All three of them stand, eyes wide and mouths hanging open.

"Get over yourselves." Evie plops into the fourth seat and looks at Bastian. "She's all yours."

He's combed his hair back into a tie, which gives me a full view of his eyes. Standing right here, lost in his gaze, I could die a happy woman. He's freshly pressed his white tunic and cotton pants, and they fit perfectly in all the right places. It's awkward inspecting him while the others watch, because he's doing the same thing to me.

"Are you ready?" he asks, taking my hand in his, a finger trailing along the curve of my palm. This means as much to him as it does to me.

"Yes." I grip his hand tighter, relishing the way I've made him sweat.

Cool air attacks my fevered body as we step into the square where it seems the entire town is enjoying the celebration. Children dance beneath the lanterns, holding hands and singing to the boisterous music. Men and women drink and congregate, laughing and talking loudly. This is a gathering the Council would never allow within the city walls.

It provides hope.

Hope of a life where, someday, people can make their own decisions and live the way they desire. In Tenny Rocks, the townspeople have tasted a sliver of this freedom. With the exception of their work schedules, they no longer live under the Council's thumb.

Holding Bastian's hand... kissing him... is a punishable offense in the city. Here, I'm free to express how I feel. I can't let

Avren's rules continue to control me from afar. Either I'm a member of the Kindred Few, or I'm Lady Raven's pawn.

He stops me, holds up my hand, and spins me around. "I don't think this dress meets the Council's approval."

I slip my arms around his neck and press my body against his. "I no longer care about what the Council approves of." My lips meet his eagerly. It feels different because the nagging voice of Lady Raven no longer fills my head.

Avren doesn't own me. I know that now.

He feels my abandonment. Growling, he slips his hand beneath my bottom and lifts me into his arms as I wrap my legs behind his back and deepen the kiss. His tongue battles with mine, trying to win the war of who wants the other one more.

The crowd disappears as he sets me on a rock wall, my dress hiked up almost to my waist. Gravel digs into the back of my thighs, but I don't care as I take his face in my hands and dive back into our kiss. His hands slip behind me, exploring my bare back before settling on my waist.

He finally pulls away, out of breath. "You don't need to prove it to me anymore. You've earned it."

I raise an eyebrow, hoping he means another chance to share his bed. "Earned what?"

"Your tattoo." His fingers trail along my hairline, lifting a tendril of hair behind my ear and tracing the shell, setting my body on fire.

"But I thought I had to prove myself... like, in battle." My emotions are in a jumbled mess. As much as I want to drop everything and become a bona fide member of the Kindred Few, I want nothing to detract from the fire about to set my core ablaze.

He rests his forehead against mine. "I said you had to prove yourself. I didn't say how." Lifting his head, he looks me in the eye. "Avren had a chokehold on you. We've watched your progress—your desensitization toward the role the city's rules and regulations play in your life. When you rejected me the other night, I knew you weren't quite ready."

"So, you used me?" Tears well in my eyes as everything comes crashing down. "You pretended to like me to see if you could get past the brainwashing?" Disappointment morphs into anger as I push at his chest, not wanting him so close.

He snatches my wrist before I can shove him again and leans into me. "Not at all, Maribel."

I wince when he uses my full name.

"This is real." He touches his chest above his heart. "You make me feel more alive than anyone I've met in my entire life." His voice breaks, revealing his vulnerability. "Before you came home with Gray, my world revolved around eating, sleeping, and training. Susan filled a lonely night here and there, but she didn't fill what was missing in my heart." He swallows, gazing up at a stray firework lighting the night sky, then brings his face close to mine. "You, Maribel Windsong. You are the one thing in my life I didn't know I was missing." Swollen lips meet mine again, perfect in both words and actions.

A hand tugs on my skirt, and I look down at a little girl with blonde pigtails, an orange kerchief covering her head, and a yellow dress. She holds a hand smeared with dirt out to me, so I slide off the wall and take it, no longer bothered by the beliefs of my past. I keep hold of Bastian as she pulls us into the crowd of people dancing in a chain to the lively music.

By the time our chain weaves through the entire square, we are both laughing and out of breath. Bastian slips a hand behind my back and leads me down an alley, meandering through stone buildings. With his warm hand in mine and the oil lamps on the stoops of this narrow passageway, I feel safe. This man could ask me to jump into the river, and I'd follow him willingly. It's crazy how a few weeks can change your perspective on someone.

We stop in front of a door without an oil lamp. Bastian raps on the surface with his knuckles, and I can feel his broad smile in the dim light.

"What are you doing?" I whisper, the words magnified in our desolate surroundings.

"Don't worry." He gives my cheek a swift pinch and turns to the door as it opens.

"Bastian Hale," a woman's voice says. In the shadows, I can't see her face. "Come for another reading?"

"Not tonight, Reviva." He drapes an arm over my shoulder, tugging me to him. "This is Maribel, the newest member of our family. She'll need a tag."

A tag? What does he think I am? A dog? A cow on his farm?

"Ahh…" The woman reaches out and touches my face. Her long, bony fingers are ice cold as she traces the contours.

I clutch my arms to my chest, unsure if I want to stay very long. The festivities in the town square are much more appealing.

"May I read your palm?" Reviva asks, her hand dropping from my face.

"No." Bastian's voice is firm. "That's not why we're here." His hand slides over my lower back, gripping my hip. "Mari needs a tattoo."

I swallow, my throat dry and my head spinning. He had mentioned that I've earned it, but I didn't think he meant this soon. The Council forbids markings of any kind on the body because they taint the pristine nature of our society. I hate how I'm still conflicted. Getting this tattoo is supposed to be my way to say *fuck you*, as Bastian would put it, to the Council.

I long for a drink, my throat now feeling like sandpaper. "I'm ready." This is more than a way to impress a man. This is belonging. This is a symbol of leaving Avren behind and taking my new role—though it scares the crap out of me—as one of the two saviors by the horns.

He lifts a hand to my shoulder, slipping the material of my dress to the side. "I thought it might look lovely right here."

Leaning down, he kisses the bare skin of my shoulder, causing a rush of heat to pool in my gut.

"Come, come." Reviva opens the door wider, letting us cross the threshold.

I'm hit with the pungent smells of herbs, reminiscent of Ben's cottage. In the city, the aromas of chlorine, bleach, and the occasional perfume were everyday. In the wilderness, I've become accustomed to campfires, moss, and the earthy smells of the life cycle. The fresh smells make me want to curl up by the fire in Reviva's hearth and fall asleep.

She leads me to a chair at the table in her kitchen. Brightly colored cards lie scattered over the wooden surface, along with mismatched teacups stained with many uses. "Are you sure you don't want a reading, dear?" Her bony fingers clasp my shoulder. "I sense your fear."

Do you think the tattoo needle might have something to do with it?

"No, I'm fine," I lie. Dancing in the square sounds like a much better time. "Let's get this over with."

Bastian crouches beside me, gathering my hands into his. His blue eyes assess me as tiny wrinkles form between his brows. "I thought you wanted this."

Yes. I want to belong somewhere. I love Levi and Grayson. Bastian and Evie are growing on me. If I need to get a tattoo to prove I belong, then I will do it. I don't know if I want the title of the savior from the prophecy. In fact, I'm pretty sure I don't.

I rest my forehead against his, desperate to find his scent hidden in the pungent incense. "Can we add a fifth circle?"

He lets out a stifled laugh. "I always thought the four-circle thing was stupid. It seems more complete with five—stronger, more resilient."

I tilt my chin slightly to take his lips in a soft kiss. "Then let's do this."

Turning around, I sit backward in the chair, resting my arms on it. Bastian slips my dress partway down my arm to reveal my bare shoulder. I shudder slightly as he traces the area with his fingernail to show Reviva where to place it. He knows what his touch does to me.

A cold, wet cloth swipes over my shoulder. Reviva dries it, then hobbles over to the other side of the room. She comes back with a brown leather pouch, unrolling it on the table to reveal her tools.

I grip the back of the chair tighter as she touches her pen to my skin. I fight back the tears as she traces the first circle.

"Talk to me." Bastian sits on the floor, watching my face. "I'm here if you need something to punch or to dig your fingernails into."

All I want to do is scream obscenities at him. Tonight was supposed to be special. I wore this dress for him—one that Evie said he would love. It feels as if this woman might burn a hole straight through my skin to my bone, and I'll be in no shape to return to the dance. Why did I agree to this? I close my eyes. "I'm... fine... Bastian."

Reviva continues to assault my skin, thinking nothing of my pain. "The last time we met, you drew the lovers' card."

"Yes." He averts his eyes from mine to look at his fortuneteller. "What of it?"

"And this is what the universe brought you?" Reviva's pen seems to dig deeper into my shoulder. "A weakling from Avren? Took you for the warrior-woman type."

I tense, ready to defend myself.

"The universe has tethered me to her. I can't help myself." Bastian still won't look at me. "It's as if she's a drug I can't get enough of."

"I'm right here," I grumble, hurt by his words. "The least you can do is say why you like me."

His eyes dart to mine as I'm held captive in the hands of the tattoo artist. "You don't back down. You strive to accomplish things that seem impossible to others. You're headstrong, not willing to let others define who you are because of your upbringing. You're a good friend to Levi. Others disregard him because he's deaf." He grabs at the scruff of his neck, dipping his head slightly. "And you're a damn good kisser."

I stare at him through the slats of the chair, no longer regarding the pain of Reviva's needle. "Then, if the magnetic connection disappeared, you'd still like me?"

He threads his fingers through mine, giving me all kinds of feels. "I don't need an unnatural bond to like you, Mari. You've reeled me in by just being you."

Reviva sets the needle on the table. She picks up a square of cloth and rubs balm from a porcelain bowl on my skin. The coolness of the salve, along with Bastian's words, calms my soul.

"My turn," he says, jumping up and brushing the dirt from the floor from his pants.

"Are you getting one?"

He already has multiple runes decorating his skin.

"I have to add a circle." He lifts his tunic over his head, revealing the hard planes of his muscles.

I hate how he makes me feel every time he takes his shirt off. It's as if the gods formed him from their most perfect mold, making the rest of us feel extremely inadequate in his presence. And yet, I can't look away. I tear my eyes away to study the glass jars on Reviva's shelves, chancing small peeks every once in a while.

When the tattoo is complete, Bastian hands Reviva a bag of coins.

She jangles it in her palm, seeming to contemplate something. "What of the three of swords?"

Bastian's face darkens, his lips pull into a pout. "I don't want to discuss that. Leave it be." He snatches my hand, and we're out the door, bombarded by the clean air of the wilderness.

I know better than to question. Instead, I'll tuck the comment away for our uncertain future.

We climb down the stairs to the river. The party on the wooden platform is as lively as the one in the square, but when we step onto the dance floor, the music slows to a haunting melody. I'm in his arms, his hand dangerously low on my back. The hypnotic sway of his hips is like a drug I can't get enough of. I stare into his eyes, lost in the way they catch the torchlight.

He dips his head, and his lips touch my ear, grazing the lobe and making me shiver. "Have I told you that you look amazing tonight? You make me forget there's anyone else here."

I shift away from him, furrow my brow, and cover my mouth to feign shock. "Commander Hale always has one eye on his surroundings."

"Like I said." His lips move along my jawline. "I can't take my eyes from you." He draws me closer, pressing his mouth to mine. We're barely moving now, only swaying to the music drifting over the dance floor.

His hands drift over the silken material of my dress as he deepens the kiss, his tongue exploring mine. Steady palms grip my hips before slipping behind my back to explore my bare skin, all while never breaking the tangle of our mouths. My fingers tug on the tie in his hair, letting the elastic fall to the ground so I can bury my hands in his long strands.

The floor beneath my feet suddenly gives way, and screams rise around us. A splash, followed by more, tells me people are falling into the river. As the entire dance floor rises vertically into the air, I release Bastian and grab onto a railing, hoping he'll do the same. I watch him slide down the planks and into the water below. My fingers ache, struggling to hold onto the wooden slat.

Screeches rise from the shoreline as humanlike creatures search the banks of the waterway. From my brief glance, I see they have hunched backs, long greasy hair, and ashen gray skin.

Miscretes.

"Mari." Bastian cups his mouth. "Hold on!" His weapons cloak is back in the room where we're staying. He swims to the base of the platform, which now teeters back and forth, stuck on two boulders. "If you drop, I'll catch you."

I glance at the creatures sniffing along the riverbank. One catches me looking. The humanness in its eyes makes me turn away. Did they cause this?

A deafening creak shakes the entire structure, and I pitch forward as the railing cracks, my feet dangling above the rapids.

"The whole thing's going to break in half!" Bastian shouts. "Drop!"

My body trembles, my fingers growing numb as I look over my shoulder at the water below. The creatures still scour the riverbank, seeming afraid to go into the water after the humans. Or are they after something else?

Bastian lifts a rock from the bottom of the river, holds it over his head, and throws it at a Miscrete getting too close to a woman and little girl. The creature dodges it and hisses at the commander.

"Mari! You need to drop," Bastian pleads.

I close my eyes, draw in a breath, and let my hands do the thing they've wanted to do for the last minute—release. Screaming, I fall to the water below.

CHAPTER TWENTY-FIVE

*B*astian is there to pull me up from the rapids before I get swept away. Clumps of hair stick to my face. Exhausted, I wipe them away to get a closer look at the enemy.

"What do you think they want?" I clutch my arms as a horde of Miscretes approach the bank, one dipping its toe into the water.

Bastian trudges through the water to assist a woman to the opposite shore from the creatures. "At first I thought the aim was more recruits, but based on their actions, it appears they have orders to find a specific person."

Two dozen eyes watch us from the edge of the river, seemingly waiting for us to exit. They growl and bark commands at each other as if hoping for the most daring to take the lead.

"What does Arazian want with us?" My legs grow numb in the cold water, and I long for nothing more than to get back to the inn and sleep.

He catches a rope from someone on the shore and hands it to an older-looking man. He lays a hand on the man's back. "Don't worry. It's only about five steps to the shore. They will pull you out when you get there." Turning to me, he wraps an arm around my waist to pull me close to his side. "Probably the same thing the fae king wants with you. To use you as a weapon against everyone else. We need a plan for when we exit the water. It won't take them long to find the bridge. The armory is along the riverbank. If I can get a sword, I can make quick work of them."

"Like you did when you went to rescue Lyden?" I regret the words as they leave my mouth, but the scar on Bastian's face serves as a living testament to the viciousness of the beasts.

He shifts so we're face-to-face as his hand cups my cheek. "I *won't* let them take you."

My dress is soaking wet from falling into the river, the bandage and salve long washed away from my tattoo. It burns like hell, and a band of mutant creatures want to kidnap me. But standing this close to Bastian, I feel emboldened, like I can take on the world. Power emanates from his every pore.

"I'm ready." I wrap my arms around his neck and kiss him like we'll never see each other again. "Let's kick some Miscrete butt."

His lips pull back into a smile of approval. "Join the group of women helping each other out over there, then follow me. The second you exit the water, they'll catch your scent."

"But how...?"

"Arazian is crafty. He was a member of the Council of Avren for a reason. Don't underestimate what he will do if he wants something." Bastian kisses my forehead. "I'll see you on the other side."

I mingle among a group of women using a thick vine to climb out of the river. It's funny to watch them try to climb up the slick bank in long dresses. Most have ditched their heels, using their bare feet to climb. I wade through the water to the woman who seems to be overseeing the operation.

"Where are your dates?" I can't imagine them taking off and leaving the women behind to fend for themselves.

She rakes her eyes over my dress now that the water is only thigh high. It is almost completely see-through.

Heat rises to my cheeks, but I don't have time to discuss the ethics of my attire.

"Swept away, dragged out by the Miscretes, or ran away like babies." She sneers at me as if I'm one of them. "And where's yours?"

"He's going to meet me on the bank." I count the women left. Five.

Rather than continue my riveting discourse, I crouch below the current lady trying to climb the vine and use my shoulder to push her ass up the slope. This proves difficult, not only because she's sobbing but because she weighs a ton.

"Help me!" I growl at the other women, losing patience with waiting my turn to climb out.

Two other women join me, and we get the first woman out and safely on the shore. She wrings the folds of her dress, tears still streaming down her face.

"It's going to be alright," I say. Hysterics will get us nowhere. "What's your name?"

"Megan," she sobs.

"Ok, Megan. You're going to stay there and help from above by gripping hands and helping pull." I point to another woman. "You'll go next. The rest of us will push from below."

Using this method, we get all the women to the bank safely, leaving me alone in the river. I dig my fingernails into the vine and climb, making it to the top without help. My training with Bastian and the shorter dress have served me well.

A deafening howl resounds from the other bank, and all Miscrete eyes fix on me. In a massive swarm of hunched bodies, they move as one toward the bridge, seeming determined to overtake me.

Bastian holds a torch, motioning for me to hurry to him. In my boots, I race over the cobblestones with surprising ease. Evie knew the footwear was versatile. We run along the river away from the bridge. I ignore my lungs desperately trying to catch their next breath as we round the corner of a darkened building.

He tries the door, but it's locked. "Hold this," he demands, shoving the torch into my hands. Without hesitation, he punches his fist through the glass on the door and reaches through to unlock it. Blood smears his hand. I swallow back bile.

"Grab what you need to defend yourself." He fills his pockets with daggers before lifting a sword from the wall. "With your scent, they won't stop until they have you."

A bow rests against the wall with a quiver of arrows beside it. I rush over and lift the quiver to my back, crisscrossing the straps over the front of my dress. Now I look like a true elven princess, but will my aim be as true?

Growls and grunts come from outside the armory, so I snatch two daggers and stuff them into my boots.

Bastian holds the torch in front of him as we creep toward the open door. The light flickers on the silent threshold, playing tricks with shadows. I lick my lips, trying to visualize my first battle as my heart pounds against my chest.

A deafening screech fills the room, and the doorway is suddenly full of monsters—crooked arms, sharp claws, and rotting flesh. Bastian takes the torch in both hands and jabs it in their direction. Their scary human eyes grow wide. The beasts are clearly afraid of the flame.

Arazian plays mind games with his creations. The humans are no longer alive. These are unnatural beings fueled by magic. If I don't do something, they'll drag me away from my family.

I nock an arrow on my bow and draw back, taking aim. It whizzes through the small space and hits a creature in the head. It falls to the ground. I swallow back more bile. My second kill is just as difficult as my first one in the woods with the werewolf. But I don't have time to think.

A daring Miscrete skirts along the wall, taking advantage of

Bastian's entanglement with the main swarm. I nock a second arrow and aim it at the monster.

"Arazian only wants to talk." The voice comes from the Miscrete, but it sounds strangely like Levi's.

I don't drop my bow, but I hesitate.

There's no way.

My upper body shakes as I keep my aim on the creature. "Well, I don't want to talk to him."

"Shoot it!" Bastian calls over his shoulder. He has the flat of his sword against the chest of a Miscrete. Using his shoulders, he barrels the creature over, knocking five others down with its body.

The Miscrete moves closer to me. "Come, come, Maribel. Imagine taking the throne as princess of the First City. We have a horse waiting for you outside to whisk you away from this place."

Arazian doesn't know me. Why would he want me to come to the First City other than to kill me because of the prophecy? I let my arrow fly straight into the lying bastard monster's heart.

Levi never calls me Maribel.

I aim my arrow at the doorway, hitting monster after monster with my arrows as Bastian takes them on with his sword. His clean white shirt is now torn and covered in gashes where the Miscretes swiped at him. Beads of sweat line his forehead. He swings his sword, making a clean swipe to remove an arm.

Blood gushes from the creature's wound, but it continues coming for me. I don't have time to draw an arrow, so I snatch a dagger from my boot and hold it in front of me. "Stay where you are."

"Maribel Nexus Winsong-Barellis," the creature says, somehow still standing on two feet while losing a ton of blood.

What the hell?

This monster sounds like Flynn. Arazian must use magic to transform their voices, but it's really creeping me out.

"Daughter of Daxon Barellis, the Northern Duke." An evil grin crosses the Miscrete's lips. "We know everything about you, princess."

"If my dad's a duke, I'm not a princess." My body shakes so badly, I'm afraid I'll drop the dagger. Hearing my friends' voices affects me more than I thought. "You better study up on the whole lineage thing. I'm nothing more than the daughter of a Citizen of Avren."

A hissing sound comes from the monster, which I assume is a laugh. "You don't give yourself enough credit. Don't tell me you haven't heard the prophecy. You're to tear down Avren, the dear city you love, brick by brick. Come with us, and you can live a peaceful life, devoid of such—" it looks down at the blood gushing from its socket— "such bloodshed."

"You're a liar." I hold the tip of my dagger to its chest. "Arazian steals humans from the wilderness and turns them into disgusting creatures like you. What's more pathetic? Violence to free a people or violence to obtain power? I choose to free my people." And with that, I drive the dagger into its heart, finishing what Bastian started.

Blood stains my hands and cream-colored dress, but I don't care. I've now fully earned the throbbing pain of the tattoo on my shoulder. Both cities need to fall—the First City, with its outright evil agenda, and Avren with its veneration of the perfect person, and its subjugation of all who fall short of perfection.

Exhausted, I turn to help Bastian just as he plunges his sword into the final Miscrete. From across the room, we stare at each other. He's killed dozens, and I only a few, but I know my role was just as important in this room.

He drops to his knees, weighed down by the toll. I kneel beside him, careful not to touch his wounds, and let him envelop me in his arms. This night, full of dancing and music, was supposed to draw me closer to him. But after fighting side by side, I can't imagine anything else to better strengthen our bond. We fought together for a common purpose. In this battle, it was to protect the savior, but in the war, we will tear down the injustice surrounding us.

"Are you hurt?" His eyes hold concern as he touches the bloody material of my dress.

I shift to inspect the gashes in his tunic. Blood seeps through the thin material. "No, but you are. We need to get you back to the inn."

"I'm not ready yet." He sits crisscross and pulls me onto his lap. His fingers trail along my hairline, sending shivers through me. "You were amazing. I heard every word those creatures said to you, trying to deceive you, but you were having none of it."

"It's a little strange." I glance at the dead bodies and stockpiles of armory around us.

"What's strange?" His fingers trail to the sensitive spot behind my ear.

I wiggle in his lap, feeling him hard against my leg. As much as I want to puke after all I just went through, the experience has the opposite effect on him. "Having a romantic moment surrounded by all this... gore. Can we go somewhere else?"

He laughs, then bites down into his lip, his dark hair hanging like a curtain around his eyes. "I know just the place."

We follow the riverbank, holding hands and getting strange looks from the few people out after the attack on the dance platform. We appear as if we've walked off a battlefield and lost. It doesn't bother me. Let them stare.

At the end of town, the river veers to the left, and a vast field stands before us. Fireflies dance among the tall grasses, and the moon lights our way to an oak tree standing like a sentinel beside a small pond.

Bastian winces as he removes his shirt. In the shimmering glow of the sky above, I can see the true extent of his wounds.

"Do you think we should go back?" I touch his chest above a deeper gash.

"Shhh..." He holds a finger to my lips, tracing over them like a cool whisper. He reaches down and lifts my dress over my head. Other than my undergarments, I'm standing bare before him.

I clutch my arms beneath my chest, exposed to both the cold and embarrassment.

He holds my head in his hands, touching his forehead to mine. Heat radiates from his skin, warming me slightly. "Don't hide yourself from me. You are the most gorgeous person I've ever laid eyes on."

My heart beats wildly, unable to contain the conflicting emotions I have inside. "But you are not my husband. Only a spouse can see another undressed."

"In Avren," he says, running a hand down my arm and weaving his fingers through mine. "Do you think I don't take this seriously? With you? My commitment to you is stronger than that of any man you might sign a piece of paper and have test tube babies with. Out here, we rely on each other. There's no one I trust more."

"After such a short time?" I understand where he's coming from. After our battle in the armory, the feelings have been magnified tenfold. I can trust this man with my life. And from what he's saying, he feels the same way about me.

He cups my cheek with his free hand, applying slow caresses over my skin with his thumb. "I'm fiercely protective of you. Even if it's over my dead body, you will come out of this alive. You've given my life purpose, and I didn't know a prophecy I'd heard on repeat throughout my life could do that." Releasing my hand, he unbuckles his pants and lets them slide to the ground in a puddle.

I don't look down out of fear he's not wearing any under-garments.

"Are you afraid of me, Mari?"

No... yes... I'm not afraid of *him*, only of my inadequacies.

He picks up our clothes in one arm and takes my hand again, leading me to the pond. I glimpse his bare bottom as he walks in front of me, and I swallow back my fear. This man wants me, and there's *nothing* Lady Raven can do about it out here in the wilderness.

Bastian lays our clothes on a rock and leads me until the water is up to my chest. The water is warmer than the air within the shallow pool. The moon and fireflies create a romantic ambience.

He lowers his head until his lips are even with the surface and blows a stream of tiny waves in my direction. Being here is so natural to him, like eating and breathing. "I'll understand if you don't want to." He lifts a wet strand of hair away from my forehead. "You told me how you felt last time in the cabin."

As an eighteen-year-old in Avren, this is about the time the Council would pick a partner for me. Until they deemed me an Undesirable, I had every hope it would be Flynn Baxter, the boy who made me feel things I'd never dreamt possible. That is until I met Bastian. With him standing before me in a pond in the middle of the wilderness, I know without a doubt there's no one else for me.

"Please show me how to do this, Commander Hale."

CHAPTER TWENTY-SIX

*B*astian takes a step closer to me, and I hold my breath. The croaking frogs, wind in the leaves high above, and the endless chirp of crickets serenade us. He's so close, the heat of his skin threatens to sear me. His enormous hands circle my arms, drawing me near, where he leans in to kiss me. I explore his lips with my tongue, taking the time to map them in my memory as his hands run along my back, lifting me by my ass so I'm straddling him.

His tongue dives into my mouth. I wrap my legs around his back, feeling him hard beneath me.

Oh, gods.

If I'm defying Lady Raven's orders simply by kissing this man, I might as well make the most of it. My hand dives beneath the surface of the water and lands between his legs. He moans into my mouth as I grip and tug, thankful it brings him pleasure and not pain. It's not like anyone in Avren gave me lessons on how to do this.

"Mari…" Bastian breaks our kiss and squeezes his eyes shut as I continue to stroke him. He lets out a stifled laugh before turning his eyes on me. "I thought you wanted me to teach you."

"You teach me by going about everyday life." I move my hand to his chest. "When you remove your shirt, your muscles flex, and you show me how to seduce you with the removal of my clothes." I reach behind me and unsnap my bra, letting it drift beside us on top of the water.

Bastian reaches up to touch me, but I block him with my hand.

"You teach me the art of seduction with your words." I press into him with my hips to show him I know how to tease. "Like when you call me 'Windsong' or 'princess'. At first, they infuriated me, but now they're like a verbal aphrodisiac."

"Don't talk dirty to me, princess." He snatches my hand, apparently tired of waiting. "I won't even tell you all the ways you've had my heart racing since we met. The way you walk through the woods in Evie's tight leather fighting gear, or the way you hold the bow like a novice just to get me close to you."

"I've been naughty, haven't I?" I flutter my eyelashes, wondering if I left the old Mari behind in the village. "But I don't want to be good anymore if it means being good without you."

His heart hammers against his chest as he sucks on my lower lip, making me arch my back. The exhilarating feelings ripping through my body make me wish we could stay here in Tenny Rocks and forget about my role as the savior. He lifts me slightly, dips his head, and takes my nipple into his mouth, rolling his tongue over the hard pebble and making the growing ache in the pit of my stomach intensify. I didn't know this is what the Council took away from us—this hunger for one another.

He moves to my other breast, teasing me with his nips and tugs, and arousing something deep inside of me. I want this man more than anything I've ever wanted in my life—more than marrying Flynn, more than becoming a dressmaker, more than becoming a Citizen of Avren.

"Are you sure you want to do this?" he asks, lifting me out of the water, my arms and legs around him like a mythical monkey

I've seen in fairytales. "We can wait as long as you need." His words say one thing, but his body and eyes say the complete opposite. He wants me—bad.

And I want him. "Show me how to do it, Bastian."

He carries me out of the water and sets me on my feet to lay his cloak on the ground. I'd always imagined my first time would be in the apartment I shared with my husband on our wedding night. As Bastian lays me down on his cloak, fireflies blink above his head, and somehow this seems just as perfect.

"What do you know?" he asks, hovering above me, his dark hair cascading down.

I know what my girlfriends told me, things we wouldn't read in any book in Avren's library. And when Flynn's hand touched my breast through the material of my sweater, he whispered secrets about what married partners do behind closed doors. He told me how, late at night, he reached beneath the covers to pleasure himself, imaging it was me.

"I think I know enough," I say, arching my hips to meet him, only the thin layer of my underwear between us. "But what if I'm bad at it?"

He chuckles, smoothing down my hair. "You could never be bad at it, Windsong."

After my confession, he's using my trigger words intentionally, and it makes me long for him more. With his expert hands, he removes my last undergarment, and I lie naked before him in the moonlight.

He sits above me, taking in every curve, dip, and imperfection of my body with a tiny, satisfied smile on his lips. "I promise to protect, love, and worship you until my dying breath."

"Please don't talk about death." I sit up and pull him to me. "I only want to know what it feels like to live for the first time in my life."

Heated kisses meet my eager lips; our hands explore each other's bodies. And he teaches me. He shows me how the swirls and flicks of his tongue in the right places can send me into ecstasy, screaming his name for all the wildland creatures to hear. He holds my hands above my head, both of my wrists fitting perfectly in one of his, and licks a trail of my sweat from my navel to my throat as I whimper, my voice hoarse from screaming.

Foreplay is what he calls it. Before he performs each act, he lays it out for me, making me more worked up from the anticipation.

After I'm as pliable as a ball of putty in his hands, his lips brush over my neck as he says, "Foreplay's over, princess. So, I'll ask you one more time. Do you want me to make love to you?" He rubs my thighs with his strong hands, starting from my knee up to where my leg meets my hip.

Sitting up, I grab both of his arms and stare him intently in the eyes. My body is slick with sweat from multiple orgasms. "If you don't, I'll kick your ass."

He taps his chin. "Hmm... I might have to take you up on that." Reaching down, he strokes himself. "But I need this more than a good ass kicking."

He positions himself over my core, and I reach out for something to grab. My fingers wrap around the root of a nearby tree. I squeeze my eyes shut and brace myself for impact, not exactly sure what to expect.

"Mari... Mari... because this is your first time, it might hurt a little at first." He kisses my neck, sending delicious chills down to my core. "But it's meant to bring pleasure. We wouldn't want to do it otherwise." Long strands of hair sweep across my collarbone as his lips touch my ear. "I'll be gentle."

Still, I'm not so sure, so I let him take over. He slides himself inside of me slowly, and the initial pain hits, causing me to wriggle my hips. Two palms grip them, settling me before he moves farther inside. My eyes remain tightly shut, not knowing what to expect.

"Mari, look at me." His voice is calm, like the air surrounding us.

I open them to stare into his beautiful blue eyes. He's propped up on his arms, so I can see his muscular chest as he moves in and out of me, setting a rhythm. It feels so strange but entangled with good. I want to wrap my legs around him, to draw him closer, but watching him arouses me as much as his actions do. He bites into his lip with each thrust and sends a jolt of ecstasy through me. I imagine we're in a bed and I'm gripping the headboard to hold on for dear life.

Heat builds from within as he pumps faster, and I'm on the brink again, unsure if I can hold out for him. Do you build up immunity if this becomes a routine? Because I want to do this every day. What did the old prude, Lady Raven, have against this?

My head spins as he shifts slightly, hitting a pleasurable spot deep within. He's an expert and knows exactly what he's doing. I really do feel like a ball of clay in his hands as he shapes the experience to his liking and, obviously, mine.

"It's going to happen again." I buck my hips to drive him deeper, not sure if I can get enough.

"That's my princess. Give into it." He's so masterful, not only with his actions but with his words.

With one artfully placed slam, we're both calling out together, filling the meadow with our cries. My whole body shakes with wonderful release. He falls on top of me, wrapping his arms around my back, his breath heavy.

His lips near my ear, he whispers, "I didn't know love could make it feel that way."

Love? He loves me? I knew our connection attracted him to me, but I thought he wanted to break it.

He rolls off me and rises on his elbow, his fingers trailing along my hairline. "I didn't think I was capable of love until I met you. You've turned my world upside down. My duty is to serve and protect the savior, not give her my heart."

"And what if one of us dies, Bastian?" I hate being the killjoy in the conversation, but we live in a cruel world, not a fairytale. "We'd be reckless to give our hearts to each other."

His fingers pause on my hairline before he gives me a light kiss on the lips. "I'd rather love recklessly than never love at all."

The croaks of the frogs and chirping of the crickets surround us as his arms envelop me, drawing me into another deep kiss. While we should go back to the others, we make love again, unable to contain the passions burning inside us, before falling asleep in each other's arms.

THE SKY LIGHTENS as we walk back to the village, passing the early morning fishermen on the river. We climb the stone stairs before reaching the armory. I turn my eyes away. I don't want to see the remnants of the carnage from our fight with the Miscretes. We walk across the square to the inn, confident in the story we've developed to tell the others.

The door to the inn creaks open. Katiana looks up from stoking the fire in the hearth as we enter and tries to suppress a grin. "You never change."

Bastian ignores her, taking my hand and leading me up the stairs. After my night with him, I try not to think too deeply about her comment either.

He turns the knob and opens the door. All three of our siblings are out of bed and dressed, loading their cloaks with their weapons.

"Where have you been?" Evie crosses the room, hands on her hips. She looks down at our clothes, covered in the remnants of the blood we couldn't wash out in the pond. "Was it you?" Her eyes drill into Bastian's. "Katiana told Gray this morning what happened in the armory after the dance floor collapsed. I *knew* this had you written all over it."

"They were tracking Mari." Bastian crosses the room and pulls off his shirt, then digs through his bag for a different one. "I kept her away from the inn last night in case there were more."

"But we could have helped you," Levi signs. He hasn't taken his attention away from me since we entered the room. It's as if he can read the lies between Bastian's carefully crafted lines.

"Leave them alone." Grayson flips a dagger and loads it into a compartment inside his cloak. "They're exploring each other for the first time. It's obvious she's just been f—"

"*Gray*," Evie warns, throwing a shoe across the room at him.

"Like I said." Bastian yanks his fresh shirt over his head. "Miscretes. That's all. It was safer for everyone if we were outside the village." He tosses me my bag. "There's a washroom down the hall. Go get dressed." His commands are so different from the soft caress of his voice the night before. It's a way for him to throw them off our scent. And his scent is still all over me.

An oversized basin sits in the room filled with suds and a bit of murky water. Though someone has used the tub, it must be cleaner than my body. Thankfully, the water is still hot as I sink down to my shoulders and let it calm my nerves. Today, I will face King Cirrus with little knowledge of the Unseelie Court or the fae and operating on less than two hours of sleep. *Levi will protect me.* I close my eyes to block out what's coming. *Levi will protect me.*

But what if I need to protect him?

I stand up in the tub, water cascading from my body as I shiver in the cold air. Levi put those thoughts in my head. In the preparations for going to Frostacre, I never once thought I'd depend on Levi for physical protection. He knows a lot more about his ancestors, so his knowledge of customs and tricks will help, but I will have my daggers with me. I have every intention of leaving with all my siblings and the prophecy.

I settle back into the suds and wash my hair and body. When I'm done, I step out of the tub, pat myself dry, and pull my clothes from my bag. Someone packed me a green velvet dress and boots with dagger sheaths built into them. An envelope is on top of the dress. I open the seal and pull out the note.

Mari,

I can't have my little sister facing the fairy king without the proper attire. Show them what you're made of.

Evie

Her note makes me smile. It's not just me and Levi entering the court. I have the full power of the Kindred Few behind me.

There's a knock on the door, so I gather a towel around me to open it. It's Grayson, looking sheepish and older-brotherly. He blocks his eyes with his hand as he enters and holds his other arm out, swinging it wildly so he doesn't bump into anything. I lead him to a bench and help him sit down.

"You don't have to cover your eyes." I sit beside him and look at my puckered toes. "I'm fully covered."

He drops his hand. "Trying to show an inkling of respect. As the only other Avrenian, I feel responsible for you." He clasps his hands between his knees, his fingers forming a steeple. "But that's not why I came in here. I want to talk privately."

"Does this have to do with where Bastian and I were last night?" Suspicion runs deep over each of my siblings' faces.

"In a way." Running a hand through his hair, he sighs. "Be careful with Bastian. I don't want to see your heart broken."

"And what would he think if he knew you were in here talking to me about this?" I cross my arms, appalled Grayson thinks he knows what is right for me. "You know about as much about our life in private as I know about yours with Evie." He said he loved me, and it wasn't the same with other women.

"There are things you don't know about him—beyond his sexual exploits—that garner my concern. Just be careful." He lays a hand on my arm.

"What things?" I don't understand why people are so damn

secretive around here. "He's your brother. Why are you so concerned?"

"They aren't things I know, only things I sense based on observations." He gives me a lopsided smile and ruffles my wet hair. "So, you can take it or leave it, but I'm usually pretty good with my intuition."

He leaves me alone again, not nearly as happy as I was when I first sank into the tub.

I enter the room barefoot; the skirt of the green dress sweeps over the floor. All eyes turn to me, taking in my formal attire for my appointment with King Cirrus. Levi adjusts the cuffs on his button-up shirt. He looks handsome in black pants and shiny dress shoes.

"Are we distracting Cirrus or going to a ball?" I tug at my sleeves, the material tighter than I had hoped.

"If we don't show up in formal attire, we'll offend him." Levi has his foot on a chair to tie his laces. "It's one of the rules. Remember, our primary goal is to keep Cirrus talking. The longer we can give the others to search for the prophecy, the better."

"What if I mess up?" My plan is to let Levi do the talking.

He crosses the room and lifts the Kindred Few necklace I've left on the table. "I've added a magical element to your locket. Besides the yarrow, it contains a spell which will draw you back to this spot if you clasp it in your hand." When he snaps the locket open, the herb glimmers with the supernatural element.

"And you added this to yours?" I nod at his locket.

"Of course," he says, turning to lift his other shoe to the chair.

With our bags slung over our shoulders, we leave the room and head out the front door of the inn, Katiana's voice calling out to Grayson behind us.

"I looked for you last night," she calls from the open door. "You must have missed me. I wore my pink floral."

"I bet you looked ravishing." Grayson tips his hat at her but doesn't slow his steps. "Next time, my love."

Katiana's face flames a color that is probably similar to the color of the dress she wore.

Bastian falls into step beside me, behind the others. It seems like a betrayal, not telling him about my conversation with Grayson. He slips a piece of paper into my hand, which I quickly crumple and stuff between my cleavage. I'll read it when it's not as obvious to the others.

"If anything happens, use Levi's locket." He's tied his hair back in a knot, and his black fighting gear is loaded with weapons. Very different from the man who made love to me last night, but still just as handsome. "We'll meet you in Tenny Rocks."

"Do you know where to find the prophecy?" From what I imagine about the Unseelie Court, it is a vast system of underground tunnels and caverns, easy to lose yourself in.

"Levi says Cirrus will keep it close—his throne room, his sleeping quarters, or where he stores his gold. While we search, Levi will poke around with his questioning, trying to get a clue from the king himself." He reaches into his pocket and removes a black box. "This is a communication device we swiped from two of Avren's soldiers. We'll have them both turned on so we can hear what's happening in the throne room."

I take it from his hand, inspecting the familiar equipment. "It's called a radio. It's part of a soldier's standard gear. They need to communicate with each other in the wilderness."

He stops, taking my arms in his hands. "Do not take any chances. We need you alive more than we need the prophecy. The other savior will reveal him or herself, eventually. But if you haven't noticed, I'm not very patient."

"I'll do my part for our family," I say, slipping the dress from my shoulder and tapping my tattoo with my fingernail.

He glances ahead before kissing my shoulder, sending all

kinds of warmth through me. "I know you will, but we need the two of you alive."

I don't know what this evening will hold, but I will make sure everyone else makes it out before me. They are my world, and I can't imagine life without any of them.

CHAPTER TWENTY-SEVEN

*T*he landscape changes as the afternoon wears on, casting shadows among the ferns and flowers. The forest isn't as heavy here as we push closer to the mountains. It's hard to believe that Frostacre is nestled in the unforgiving world of the tundra high above us. As we start on the trail into the foothills, I throw my cloak over my shoulders, feeling the chilling effects of the altitude and the setting sun.

"We don't have to worry about other Supes up here." Evie walks beside me, a red scarf tied loosely around her neck.

"Do you really think he knows we're coming?" I look up at the snow-covered mountains, trying to make out where Frostacre is located.

"There's no doubt he senses you. We deal with your magnetic attraction crap all the time." She gives me a sideways glance and a smirk. "Grayson's taken to spending the nights in my bed to deal with it. I'm surprised Bastian held off for so long. And Levi...?" She sighs, glancing behind us at the others. "I'm afraid that boy would do anything for you."

"But if we can break the magnetic connection, everything will be better, right?" There's nothing I want more than to know for sure what Bastian feels for me is real.

"It's not something we can break, Mari." She bends to pick a flower from the ground. "It's like this flower. You can remove the flowering bud, but it will grow back. It's part of the natural cycle. You need to pick the plant from the roots—or kill the savior—to break the connection."

All my hopes of freeing myself from magical shackles are lost. It's something I'll have to live with until I die. I look over my shoulder at Bastian. He's listening intently to Grayson talk as Levi moves silently beside them with a tall walking stick in his hand. From this distance, I can almost make out his fae features— his slender build, green eyes, and beautifully angled jaw. He wears a wide-brimmed hat, pitched to the side, and an oversized poncho-like coat.

He lifts his face and smiles, as if sensing my stare.

I don't want him to suffer because of my stupid magnetism. If the fae king can tell me how to break it besides dying, I'll find a way.

The higher we climb, more and more of the trees disappear, replaced by bushes. Every couple hundred feet, I stop to catch my breath. The air is not only cold but thinner, making it difficult for my struggling lungs to keep up. I rest my hands on my knees and draw in shallow breaths. "Are we almost there?"

"It's not long now, Windsong." Bastian taps me twice on the back as he passes. "We'll separate at Fox Glove Crossing. An interception by Cirrus's guards is imminent after that point."

I hustle to keep up, though it all but kills me. "And how will you get in?"

"We have our ways." He scans the landscape for a hidden enemy. "Ways I won't tell you now. Spies for the king lie in wait everywhere. You go in and do your job and we'll do ours."

"Please be safe." I speak low so the others won't hear. "The thought of losing you makes my heart heavy. I can't imagine losing my mother and my..."

He twists his lip and taps it with his finger. "And what do you call us, Mari? Care to define our relationship?"

Heat rises along my neck to my cheeks. I shouldn't feel so self-conscious around him. "Friends?"

"Hardly." Tendrils of his dark hair splay against his hood as he moves forward through this wind-swept world.

There are words I don't want to say in case he doesn't feel the same way. He tells me he loves me, says I'm more than a one-night stand, but do I dare speak my own feelings aloud?

"Lovers?" He keeps his eyes forward and a slight tinge of pink stains his cheeks.

The relationship conversation bothers him as much as it does me. I'm happy with our stolen moments and swollen kisses. The thought that I can make his heart nearly beat out of his chest causes my body to overheat—or is it the exhaustion from climbing this massive hill?

"Have you read my note?" He pinches the bridge of his nose, probably trying to hide the remaining pink on his cheeks from Evie, who looks back at us.

"No." I trudge over the rock-laden path, each step a pure act of willpower. "It's not like I've had any alone time. I don't want the others to tease us relentlessly with unwanted jokes."

"Do you think I care?" He lifts me over a large boulder, then skirts a mud puddle. "The way we feel about each other is written all over our faces. We don't need to hide it anymore."

Every reluctancy that weighs me down always stems back to Avren. An unmarried, intimate relationship is cause for expulsion. Deprogramming the marks carved deeply into my essence will take time.

He takes my hand, long fingers entwining with mine. "You're worth waiting for. From the glimpses of the real you I've seen, I can't imagine what it will be like when nothing holds you back from your true potential."

I draw my hood close to my face to hide my smile.

The bushes grow smaller and eventually disappear as we cross the tundra dotted with arctic moss and tiny purple flowers turned inside out in the heavy winds. We follow the path down into a valley where a high mountain stream runs over a cliffside and into a pool below. The magic I felt when Levi and I were near Mafekadi fills the air in this secluded ravine. Mist pricks my exposed skin, having the opposite effect of what I expect. It warms my chilled bones.

Grayson and Evie stop, crouching to fill their canteens in the pool.

"This is where we must part." Bastian grips the hilt of his sword, keeping his gaze on his boots shuffling in the dirt.

Levi stands beside me, his head held high as Grayson approaches us.

He adjusts each of our cloaks, brushing dirt from our shoulders. "I can't believe we're sending our two babies to confront the king of the Unseelie Court."

Levi swats Grayson's hand from his shoulder, narrows his eyes, and wrinkles his nose. "Baby" isn't the word I'd use either.

"Kidding aside..." Grayson tugs on my earlobe and swats Levi's bottom. "Don't do anything I wouldn't do. Keep it on the down-low. Let Cirrus do the talking because you know how much he loves to hear his own voice. The longer you can keep him talking, the more time we'll have to complete our part of the mission." He throws an arm around each of our shoulders. "Make sure you don't get trapped. Seriously. I hear ten thousand years buried beneath the ground really does something to your complexion."

Levi signs to Grayson without speaking, but I can tell by his face it's probably a profanity.

"No need to use your potty hands with me." Grayson takes a

swig from his canteen, and his skin changes. Every imperfection —acne, redness, and fine lines—is smoothed over with one drink from the pool. Is it a fountain of youth? "I'm your favorite sibling."

"Yeah, right," Levi signs, turning his back on Grayson.

As much as Grayson is kidding around, I don't want Levi going into the fae world hot-headed. I'm the one who's supposed to be the savior. I need to take on my role, despite my "baby" status.

"We're all on the same team." I take Evie and Levi's hands.

Bastian follows my lead, snatching Evie's other hand and then Grayson's.

Levi won't look at Grayson as they complete the circle.

Standing here in Fox Glove Crossing, I believe together we have the power to accomplish any task thrown at us. The energy in our circle is palpable, as if the gods of the wilderness are looking down on us, intent on helping us succeed.

"We'll meet you tomorrow morning in Tenny Rocks with the knowledge we need to take down Avren and the First City." I hang my head, unsure if I should bring up the one thing that's bothered me for a while. If the other savior is from the First City, will they really be on our side?

"If you're not back there by ten, we'll come to get you. Don't think for a moment we'll let you rot away in Cirrus's prison." Bastian looks from me to Levi.

"Don't worry, Dad," Levi drops his brothers' hands to sign. "I'll have her back by curfew."

Bastian draws me into his arms, where his weapons impede our embrace. I wince when the hilt of a knife presses against my chest. He takes my chin between his fingers, so I focus my attention solely on him. "Don't take any chances in there. Find out what Cirrus wants, keep him talking, and leave. Keep the radio in your pocket turned on so we can hear everything." With a dip of his head, he kisses me, slow and sweet, showing me he doesn't care what the others think.

And then they're gone, leaving Levi and me in the ravine alone with the sound of the waterfall surrounding us.

"This way." Levi taps my arm and motions to a trail running along the side of the pond.

We follow the narrow path, one behind the other and cling to the wall to prevent an accidental fall into the water. Behind the falls is the entrance to a darkened cave, which must be the way into Frostacre. Two pairs of glowing eyes confirm my suspicions.

The fae guards step out of the shadows and onto the path, blocking our entrance by crossing their spears. One has long blond hair like Quinn and the other, braided silver hair. Both are painstakingly beautiful, sure to lure in unsuspecting travelers.

"State your business," the blond guard says, seemingly trying to keep a straight face.

The path is wider here, so I step in front of Levi, not wanting the guards to know about his deafness. "We're here to gain an audience with King Cirrus."

"Do you have an appointment?" As much as the blond guard looks amused, the silver one appears bored, loosely holding his spear. "The king sets his meetings on Mondays, Wednesdays, and the occasional Fridays. Today is Thursday, so you'll have to come back with an appointment."

This is worse than going to a healer in Avren.

I straighten my back, trying to bolster my self-confidence. "Can you tell King Cirrus that Maribel Windsong-Barellis is here to see him, and I only grant an audience with monarchs on Thursdays?" I wink at the silver-haired fae, and his eyes widen. "I also helped assassinate Quinn Malum."

Levi's heel slams down on my toe, but I miraculously keep from crying out, though it hurts like hell. He signs, "She means she saw him assassinated when thieves attacked them on their way back from Mafekadi."

The blond, who can't seem to keep from turning his lips up into a creepy smile, circles us. "You're Levi Crassus, Bracken's cursed nephew." He lifts his spear and leans on it like he's having a casual conversation with friends. "Best day of my life was when I helped escort your betrayer mother out of this place. You're nothing but a symbol of her turning her back on our race."

"Great." I rub my hands together, feeling the damp cold of the waterfall. "We're all friends."

"Heard the Miscretes took care of Lilibeth when you were nothing but a snot-nosed kid." The blond's cruelty has hit a new level, making me want to remove a dagger from my boot.

Levi rests a hand on my arm, unfazed by the insults. "Maribel needs to see King Cirrus." His level-headedness is amazing to me, but he understands the fae more than I ever will.

"The king will want to see the girl," the silver fae says, holding his spear in front of him. "Looks like they come as a package deal."

The guards each grab one of our arms and drag us into the cave beneath the falls.

I struggle against the silver one's hand. "You don't have to hold on so tight. We want to go. Remember?"

To my relief, he releases me completely.

I expect the cave to hold the moisture from mist, but it is dry. Torches every twenty feet or so help warm the tunnel as strange music echoes from the walls.

The blond fae rambles on about union benefits and the need for quicker transport from the outer reaches to the court. "I mean, I'm one hundred and ninety-eight years old. I shouldn't have to walk a mile every time someone shows up who wants to see the king. No regard for the little fae."

The silver-haired guard ignores him, never showing an ounce of amusement on his face. It makes me wish I could delve into the inner workings of his mind to see what is really going on in there. Probably a yes-man following his orders and not wanting any trouble. There are a lot of guards in Avren like this—wanting to please the Council and earn higher rankings. "Head back to the entrance. I'll take it from here."

A few minutes after the blond guard leaves, the tunnel opens into a massive cavern. Luminescent moss and glowing crystals line the walls of the cavern lighting Frostacre. Labyrinths of twisting tunnels branch in different directions from the massive four-story city. Twisted trees with branches that reach for an unseen sky dot the underground landscape, their roots intertwining with the dark earth. Unseelie fae flit through the shadows with ethereal grace, their eyes gleaming with otherworldly light.

I look at the guard beside me, shaking. Beneath the surface, his eyes glow, giving him an almost alien appearance. This is the person I need to trust to get me to King Cirrus, but will it bring him more delight to lead me astray through the twisting passages? The corner of his lip bends upward as if he suspects my mistrust.

Time seems to move differently here, and the boundaries between dreams and reality blur. Intricate illusions dance along the city's edges, playing tricks on me. At the entrance of a tunnel, I see three guards holding Grayson, Evie, and Bastian bound and gagged, but when I shake my head, they're gone. In the center of the cavern, by a fountain, I see my mother sitting by the cool water beckoning me to come take a sip. But Levi warned me about Frostacre's food and drink. The tricks are intense, setting my body into a flurry of emotions, caught between wanting to give in to the dreams and keeping a foot firmly in reality.

To keep with the fluidity of the dreamlike atmosphere, my guard slips an arm around my waist, transfixing me with his eyes. "The king prepares a feast for you, Maribel. He invites you to his private dining quarters."

Sharp nails dig into my arm, but someone swiftly removes

them. I hear Levi's voice like it's miles away, drifting through the cloudiness in my brain. "Block him out. You can do it, Mari."

I inhale sharply, trying to clear my head, and rip my eyes away from my guard. "I will go meet the king, but Levi goes with me."

The silver-haired guard lifts a finely manicured eyebrow above his glowing eyes, seeming bored again. He must get a rise out of torturing humans in the dream world. "Very well."

At the far end of the city, we face another cavern, its entrance covered in a material that moves like liquid filled with a sparkling life of its own. The guard holds up a palm, and it parts for us as we cross the threshold.

When I reach a finger to touch it, Levi snatches it away.

"Touch nothing," he hisses.

Within the chamber, an elaborate dining table is set with piles of food, making my stomach grumble. Between the candelabras are piles of meats, fruits, breads, and cheeses. Towering chocolate cakes, strawberry cheesecake, and vanilla pudding make my sweet tooth cry out. These are some of my favorite foods I haven't tasted since I was in Avren.

"He's playing with you," Levi whispers in my ear just before the guard hits him on the side of the head with his spear, knocking him to the ground.

I want to go to him but don't have a chance as King Cirrus enters the room. He's the most beautiful creature I've ever seen, with long, flowing white hair and an almost equally pale skin. And he has the most perfect male face I've ever seen—almond-shaped eyes, chiseled jawline, prominent brow. Despite all the white, he's shrouded in darkness and draped in black robes that move as if they have a life of their own. His piercing green eyes stare at me, not glowing like the others. "Welcome to Frostacre, Maribel Windsong. I'm glad you finally accepted my invitation. I've been dying to meet you."

CHAPTER TWENTY-EIGHT

A small creature wearing a blue pointed hat pulls out the king's chair at the head of the table. Never in my life have I witnessed something so graceful and mesmerizing. He makes me forget about Levi lying on the ground near my feet. I pinch my arm to tear my attention away from Cirrus and back to my friend. A welt about the size of a walnut protrudes from his forehead.

Levi rises to his elbows and takes my hand so I can help him to his feet. If a guard dares to hit him again, I'll drive my iron dagger into his heart.

"Are you ok?" I ask as we walk to the table.

He keeps his lips pressed together and nods. The fae in Frostacre scare him senseless, but I don't want to do anything to make things worse for him.

Cirrus holds an open palm toward the chair to his right. "Come sit beside me, Maribel. I've never had a savior in my court before, and the mere thought of it intrigues me."

The pointy-hat creature pulls out my chair, and I sit, feeling the heady magic pushing at me from all sides. Levi takes my hand beneath the table and squeezes, as if trying to keep me tied to reality.

A fae woman with hair as white as Cirrus's and dressed in a gossamer dress fills the king's goblet with blood red wine. She seems to float over to me, filling my cup and then Levi's before leaving the room.

"Tell me what it's like." Cirrus folds his long fingers together as he leans his elbows on the table, pitching closer, as if I'm the most fascinating creature he's encountered. "The strange juxtaposition between playing the role of the savior of the wilderness and growing up in Avren."

As much as I don't want to play into any of his traps, this is my job. I need to give the others time. "I find it exhausting. To grow up in a pampered world where I'm taught to sew and to live the life of an influential society woman only for the Council to thrust me into a world of unforgiving conditions. It's enough to make anyone give up. And then to find out you're a prophesied savior, foretold to bring destruction upon my friends and neighbors, well, honestly, it makes my head spin."

"I see." A flash of light crosses through his eyes as he sets his chin on his folded hands. "What if I told you I can take all this pressure away—so you never worry again about which dagger you need to kill which creature?"

"Then I'd tell you I'd be forever in your debt." Our conversation is getting too close to the king placing me in a cage and keeping me as his personal pet. "Tell me more about what it's like living in Frostacre."

The king slides his hand the short distance over the corner of the table and takes my free hand in his, sending icy chills through my veins. I swallow back the bile as Levi continues to caress my right hand to keep me sane.

"It's an absolute dream. Imagine dinner spreads like this every night. Grand balls where the most handsome fae fight for the chance to seduce you. Midnight swims in the underground hot springs. And your own private suite, complete with a canopy bed and satin sheets." His fingers trail along my skin, sending images of his descriptions flickering through my mind.

"And your queen? What is she like?" I don't remember Levi ever mentioning a queen, but if there is one, and it keeps Cirrus talking, I want to know.

"Insufferable." The king's lips fall as if I've brought up a sore subject. "Had to lock her away in the deepest part of the dungeon after she took issue over my affairs. Can't have a queen who won't let me have a little fun. Might let her out in another hundred years."

"How did you fall in love?" It's personal, but it makes me think of Bastian creeping through the magic-filled tunnels, searching for the prophecy. If I focus on my reality, I might make it through this.

"Love?" The king appears as if he might burst out laughing. "Maybe a bit of lust at first, but the purpose of our marriage is to link two full-blooded families. I didn't marry for love." His fingers slide along my hand to my wrist and then to my forearm as if he's admiring my skin. "What about you? Are you in love?"

I grip Levi's hand tighter. As much as I want to learn about my connection with Bastian, I want to protect him. The fae don't tell lies, but diversion using a good story might work. "There was a boy in Avren who captured my attention. More of an obsession than love. How far could we take our heated encounters without the Council knowing?"

"And what became of this boy?" The king stops his slow crawl up my sleeve to listen to my response. I don't dare shake my arm free, knowing Cirrus's power.

"He's a soldier in the Avren guard. I guess he's my enemy." The thought of it leaves a hollowness in the pit of my stomach. Flynn did nothing to hurt me. He wanted to bring me back into the city.

"I can make you forget about him." The king grips my elbow, massaging it and filling me with a betraying need. I close my eyes and inhale the magic surrounding me. My thoughts wander to an enormous bed covered in mounds of pillows. Images of Cirrus above me, moaning my name, make me squeeze my legs together. Above him is a frame containing a parchment with ancient script. *The prophecy?* If I accept his invitation, maybe I can get it myself and use my locket to get back. That is, if I'm strong enough to resist the king of the Unseelie Court.

Heart pounding, I open my eyes to see the king holding a strawberry between his slender fingers. "Taste, Maribel. Accept everything I offer."

Levi's fingernails dig so hard into my palm, I'm sure they're drawing blood. He's reminding me not to eat the food. The king's eyes flash to my companion's as if it's the first time he's noticed him in the room.

"The son of Lilibeth Swallow. What are you doing here?" His grip tightens on my elbow. "Didn't I banish you with your whore of a mother?"

Based on what the king has told me, he shouldn't point fingers on this matter.

Until this point, Levi has shown decorum and respect for his people. Any misstep might ruin the mission. I hear the tightness in his voice as he growls, "My mother did nothing wrong except fall in love with a human."

"That's fine, but to marry the creature?" Cirrus turns up his nose, unable to contain his disgust. "And procreate with it? To weaken Frostacre's bloodline is an act of treason. You and all your descendants deserve the curse put on you by your mother's insolence." A flash of light crosses the king's eyes again as he assesses both of us. "But if you were to leave, letting this fine woman stay with me, I'd repay you by lifting the curse."

Levi's body stiffens as my hand tingles from his iron grip. This isn't the plan. But the visions Cirrus placed in my head have me seeing things differently. I can snatch the prophecy and use the necklace to get to Tenny Rocks. My brother will be free to walk out the door without a hair misplaced and possibly with his hearing.

"I will *never* leave her with the likes of you." Levi's eyes narrow with such fire, I'm afraid he might knock Cirrus to the ground. "You call it a curse, but in reality, it's a blessing." He holds his thumbs up to his lips and throws his hands out, palm down, in front of him.

"Oh, my. You know her life in Frostacre will be a million times better than shacking up in the wilderness with you." He touches my cheek with his long fingernail, sending delicious quivers through me.

I hate how his magic affects me. I'm not sure if I can even get Levi to leave.

"That's where you're wrong, Your Majesty." Levi drops my hand and stands, holding a shaking iron dagger in his other hand. "The Kindred Few have one thing you'll never have."

"And what's that, fool?" Despite the weapon pointed at his head, the king looks calm.

Levi steps around my chair, moving closer to the king.

I want to snatch the dagger from his hand, but it's out of reach.

"Love." He crosses both hands over the center of his chest, keeping hold of the weapon. "You keep people close for power and greed. We'd lay down our lives for our brothers and sisters because we're family. That's what my parents did for each other."

This wasn't part of the plan. He was supposed to get the king to give us clues as to the whereabouts of the prophecy, not antagonize him. I wish I could let him know the king clued me in already with his mental invitation to his bed chambers.

Cirrus's face tightens and turns a strange shade of pink as he plucks a grape from the table and pops it in his mouth. He assesses us while he chews. "Let's put that to the test." With a flick of his wrist, the dagger in Levi's hand falls to the floor. He leans his elbows on the table, the arms of his robe slinking downward.

"If I promise to let this *human* go after she entertains me for a while, will you let me kill you where you stand?"

The blood seems to rush out of my body. The king must be joking. Levi and I are both walking out of here with the prophecy. I won't have it any other way.

"Let him go." I touch my brother's arm before rising and standing between them. "Do what you want with me. He's done nothing wrong. Haven't you punished him enough because of what you consider to be his mother's sin?"

Cirrus leans back in his chair, crossing his arms and one leg over the other. "No. I've made up my mind, and it takes an act of monumental effort to change it." A final burst of light flickers through his eyes. "Forfeit your life for the girl's."

A lone finger links with mine as my best friend turns to me with a sad smile on his lips. He mouths, "You are kin."

The iron dagger rises from the floor, flips two times in the air, and drives itself into Levi's chest. He falls to the floor in a heap, and this time, there's no saving him. I crouch beside him, intent on holding it together despite the rage and heartache threatening to tear me apart. The dam keeping back the massive wave of sorrow holds fast. There's no time for tears.

I slide my hand into my boot, my fingers wrapping around the smooth handle of a dagger.

"You will learn eventually that life's temporary, dear Maribel. Friends, enemies, and lovers come and go." He's still reclined in his chair, acting as if nothing happened. As if he swatted a bug with his hand.

I want to rip his fucking head off.

Finally, he moves to crouch beside me, lifting my chin with his fingernail. "You need to learn to feel no emotion. I learned this in the first decade of the five centuries I've lived in this world."

Hating every melodic note of his voice, I squeeze my eyes shut, wanting to block him out, but also knowing what I need to do. "Take me to your room. You'd better follow through with your promise to him and let me go after we... let's get it over with." Everything inside me is screaming to kill him right now, but I'm not sure how to get to his bedchambers. Killing him might set off a series of events that will keep me from finding the prophecy. Burning tears sting my eyes, so I brush them away with the sleeve of my dress. As much as I want to curl into a ball and cry, I need to stay strong for Levi.

The king wraps his slender arm around mine and holds me close to him, leading me through the narrow corridors of his underground lair. Images of Levi working in the sunshine of his garden fill my head. He lifts his eyes and smiles, holding a plump tomato in his hand as I approach. I need to swipe the images away to keep my composure. There's no guarantee I'll ever leave this place.

At an enormous gold door, Cirrus removes a key from around his neck and unlocks it. He pushes it open and ushers me in. My attention is immediately on the wall behind the bed. It's a bit startling to find that it's an exact replica of my vision. I hope that doesn't mean I'll soon be in bed with the fae king.

"Make yourself comfortable." Cirrus removes goblets from a glass cabinet. He pops the cork on a bottle of wine and pours two glasses, then carries them over to a table. "There's a bath behind the double doors."

"Can you draw it for me?" I sit on the edge of the bed and cross my ankles. "Maybe we can take it together?"

I'm not sure how much of this act he's buying. He must feel the aura of my all-out rage.

"Very well." Cirrus picks up a wine glass and carries it into the bathroom.

I climb onto the bed, taking the frame down from the wall and laying it on the floor. With my dagger, I make quick work of the bindings and free the parchment from the casing. My hands sweat. I don't like that I can't hear Cirrus over the running water in the bathroom. If he catches me, I'm not sure what I'll do. I fold the parchment, tuck it into my corset, and shove the frame under the bed.

Cirrus appears in the doorway, nose in the air and glass of wine in hand. "My father used the dwarves to dig out Frostacre in the sixty-seventh century." He pauses when he finally looks at me. "What are you doing on the floor?"

"I dropped my ring." I swipe my palms over the thick carpeting frantically. "Oh, never mind. I found it." I hold up the ring, I'd slipped from my finger moments before at the sound of his voice. "It's a size too big and keeps coming off."

He stares at me as if he can't believe the prophecy picked me to assume the role as savior. "Your bath is ready."

I scramble to my feet, trying not to trip on the skirt of my dress, and hurry into the bathroom. Knowing nothing about the king, I'm not sure how observant he is. It might take him two minutes or two years to notice the frame missing from above his bed.

With my limited time, I roll up my sleeves and remove the dagger from my pocket, ready to force myself into a mindset where I can kill the fae king in cold blood. The weapon shakes in my hand as I take in shallow breaths, contemplating my next move. Every creak of the floorboards beyond the door sets my heart into wild palpitations. It's a strange game of who will open the bathroom door first.

To both my dismay and relief over not drawing it out any longer, he makes the first move. As the door opens, I hide the dagger behind my back, carefully slipping it into my pocket.

"Can I help you with your dress?" He moves behind me, not waiting for an answer, his lithe fingers sliding the buttons through the eyelets. Cool air hits the bare skin of my shoulders.

My heart is now in my throat. I don't want it to go any farther, and if I don't stop him, we'll end up in bed like the vision he implanted in my mind earlier. Without a word, he slides the green velvet from my shoulders, his cool hands skimming along my skin. He's an expert in using his glamour, threatening to make me forget all about the dagger in my pocket.

The garment slips from my hips to the ground, and I'm standing exposed in my corset and underclothes. The weapon seems impossibly out of reach.

His lips brush my shoulder, stopping to nip the sensitive spot where my neck meets my collarbone, and work their way up to my ear. "Join me, Maribel. Make Frostacre your home. As my pet, you'll never need to lift a weapon again."

In my clouded judgment, it sounds so inviting. This drop dead gorgeous fairy wants me around. He'll protect me from Arazian and Lady Raven. I drift into his dreamworld as I feel his fingers working the ribbon on my corset. There's some reason he shouldn't do that. There's something hidden, but I can't remember what.

He stops long enough to pick up a glass of wine from a small wooden ledge beside the tub. "Here. Have a drink. It will relax you."

I hold the glass of wine, staring down into the red poison.

A voice calls out in my head. *Don't eat or drink anything. Fae food and drink will drive you into madness.*

Levi.

I turn and throw the contents of the glass into Cirrus's face before diving to the floor to find my dagger in the dress.

"You'll pay for that, you Undesirable wench." His slender fingers turn from gentle to unforgiving as he grips my hair and drags me across the bathroom floor.

I keep hold of my dress, patting the folds for the hard iron. There's too much material. My scalp cries out where his fingernails dig into flesh.

Using my hair, he lifts me to my feet and shoves me against the wall, holding me by the shoulders. His eyes are wide, and dark lines threaten to burst through his pale skin. In anger, he can't hide his true self behind his glamour. "You're going to die like the miserable half-blood lying on the dining room floor. It will take my staff weeks to get the stain out of the marble."

My searching fingers finally hit the hard object in my dress, so I plunge them into the pocket to retrieve it. Hands no longer shaking, I stare at the king as his hands slide from my shoulders to my throat, trying to choke the life out of me. As my head spins, I use everything within me to thrust the weapon's blade into his side.

He staggers backward, staring down at the projectile protruding from his waist. For most, this wouldn't be a fatal blow, but he's fae and the weapon's iron.

"What have you done?" He yanks the dagger out and tosses it to the ground as the black lines on his face become more pronounced. "You're a human. Mortal. You're weak. I'm the king." His skin morphs from its usual perfect ivory to ashen as he stumbles, trips, and lands in the tub. His head lolls to the side as he gets the bath he wanted.

I just killed the king of Frostacre.

CHAPTER TWENTY-NINE

*V*oices come from the bedroom. Have the fae discovered my crime so quickly? I throw my dress over my head and crack the door open to peek into the other room. A shadowy figure stands beside the king's dresser, rifling through the contents. Another is on his hands and knees searching beneath the bed.

I rush into the room and throw myself into Bastian's arms, catching him off guard as he rifles through papers on Cirrus's table. I'm lucky he doesn't pull a weapon on me.

"Mari?" He's surprised to find me here. The plan was to keep to the dining room and distract the fae king. He leans back and inspects my state of disarray.

My dress is unbuttoned, my hair loose from the pins, and I probably have blood on my hands and face.

Grayson and Evie come to join us, both looking concerned.

"Where's Levi?" Grayson turns his head toward the flickering oil lamp in the bathroom. From this angle, he can't see Cirrus. "We lost contact with your radio underground."

The tears flow as I break into sobs. The traumatic events of the last hour finally unload on me. My knees buckle, but Bastian catches me, holding me up in his powerful arms. All I want right now is to be back in my room in the cabin with Levi lying in the other bed.

"He's dead," I say between my sobs. "And Cirrus is dead, so we need to leave."

"What?" Grayson acts on his suspicions and swings open the bathroom door. "You killed the king?"

"He killed Levi." Saying those words seems impossible. I swallow back fresh tears. "He killed one of his own."

"We need to leave." Grayson heads toward the door, dagger drawn. "It won't take them long to find out."

"We can't leave here without the prophecy." Evie's usually stoic face is stained with tears. She gathers her red curls into a tie before lifting her bow. "If we do, Levi's death will be in vain."

I manage a slight smile and remove the folded parchment from my corset. "Is this our ticket out of here?"

"Holy shit, Mari." Grayson crosses the room, lifts me, and spins me around. "You're amazing. I'd ask how, but we need to leave."

The sound of marching boots echoes outside the door as graceful as the flutter of birds' wings, setting an ominous tone to the atmosphere. Through some type of telepathy, they must know their leader's dead. The guards are here to kill the one who assassinated the king.

"Through here," Bastian calls, opening a door at the rear of the room.

It leads into a tunnel probably used by the king for emergencies like this. I jog behind Bastian in the dim light of luminescent vines. Tree roots and occasional stairs prevent me from running.

Ancient stone steps lead upward, but daylight is nowhere in sight. The sounds of frighteningly light footsteps and the flutter of wings surround us, making me wonder if I'm going mad as they run on repeat through my head. It must be a fae trick. The art of convincing your enemy she's insane has kept Frostacre on the map for centuries. I killed their king, I have the prophecy, and there's blood to pay.

But today, it won't be mine.

I keep up with Bastian as he ascends the crumbling escape route. It's a miracle the others are blocking out the faes' attempts to paralyze us with fear. This is what they've trained for, and they'll face much worse in Avren and the First City.

"Do you hear them?" My voice comes out choppy and short. "The soldiers?"

"Of course." Bastian keeps his pace, not slowing down an iota. "We need to trust each other. It's the only way we'll survive." He reaches back and takes my hand, pulling me alongside him. "We've lost one brother today. That's one too many." There's an unrecognizable hollowness in his voice, one I hope I never hear again, though it resonates through my own empty chest.

The higher we climb, the louder the sounds echo against the stone walls. Grayson and Evie keep watch behind us while Bastian holds a torch out in front.

When we reach a wall at the top of the staircase, the sound is almost deafening. I cover my ears, close my eyes, and crouch down, unsure if I can endure it. I'm almost certain they're surrounding us, ready to slice out my heart and feed it to a werewolf.

A hand rests on my shoulder, warm but firm. "Come on, Mari," Bastian says. "It's our way out."

There's a narrow tunnel beside the wall. I need to sidestep through it, sliding one foot along at a time. It's a wonder Bastian fits into such a tight space. Within minutes, we're stepping out into an enchanted wood beside a pool. Tiny fairies, wood nymphs, and lightning bugs scatter as we stumble out, some into the trees, and others beneath the lily pads in the water. Despite our climb out of the city, we're much lower on the mountain than where we entered Frostacre. Earlier, I'd been so fascinated by every detail when accompanied by the two guards that I'd hardly noticed our descent. Here, no fae stand guard.

My heart's heavy with the thought of leaving Levi behind, but there's no time to grieve. We have what we came for and need to return to Tenny Rocks before dark.

"Use your locket." Bastian's gaze is on the silver chain around my neck.

"But you..." I don't want to run away and leave the others behind.

"We'll be fine." He glances at Grayson and Evie, both nodding in agreement. "The goal is to protect the prophecy. Wait until we get there to open it."

"And Levi? We can't just leave him."

"We must for now." Grayson skirts the pond, running the tip of his blade through the murky water. "Without the prophecy... without the full strength of the rest of the Kindred Few... all will be lost. He knew the risks of coming here."

And now the rest of us must live without him.

In a month, I've lost two important people. I've learned to live life without my mother. I can do the same with Levi. But the constant reminders of him in the cabin, the garden, the meadow, and the woods, will stay with me always.

I look into Bastian's eyes, unable to contain the grief any longer as I bring the tips of my fingers up to the locket and disappear.

WITH A THUD, I land on my knees on the hard wooden floor of our room in Tenny Rocks. My head spins, so I crawl over the floor, scrape a tin basin out from under the bed, and throw up. I roll onto my back, not caring that I'm still on the floor, and stare up at the thatched ceiling. Numbness overtakes my mind and body.

With Levi gone, did any of this even matter?

I drift to sleep. The others will return in an hour or two, and I don't have the strength or desire to leave this very spot.

THE DOOR SLAMS open and Grayson enters, followed by Evie and Bastian. "And I say elves have it two-to-one over pixies. Who ever saw a drunk pixie?"

I groan, grab a pillow from Bastian's mattress beside me, and throw it over my head to block the inane nature of the conversation. It's Grayson's way of dealing with his grief, I know, but to me it mocks Levi's memory. I don't know what I expected. A grand parade through the village with flowers and a chorus of mourners?

No.

Levi wouldn't want that. I don't want that. What I want is space and time to live in my grief, not Grayson bombarding me with his overtly jovial nature.

The room grows quiet as the others settle onto the beds, their eyes boring holes in the pillow over my head.

"We loved him too, Mari." Bastian's voice cuts through the pillow and into my soul. His footfalls creak along the floorboards, and then he's sitting beside me, rubbing my back. "He'd want us to go on." He sighs, and his hand pauses. "None of us are saying you can't feel what you're feeling. It's real and raw." His slow sweeps begin again at my shoulder and run down my back. "But this is larger than us. You have a role to play in this bigger war, and I'm not sure how many more we'll lose. Levi's death gave us the prophecy."

The prophecy. Folded paper wedged between my stiff corset and soft skin, ready to reveal to us the secrets of the world.

I roll onto my elbow to prop myself up and look at him—at them. Like Levi, this is my family now that my mother's gone and my father disowned me. My face is a mess. I can feel the sticky residue of tears on my cheeks. "I'd trade Levi for the prophecy in a heartbeat. The other savior will reveal themselves eventually. That's how you found me."

Grayson walks over and sits cross-legged beside me, placing his hands in his lap. "Levi once told me he knew he'd die at the hands of the fae. He knew too much. Deep secrets ran through his bloodline that the king thought died with Levi's mother. His human side posed a danger to Frostacre because they knew he held more loyalty to people than to the fae." He reaches above him and rests his arm on the footboard of the bed. "You say you had a vision placed in your head by Cirrus. Maybe it was really Levi."

"Was he strong enough to do that?" I piece through my vision, trying to find clarity. "His limited magic couldn't save him from Quinn Magnum. And why would he place an image of the king and I..." I stop. Heat flames my face, but they need all the details. "In my vision, I wasn't just in the bedroom. I was underneath Cirrus—in the bed."

"Levi told me before we left that if he could get close to the king, he might be able to delve into his mind." Grayson drops his eyes, staring at the floorboards. "Cirrus must have felt the intrusion, seeing him as a threat. Thankfully, Levi planted the image in your mind before he died."

Bastian furrows his brows, probably trying to block out the image my recollection brings. "The fae have interesting ways to convey messages—even Levi. The king was too smart to reveal the exact location of the prophecy, but it's obvious he couldn't resist taking you to his bedchambers."

"Are we going to look at this prophecy already?" Evie lounges on the bed as she tosses her dagger up into the air, catching it by the handle each time. Will I ever be so brazen?

Sitting up all the way, I reach into my corset, but Bastian stops me, his coarse fingers wrapping around my wrist.

"Let's wait until we are home." He helps me to my feet, my muscles aching from sleeping on the floor. "I'll feel better when we're behind the safety of our wards. I'm afraid we've made enemies with all of Frostacre."

We gather our things, stuffing clothes and weapons into our bags and cloaks. The setting sun blinds me as we step out of the inn, ready for the long trek home. There's the fear of the other Supes trying to take advantage of our nighttime journey, but I'm confident in my companions. We need our own beds and the familiarity of Levi's loving touches in the cabin. It will give us a space to grieve.

THE DARKENED sky still hangs heavy over our cabin when we arrive in the middle of the night. Familiar chirps of crickets and other creatures fill the air. Only two werewolves and one vampire meet their deaths along the way, my kin making quick work of them.

I stagger over the threshold, no longer sure of my footing. The heavy shroud of this day weighs my shoulders down like an oppressive fog. A strong hand catches my elbow, leading me not to the room I shared with Levi but to the stairs.

Bastian rolls down the comforter, fluffs the pillow on the side closest to the wall, and waits for me. I slip into his bed and lay my head down, letting his scent surround me as he wraps me in his arms. "We'll honor him." He speaks so softly, I wonder if I made the words up myself.

"He didn't deserve to die." My words come out pale instead of being the powerful statement I want to convey. "He saw the good in everyone."

His fingers trail along my hairline. "We all loved him. He understood what it was like to grow up in the wilderness—to fend for yourself. We both lost our families. Those shared experiences create strong bonds. Though I don't show my emotions too often with tears, there's a gaping hole in my heart that will probably never mend." A feather-soft kiss graces my cheek before he settles onto his pillow.

I stare up at the ceiling. A storm rumbles in the distance, echoing through the valley. Flashes of light illuminate the shadow of trees on the wall. The parchment scorches my skin beneath my dress as if it's unable to contain its secrets any longer. But like me, it will have to wait a few more hours until we can all open it together.

CHAPTER THIRTY

"*A*re you ready to do this?" Bastian stands beside the bed holding a croissant in his hand. "Grayson thought he'd lure you out with warm baked goods."

I grumble an obscenity and throw the blanket over my head. As hungry as I am from not eating at King Cirrus's table last night, sleep is more of a priority. Getting in late and staying up thinking about Levi and the prophecy have me spent.

The mattress bows at his weight beside me. His large, comforting hand caresses my shoulder. "Aren't you curious at all? We waited for years for you to come along and now we'll know the identity of the other savior. Imagine another person like you out there with First City lineage."

I sit up, knowing I've lost the stay-in-bed fight. "That's what scares me. What type of person, or creature, comes from the First City? The only ones I've seen tried to kill us in Tenny Rocks."

He stands and walks to his desk, picking up a piece of paper. "It is written. There's not much we can do to change it. You have us, and we'll do everything in our power to protect you. But we can't guide the hands of fate. We can't change your destiny."

"Give me the damn croissant." I slide my feet over the side of the bed, let them touch the cold floor, and shiver. The insurmountable mountain I must climb keeps growing—Supes who want to kill me and a prophesied mutant fighting buddy. Worst of all, my best friend is dead. I hate waking up on the wrong side of the bed, but it's getting to be too much.

After stuffing the roll into my mouth, I pad down the stairs behind Bastian to join the others. I've already removed the prophecy from my corset, and I hold it in my hand. Grayson and Evie sit in the living room with mugs of coffee. They stop their conversation when we appear.

Grayson smiles. It's way too chipper for my tired head. "Looks like it was a rough night."

Evie shoots him a warning glare before looking at me. "Is that the prophecy?"

I hold the paper in my hand out to her, not wanting the responsibility of reading it. With its fae magic, it's practically burning a hole in my palm. "Do you think we should read the first half?" I only heard it the time Levi recited it out loud from memory.

"Got it here." Grayson lifts an open book from the side table next to his chair and runs his fingers along the words.

Bastian and I sit at the table.

"Two cities loom above us all,
one veiled in beauty, and the other darkness.
Both hold death within their walls.
For those saved by Mahogany's gaze
dance among the fairy rings and a fire's blaze.
The great wilderness protects the hidden.
Two will rise from the cities' walls—young and brave and true.
Their sacrifice will save us all
and end the evil reign
of both great cities."

Evie unfolds the parchment, her hands shaking. Unlike me, those raised in the wilderness have waited years for this. Her eyes flick from Bastian to Grayson to me.

"A seamstress born and raised
among the privileged few.
Abandoned by her father.
Orphaned by her mother.
She'll learn to fight with
grace and ease, facing friend and foe.
An orphaned son of power
taken well before his time.
The precious babe laid in the hands
of a farmer and his wife.
Torn between two worlds,
the boy becomes a man,
ready to rip the fabric of two cities
to save his precious land."

Evie stops reading. Her voice is low as she says, "There's one more part."

We already know, but we don't stop her.

"Maribel Nexus Windsong-Barellis and Bastian Aidan Hale.
Both from different worlds
and destined to tear each other apart."

The room remains silent, letting the prophet's words spin in our heads. A million thoughts fight for my attention as I struggle to grasp one. Our connection. It's so obvious. We're drawn together because of fate. We need to work together to take down the cities before we turn on each other. And he's from the First City—the enemy. Has he been playing me all along, knowing I was the second savior? I want to scream and roll up in a ball at the same time.

I narrow my eyes, struggling to look him in the face. "Did you know?"

His skin is deathly pale as rare tears well in his eyes. He's putting on a good show if he knows something. "No." He leans forward, holding his head in his hands.

Grayson stands and paces in front of the fireplace, arms folded. "We can't start pointing fingers. He's our brother. If he says he didn't know, we must believe him." He stops pacing and approaches the table, resting his hands on it, and leans forward. "But if I find out you've played us all this time, you'll wish you were dead."

Bastian scrapes back his chair and storms out the back door, letting it slam behind him.

Evic sits on the table beside Grayson. She runs her hand up his arm. "Think about what he's going through. Not only is he the second savior, but he's just found out his whole life's a lie and he's from the First City. Who's his father? Who's his mother? I've never heard of children in Arazian's realm."

My mixed emotions tug at me from all sides, threatening to tear me apart. All the hope I had before we traveled to Frostacre, smashed to pieces by the fae. And in all this, I thought I knew Bastian. He connected with me in a way no one else could, even Levi. How I long for my friend's advice.

Grayson looks out the rear window and then the front one, most likely looking for Bastian. "We've got trouble."

"What is it?" Evie joins him at the window, hiding behind the curtain. "What does he want? He's carrying something."

I push back my chair to join them, curious. A tall fairy with long, dark hair stands on the border of the protective barrier. In his arms, he holds a body. He stares at us for what seems like hours before laying his load on the ground and walking away.

"Bracken." Grayson lets the curtain fall and heads for the front door. "He's returned Levi's body."

Evie and I follow him outside as he jogs across the yard and lifts our brother to his chest. Seeing his lifeless form, Grayson lets out a sob, clutching him closer as tears run down his cheeks.

In my life love leads to loss. First my father, then my mother, and then Levi. Who else will I have to lose to bring freedom to the wilderness? I turn to see Bastian standing by the corner of the cabin.

As much as each loss in my life has torn me apart, I'd rather love someone with every fiber of my being and lose them than never love at all. I want to run to him and throw myself into his arms, lose myself in him, but I refrain. We need to bury Levi.

Grayson and Bastian dig a hole beside our brother's flower garden while Evie and I wrap his body in a blanket. Before covering him up, I take one last look at his perfect face. His glasses were lost somewhere along the way, and bruises cover his skin, but he still has a kindly pout on his lips and dark wisps of hair contrasting with his deathly pale skin. Knowing his soul is no longer with him, I fold the blanket over his face, tucking it behind his head.

Bastian shovels the last bit of dirt over the grave while we sprinkle flower seed over the freshly turned soil. With a watering can, Evie provides moisture to the plot, and within minutes, flowers pop through, brimming with new life.

Leaning closer to me, Grayson says, "Fae magic."

"I'd like to speak first." Evie crouches beside the grave and runs her fingernail along a petal on a purple flower. "Levi Crassus taught me everything I know about acceptance. As part of the deaf community, he understood prejudice, hatred, and rejection by his own people. He could have turned this into bitterness, but he loved more than anyone I've ever met. I'm eternally grateful for what he's given me." She stands and steps back, the purple flower in her hand.

I swallow back the lump growing in my throat. Tears sting my eyes for what seems like the hundredth time since we left Frostacre. The thought of entering his room—our room—makes me want to give up and fight harder at the same time.

Bastian watches me as if I'm a rabid werewolf, ready to lash out. It's not his fault, but I'm not sure what it means for him or for us. The thought of fighting together to take down the cities thrills me, while his lineage scares me senseless. After all I've heard of the First City, what good can come from it?

"I'll go next." Grayson picks a red flower from the gravesite and sticks it behind his ear. "When I first arrived in the wilderness, I barely knew what a knife was, let alone how to use one." He glances at Bastian. "After bringing you into the fold, you were so drunk all the time, you couldn't be bothered with an Avrenian. 'Useless piece of fodder,' I think you called me." A boyish smile crosses his face at the memory. He holds up a hand. "No worries, I've forgiven you. But Levi taught me how to throw a dagger with deadly accuracy. Must have killed twenty trees." His lip quirks as he bites it and averts his gaze to the sky as his voice cracks. "He's one of the best damn men I've ever known."

It's getting to where I don't know if I can hold it together enough to speak. But I need to for myself and Levi. "He was the first to call me kin, to accept me as the prophesied savior, and to consider me his friend. Never in my life have I met someone so accepting of a person he's never met coming from a city he despises. He was a walking example of something my father told me a long time ago: a true friend lays down his life for those he loves." I stoop and pluck a white flower from the grave, twisting it between my fingers.

Bastian hasn't spoken since the reading of the prophecy—at least not to me. Hooded eyes stress his sullen face, causing a stirring inside me. If he really knew nothing about his heritage, he's dealing with multiple hefty loads at the same time.

"Levi moved to my house when he was ten years old, and I was twelve. My mother was kind to a little boy whose world had just been ripped apart. She baked him my favorite cookies, let him sleep in late, and brought him home a pet kitten. I was so jealous of her doting on him, I turned to bullying. At school, I'd tell the other kids he wet the bed and made fun of his signing behind his back." He inhales sharply and looks to the side. "It wasn't until one night, when we had a big storm on the farm and we couldn't find him, that I realized how important he was to me. He'd fallen into the stream and was swept away by the rushing water. Fortunately, he grabbed onto a tree root, pulling himself to safety. We found him the next day, a frickin' muddy mess but alive. I swore that day I'd never bully him again, I'd defend him to my dying breath, and I'd never be jealous of what he had." He looks at me, his crystal-blue eyes drilling into mine. "Until I saw him with you. It came so easily to him." Instead of picking a flower, he scoops dirt into his hand, letting it sift through his fingers onto the grave. "Rest in peace, little brother." He turns and walks down the path to the Grove.

My heart aches listening to his story, seeing the anguish on his face, and watching him leave. I want to go after him, to tell him everything's alright between us, but he deserves his space.

Grayson wraps an arm around my shoulder, squeezing. "It makes sense, doesn't it? That Bastian would be a savior. To me, he's always seemed a bit unhinged. Maybe it's the Miscrete in him."

I twist out of his arm. "Bastian's not a Miscrete. Besides Arazian and his mutations, who else lives in the First City?" Images of a towering black castle with dungeons, bats, and screaming always fill my head when I think of Arazian's lair.

"We don't know." Evie clasps her hands behind her back as she walks toward us. She's lived in the shadow of the First City longer than us, so she's heard the bone-chilling tales of what goes on behind the monstrous walls. "There are rumors." She tilts her head as if assessing whether she should share them with me. "Rumors that the Northern Duke keeps company with Arazian along with other former Avrenians he chooses not to mutate."

The sound of his title makes me pause. A distant melody plays in my head, its tinny notes making me long for my father, not the powerful leader who associates with the man who mutates humans. "Then maybe it's about time we find out."

BASTIAN'S LETTER to Mari is included in book 2, The First City. Can't wait and want to read it now? Sign up for my newsletter and get early access:

heatherkindt.com

ALSO BY HEATHER KINDT

They thought it was just a game.

Meg wants one thing. For her best friend to be happy. If it were up to her, Brek would leave their hometown, attend college on a scholarship, marry the woman of his dreams, and have two-point-five kids. That is until they see the flyer for the game.

Brek doesn't only want Meg's happiness. He wants her. Even if it means putting his own life at risk by playing a game with unknown dangers. And the game has built-in consequences, testing their moral compasses and friendship to its limits.

Because opening the Green Door is not only a game, but a one-way ticket to something much more deadly.

Read the entire Eternal Artifacts series now

ALSO BY HEATHER KINDT

Most writers choose the endings to their stories . . . Most writers are not Weavers.

When the antagonist in the book Laney's writing shoves her down the stairs of the subway station, she learns she is a Weaver--a writer with the ability to bridge the narrow gap between fantasy and reality, bringing her words to life.

She soon meets William, the character she's had a mad crush on since her pen hit the paper. But he's in danger as her antagonist reveals a whole different ending planned for Laney's book which involves killing the man she loves. She must use her writing to save the people closest to her by weaving the most difficult words she will ever write.

Read the entire Weaver Trilogy now

ALSO BY HEATHER KINDT

The shadowy folds of Mo capture both souls and secrets.

Catron's father intended to scare her with his words. After all, her mother traveled far from home, losing herself to both the shadows and her wayward spirit. But instead of heeding his warning, Catron longs for more than her life as a glass blower's apprentice. When Dawkin, a member of the King of Mo's illustrious guard, offers her a place at the Vradian Academy, she willingly accepts.

Fivlon would rather gouge both of his eyes out with an iron stick than attend the Vradian Academy. Messing around with his friends is a lot more fun than attending school with a bunch of stuck-up future leaders. Following in his father's footsteps as the head of Ferox isn't a priority. Until one of his friends disappears.

Now at school, Catron and Fivlon face a much larger task than their ethics homework. As students and staff disappear from the academy, they must figure out who is behind it before they become the next victims.

Read the entire Vradian Academy series now

ALSO BY MIDNIGHT TIDE PUBLISHING

SOME ARE LED BY DESIRE,

After the mysterious death of the kingdom's queen ushers in a deadly plague, Carnaxa, Princess of Antalis, is promised to a rival kingdom. As ancient prophecies unfold, not only is Carnaxa in danger, but the fate of her kingdom as well.

Meanwhile, Anara, a gift of sorts and nothing more, was taken from her homeland. She didn't realize giving her heart away would keep her emotionally shackled, mirroring the physical chains she wore.

OTHERS ARE LED BY DUTY.

Captain Thylas has guarded Carnaxa since the day he washed ashore. When he's asked to accompany her to marry another, he finds himself torn between serving his kingdom and the desires of his heart.

Ereon, the Prince of Shaston, was raised in blood and battle. Faced with an uncompromising demand, he must choose between his birthright and his destiny.

WHEN DESIRE AND DUTY CLASH, LEGENDS ARE MADE.

ABOUT THE AUTHOR

Award-winning author Heather Kindt lives in the mountains of Colorado with her husband and two fur babies, Maggie and Bruno. When she's not writing, she's teaching fourth grade, hiking, skiing, reading, and cheering for the best team on earth: the Denver Broncos. She loves traveling and strives to include a sense of place in her stories.

In fifth grade, Heather was chosen to be in a creative writing club and still holds onto the book as a cherished relic today. She reads these stories to her students to show how terrible they are. As an adult, she wrote her first book after finishing her master's degree in teaching but didn't publish it for ten years. Her second book, Not Quite Dorothy (formally Ruby Slips and Poker Chips) catapulted her career when it won first place in a writing contest. Since then, she's written in both the fantasy and romance genres.

www.ingramcontent.com/pod-product-compliance
Lightning Source LLC
Chambersburg PA
CBHW020726210626
46807CB00016B/174